ANGEL ASSASSIN

REV CARVER SERIES BOOK ONE

PAUL SATING

Paul Sating

Cover Design: A massive Rev Specialty for Natalie at https://www.original-bookcoverdesigns.com for this amazing Rev cover. Thank you for bringing him to life!

ISBN-13: 979-8-9857203-7-2

THREE FREE NOVELLAS

Free Fantasy!

Sign up for Paul Sating's newsletter at
paulsating.com and receive THREE novellas for free!

To Tim Forbord. Rev wouldn't be half the executive chef he is without you.

REV CARVER SERIES

There are more Rev Caver books!

Book 1 – Angel Assassin
Book 2 – Angel's Creed (Coming March 2023)

WANT YOUR WINGS?

Be a good mortal. If you enjoyed the book, leave a review on Amazon, Goodreads, and/or Bookbub. Remember, the head cheese is watching your good deeds!

1

A HELL OF A RIDE

"CAN ANGELS ACTUALLY DIE?"

I chuckled at my beer at the question that pulled me away from my job. I was supposed to be keeping a demon under surveillance, not discussing immortality. My beer didn't return my joy. Such was the way of things.

"Sure," I answered too quickly. "Well, no. But, yes."

Billee shook her head, the mass of black and tan curls swaying like a floating device caught in the corner of a wave pool. Back and forth. Back and forth. Moving with the unseen forces working against it. Her smooth brown cheeks cracked when she smiled. "I don't get you, Rev."

"Trust me, most don't."

"Do angels?"

"Fewer than you'd believe."

"Can you blame them?" She turned on the bar stool, crossing a blue jean-covered leg over the other. Her foot dangled, and she bounced it in time to the music from the digital jukebox piped through the entire bar at an annoying volume. It made me miss the old days when jukeboxes played a handful of records and the sound came from the device itself. That way, if you didn't want to have horrible tunes plow into your ear holes, you just had to sit farther away and talk louder. No amount of volume could drown out the terrible song about Alabama and 'sweet homes.'

"God, I hate that fucking song," I grumbled. If I was alone in the bar, away from mortal witnesses, I would have pulled out my .327, who I named Maggie, pushed some Angelfire into the chamber, and put the digital jukebox out of my misery.

"What?"

I shook my head. "Nothing." Hunched over, I directed my question at Billee but aimed it at my half-empty mug of the Pacific Northwest's finest stout. "Blame them?"

Billee's face scrunched. "Well, you're a hard guy to get, Rev."

"How so?"

"We haven't known each other long, and yet I've got a good sense of who you are."

"Oh? And who am I?"

"You keep things too close to the vest," Billee said, still tapping her foot to the annoying song's beat. I swear, it's the longest song ever written. "You don't open up, not even to your partner."

"I open up." I wagged my pinky, not wrapped around my beer mug, at her. "And we haven't been partners long."

As a mortal, Billee didn't possess any magic. Still, she wiped all life from her dark eyes, going as flat as the Kansas landscape. "Well, we're going to agree to disagree on that one." I thought her flat eyes were unsettling until she narrowed them and quietly analyzed me.

I turned back to my beer, her scrutiny hovering.

The annoying song went on and on about blue skies. If my bosses ever wanted to punish me, they didn't need to kick me out of Heaven—which we call the Upperworld. All they had to do was lock me in a room and play this song on repeat. No worse hell existed.

I'm sure you picked up on it by now, but I'm not mortal. I'm an angel. Literally. Trust me, if you saw the way I drank and smoked, or pried into my brain to see some things I thought, you'd see I'm far from angelic.

I'm also a Reaper. *The* Reaper, many would say. A grim one, at least according to a few of my peers.

An assassin.

A monster hunter.

A killer of demons.

An immortal mop bucket, cleaning up everyone's mess.

Manager-extraordinaire of the crew who accompany mortals across the divide between the mortal and immortal planes and into their eternity.

Jack-of-all-trades kind of guy.

And right now, I was miserable. On assignment with Billee, my mortal familiar, we sat in a not-so-corporate-feeling bar, keeping tabs on my newest target. One of the most important targets I'd been assigned in decades, if not longer. I stopped keeping track a long time ago. We weren't supposed to be talking about whether angels could die, especially not in public, but Billee could be determined when she set her mind to something. An excellent familiar, one of the better ones I'd had in a few centuries, she was skilled at prying open my skull and peeking inside. Almost too good.

"Yes," I said after a while.

"Yes, you agree we will disagree?"

"Yes, angels can die. Demons can. Gods can." I heard a sharp intake of breath come from my partner. Squinting my eyes shut at my brashness, I craned my head to look at her, reminding myself that Billee was intelligent and insightful, but she was still mortal. Twenty-eight, or was it twenty-nine? I couldn't remember. Either way, she wasn't yet thirty. I had boxers older than her. Sometimes, in that context, it's best to slow-roll information. Even if it's background stuff. Especially when it's a mortal asking about the nature of immortals. She

4 | PAUL SATING

hadn't been a familiar for long. It took most years, sometimes decades, to grasp the responsibilities of the job. She was picking up quickly, but it would be some time before she accepted the reality I'd slowly reveal to her. "Sorry, that was a little heavy-handed."

"You don't say?" At least that was delivered with a wink.

"Everything dies, Billee," I said before straightening my back and barking, "except for this song, apparently."

That drew curious glances from two old men who sat as far apart at a table as possible. Not the real friendly type, by first looks. But since we were in a relatively upscale bar, at least for Olympia, Washington, I didn't have to worry about southern pride and the need to defend isolationist cultures precipitating a bar fight. Those rarely ended well. Plus, the patrons were safe. At least from me. My third eye saw their individual futures. None of them had to worry about crossing paths with me. All but one old guy in a corduroy jacket, drinking alone in the corner, would outlive this bar, which was sad. I dug the place. The staff was clean and professional, quick to serve drinks—which was always a plus. My third eye saw the owner had nearly bankrupted herself to secure the business through downtimes. All for nothing, because she was going to contract an illness in about five years that would take her attention away from business. Without her running the show, it would begin a slow decay and finally become insolvent. What a shame.

Billee chuckled. "It's a long one."

I slapped my thighs with the flats of both hands and shot her a playful look. "So, if you feel like I'm holding out on you, I'm sorry. I don't mean to. I've been doing this for a long time." As smart as Billee was, asking her to wrap her head around the fact that I'd been a Reaper for the past eight thousand years might be a step too far in the 'let's see how much Billee is ready for' game. "Do me a favor if you think I am holding anything back."

"What favor?"

"Call me on it."

She rubbed her hands together. "Oh, I'm going to enjoy this."

I smirked, raising my finger to get the bartender's attention, circling it at my beer when I had it. "Want another?" I asked Billee. She shook her head. I gave the bartender a thumbs up and he moved off to his task.

"You don't have to go into specifics," she said, casually glancing toward our young target, sitting alone at a table in the middle of the bar. "But how can you tell?"

"Tell what?" In front of our guy sat a pile of small bones, the remains of two orders of chicken wings that made the ultimate sacrifice. Dark sauce smeared the wax paper-lined basket, looking like the blood of his victims, if I was to play up to demonic stereotypes. His mug of beer was still full. Scrolling through his phone, he wasn't aware of our attention.

"That he's a demon," she said matter-of-factly, as if asking how I could tell a truck was indeed a truck. "I don't see '666' tattooed on his head. He's as pasty as any white person living in the Pacific Northwest. No red scales. Don't see horns, even with that terrible haircut. So, how can you tell?"

I laughed and didn't temper it.

At my outburst, Billee looked away from the target, probably hoping he hadn't caught her looking. "What's so funny?"

"It doesn't work like that." I gave a nod, complete with a goofy grin, to the bartender when he delivered my newest mug and waited for me to polish off the one sitting in front of me. No experienced bar patron ever goes drink-less, and I'm definitely not a rookie. When the bartender moved away, I clarified. "That whole red skin and horns thing is a recent creation. Well, recent for immortals. For you mortals, it's a tale as old as time, but trust me, that's far from the truth. Just made-up shit to scare ignorant people into compliance." I shifted my back toward her. "I mean, do you see any wings on me?"

"No. But that's because you're always wearing that stupid leather duster," she said with a smirk. "And I didn't mean literally. I wasn't expecting him to look like something from an eighth-century Roman painting, but... *that*? He's so young."

"Mmm, relatively speaking. The report says he's about six thousand years old in human years. A pup. To you? He's been around—"

"He's older than the pyramids at Giza?" Billee's disbelief made her voice raise a little too loudly.

"Settle yourself, Sparky. Don't want to grab attention. These other mortals aren't as equipped as you. Our conversation would make their brains implode."

Her gaze swiveled side to side as she checked her surroundings. I already knew no one noticed her comment— one benefit of being very good, and very experienced, at my job. She leaned closer. "I know, I know. But to be the next Lucifer? That can't be true. Is it?"

I shrugged, constantly checking on the target. He was still fixated by his phone. Stupid younger generation. "That's what they say."

"Who says?"

"Our spies' reports."

Billee sat up straight again, her eyes threatening to go flat again.

"I'm doing it again, aren't I?"

Her crossed arms told me I was. "Yes, Rev. Don't make me pry. I'm a clinical social worker. I'm good at asking questions and getting to the root of things. Unless you enjoy me searching through your gray matter, it would behoove you to willfully answer instead of making me inquire."

"'Behoove,' huh? Fancy."

"Comes with higher education and tens of thousands of

dollars in tuition debt I'll never pay off. Now, out with it." She poked my elbow.

"We get reports about the goings-on in the Underworld. I barely see them. Need-to-know basis. Keeps things safe. But even what I'm privy to amounts to a good bit of information, so I can only imagine how much the Upperworld really knows about demonic politics."

"How? I'm sure demons don't just hand over sensitive documents."

"Spies. Lots and lots of spies."

She leaned forward again, planting her hands on her legs, which made her narrow shoulders rise to ear level. "You have spies in Hell?"

I nodded. "And they have spies in the Upperworld too. See? We're not that much different from you. Well, you're not that different from us I should say, since we've been around a lot longer. But yes, our spies operate in the Underworld. We know about their politics, problems, and advantages. You name it." I turned to the bar, grabbed my mug, and put it to my lips as I rotated the stool outward and faced the tables. Most were empty, but enough patrons were looking for an afternoon meal or secret flirty rendezvous that I wouldn't draw any attention from the target. If he caught me looking, which I doubted because his tiny screen had him so transfixed, he would have seen nothing but a guy looking around a bar. "We've learned he is a very promising young demon. Though we have conflicting reports, I'm told he is being positioned to become the next Lucifer."

Billee shook her head, her black and tan curls swaying. "In all my life, I didn't know Lucifer could be replaced."

"Want your mind blown?"

"Do I?"

"Yahweh can be too. *Has* been, actually. Unlike Lucifer. That fucker is still hanging on somehow."

Billee slapped my elbow this time. "Wait. God... He is. He's not..."

The struggle was charming, but this was serious shit. You can't just drop news like that in a mortal's lap, not after the past two thousand years of conditioning committed by their various churches, synagogues, mosques, and temples. "Not the same one as time immemorial? No. Remember when I said everything dies? Yeah, Yahweh falls into that too. So does Lucifer. And that's what's supposedly going on with this young 'un over there. Someone is setting him up to be the first in line when that title is vacated."

"Is that a bad thing? I mean, hasn't the current Lucifer given Heaven enough problems?"

"Sure. But better the enemy you know, right? At least we can deal with the current one. He's pretty lame. Word is he's exhausted, which I can absolutely relate to." Subtly, I tipped my mug at the demon with jet-black hair, a firm jaw, and the problematic weapon he kept hidden under his table. "But someone that young? With energy and ambitions?"

"Could cause a lot of problems."

I nodded. "Plus, he supposedly doesn't have an Ability."

"A what?"

"You'd call it magic. We call them Abilities."

The skin between Billee's eyes bulged as she scrunched her brows. "Why is that a problem? Seems like it'd be an advantage?"

"Maybe. Maybe not," I said as honestly as I could. In the Upperworld, there was no such thing as an angel without magic. The way I understood it, the same was true of the Underworld. With one exception. And that made this Ezekial Sunstone, possible future leader of that realm, a dangerous demon. "Can't know for sure. But we know he's done incredible things already, and he's not someone we can take lightly." I turned and set the mug on the bar with a thunk before I faced my partner. "This is a dangerous task, Billee. It's my fault you aren't better prepared." I stopped, focused on the rim of my mug as dark thoughts swirled. "I've been going through some shit, and that's why the Order hasn't assigned harder cases in the time we've been working together. But they know my record. This spry fellow, special as he may be, isn't my first demon and he won't be my last. But he's yours, and I won't put you at risk. Not if I can help it."

Billee's arms crossed. Damn. Thousands of years of interacting with mortals and I still had a knack for pissing them off. "Are you saying I'm not up for the job?" she said in a tone that was clearly hinted—no, this was no hint, this was a message blared over a megaphone—that I had better answer carefully.

I tried not to smile. "You're more than capable. What I meant to say is that I won't ask anything of you I'm not willing to do myself. That's why we're here, enjoying this beer. You're really missing out, by the way. This is recon, nothing more. If this Ezekial is as powerful as reports say, I'm not moving on him until I'm ready."

"Won't you get in trouble with your superiors if you wait?"

I bobbed my shoulders, truly not caring. "On my terms. If they don't like it, they can fire me and fight this startup on their own."

"I'll support you how I can, Rev."

I looked at Billee. So damned young. A full life to live. Tasked with being a familiar before her thirtieth birthday, before she had the chance to marry and understand what the antonym of 'bliss' was, or even before she held her own child in her hands.

Damn the Order for doing this to her. To any mortal. Damn the agreement between angels and demons that forced us to be escorted around this realm, being babysat.

Almost as if they were spying on our conversation, I heard a faint tinkling.

"Dammit."

"What's wrong?" Billee asked, even as I spun and hunkered over the spot of the bar that I'd claimed as my real estate for the past hour.

I ringed the area around my mug with my arms and lowered my head, allowing my long hair to fall and hide the supernatural event about to occur in this very natural setting.

"I'm getting a scroll," I mumbled, ready for it to materialize.

Small sparks of white light formed in the restricted space between my face and the polished wood. They danced and swirled, accompanied by the pleasant sound of faint chimes, almost inaudible. Faster and faster, the white sparks swirled until coalescing into a scroll no longer than a hoagie roll, just much thinner. As soon as the scroll materialized, I swiped it off the bar and dropped my hands to my lap.

Billee slid off her stool to stand beside me.

"This is why I wear the duster, by the way. Helps eliminate awkward questions when my bosses send missives at the worst time," I said as I looked at the seal and groaned.

"What's wrong?"

"It's from Jericho."

"Isn't he the one you don't like?"

"Few members of the Order get Christmas cards from me, but yes, he's the worst." I tapped the scroll against my palm.

Jericho Judas was a spoiled brat. Not even thirty-thousand years old, he was already an influential member of the Order of Thirteen—the governing body responsible for overseeing Reaper operations, among other things. Politicians, all of them. Too many Order members were barely sufferable for more than a staff meeting at a time. Then there was Jericho. Obnoxious. Entitled. A benefactor of nepotism. A dude with such a limited range of emotion, you honestly had to wonder how many bodies he had hidden in his basement.

I unrolled the scroll, read the missive, and sighed.

"What is it?"

"Another task," I said. At least Jericho wasn't so much of an ass that he waxed poetic when giving me yet one more assignment. I read the details before handing it to Billee.

A new familiar she might be, Billee knew how to be a good teammate. The scroll pinched against her body, she unrolled it enough to read the message, shielding it from any stray gaze. Her head snapped up. "A runaway demon?"

"Apparently so."

"But we already have a target. A demon target."

My beer was getting warm. No sense in abusing alcohol like that. I took a long swig. "The Order doesn't give a damn. The sooner you realize that about them, the better off you'll be. Don't be surprised if they add a third demon to the mix just to entertain themselves. Especially if Jericho is the one in charge of dishing out assignments to the Reapers now."

"They'd give us a third case?"

"Wouldn't put it past them."

"But if—" She caught herself, lowered her voice, and slid closer. "If Ezekial really is in line to become the next Lucifer, and if we have to find a runaway, how are we *also* going to investigate these disappearances?" She smacked the partially opened scroll with a finger. "Plus, this traitor, whatever that means?"

"Welcome to the job, kid. It's a hell of a ride."

2

PIROSHKIS AND PROBLEMS

SEATTLE IS A GREAT CITY. A LOT OF FUN. JUST THE RIGHT LEVEL of debauchery to keep an old angel like me entertained. What Seattle isn't is fun to drive to from Olympia.

Sure, mortals have done a wonderful job carving out the planet over the past century. Honestly, sometimes I'm amazed at what they've accomplished, especially when you consider how long it took them to figure out that an agrarian life is far easier than trekking all over the land to hunt their next meal. But, once dwellings started reaching toward the sky, our kind knew the good times were ending. Even though mortal lives have become easier, they still haven't slowed down on the whole reproducing thing. There are more of them every day. If there's an end, it's not in sight. More mortals mean more cities. Larger cities. And vehicles. So many damned vehicles.

The *one* mortal Ability, called Technology, is a blessing. Even angels are in awe of it. How can we not be? Awe sprinkled with a light cover of envy, if I'm honest. As Technology Ability permeated the mortal world, it put somewhat of a damper on our relative importance. Thus why we can't help but feel a little jealous. I mean, your cars can drive themselves! If that's not magic, I don't know what is!

But it sure as hell doesn't make getting to and from wonderful cities any easier.

"Breathe," Billee said from the passenger seat.

She wasn't faring much better, not if the way she leaned against the window, her ball of poofy curls flattened against the frustrated palm supporting her head, was a sign of her mental well-being. I-5 does that to the most patient of drivers.

"You're one to talk," I risked saying, waiting for Billee's wrath. It never came. Kudos to her. The traffic jam made me want to punch the steering wheel. She simply looked like someone waiting for her doctor to see her. "I guess I could call Pher and see what he knows about this runaway while we wait for everyone to figure out which pedal is the gas and which is the brake."

Billee extended her arm toward the windshield and the horizon of red taillights. "You might as well. We're not going anywhere. Plus, we'll need to stop soon."

"Why? Don't tell me you're hu—"

"I'm hungry." Billee cocked her head and winked. "A girl's got to eat, Rev."

"You're always eating. One day I'm going back to the archives in the Upperworld and flipping through your genealogy. I have to find out how you can eat so much and still be the size of a Pez dispenser."

"Come work out with me sometime. Trust me, you'll learn."

"Ha! No thanks. My gyms and I aren't on speaking terms. All my curls top out at sixteen ounces. Thirty-two on a good day. Forty-eight if I'm at a party."

Billee snorted. "Let's see what Pher has to say."

Pher isn't actually my boss. He's more like the only member of the Order of Thirteen I trust. And I just knew he was currently in the Overworld, doing work on something important that I was sure would land in my lap as another job one day soon. Being together in the mortal realm meant we could take advantage of mortal Technology Abilities. I pressed the button on my steering wheel to activate the car's voice commands and told it to call Pher. Told. My. Car. Mortals, man. For being able to botch up just about every chance they get to treat each other with decency, at least they're on their A-game when it comes to Technology.

The phone rang three times before Pher picked up. There was a *clink* and *thunk* as he dropped it. Billee winced.

"To what do I owe this honor?" the rusty voice on the other end of the line said.

Christopher "Pher" Montjoy was old. The type of old that probably had him sitting with a bowl of popcorn in his lap as he witnessed mortals crawling out of the brush of Africa, only to send satellites out of their solar system later during his lifetime. What I'm saying is, Pher's been around the block.

"Hey, boss."

"Revelation Carver, do my ears betray me? Is that really you?"

I grimaced slightly as Billee chuckled under her breath from the passenger seat. "I hate when you use my full name."

"Which is exactly why I enjoy using it," Pher teased on the other end of the line. His voice carried through my sports coupe via at least a dozen speakers, half of which I didn't need. It seemed like just yesterday when cars didn't even have radios. "What can I do for you? I'm sure this isn't a social call, since it sounds like you're in the car."

"I am."

"Alone?"

"Nope."

"Hi Pher," Billee said, her head still stuck to her palm as we crawled three feet forward before being forced to stop again. At this rate, we might make Seattle before Billee had grandchildren.

"Hey, Sunrose!" Pher said, sounding far more delighted at her inclusion in the conversation.

"Why does she get an affectionate name and I get my formal?"

Pher chuckled. It was a rich sound. "Don't whine. You're too old for that."

"So does someone your age giving flirty nicknames to a mortal who could be your great-great-great-great-great-great—"

"Yeah, yeah. What did you need?" Pher said behind his laughter. "Some of us have work to do."

"This new target. Any tips?"

"He works at Pike Place. Sells trinkets in one of the small shops."

I was already nodding. "We've got that much. Jericho sent the tasker."

Pher mumbled something that sounded like '*ummhummm*' and then said, "Don't have too much more than what he probably told you then. Squirmy bastard, the way I understand it."

"The target or Jericho?" Sorry, I can't help myself.

"Real name is Naaman. Been a spy for the better part of the last five thousand years, so he's got experience. Not much of a fighter, but pretty resourceful. You'll have to be careful. Wiry bastard, from the way I hear it. Can talk you out of your pants before you feel the breeze on your balls."

"Gross, Pher," Billee chastised, wearing a smile.

"Apologies Sunrose. Rev brings out the worst in me."

"Sure, blame me, you Neanderthal."

"Hey, I had dear friends who were Neanderthals. They could have taught you a thing or two, Mr. Carver."

"I'm sure." The lane opened just long enough for my spirits to rise before a battery of newly pressed brakes filled my view. "What's the real reason he's so important? Why can't the demons come get him if we know where he is? Or is this runaway thing a ruse?"

The response came with a graver tone than I expected— the type of tone that shouted what you knew was only half the story. The tone that signaled a friend was trying to take care of you the best they could, even against their own interests or benefit.

"Something big is going on. Just can't quite put my finger on it. The order to nab him came from higher up, but no one is saying why."

"How high?"

"Even the Order has no answer."

I whistled. Billee had pulled her head away from the window.

"Seems odd, for a demon posing as a trinket salesman," I said, staring at the phone icon as if it'd allow me to peer into Pher's eyes. At least that was a welcome reprieve from staring at endless brake lights.

"Same thing I'm feeling, my friend. Something isn't right." Pher sighed.

"Pretend I don't understand the mortal realm," Billee said. "What does a runaway demon have to do with an unnamed angel the Order considers a traitor?"

Silence followed. Billee had Pher thinking, or debating, whether to share something we weren't supposed to know.

"Boss?" I said, bringing my head closer to the car's microphone as if it would encourage Pher to answer.

Another sigh from Pher's side. "Over an open phone line, I can't, I won't, say. Let's keep it at that. But I don't want either of you walking into a mess. Especially when that mess could be a lot messier."

"Eloquent," I said. "Now, what's going on? This isn't just any demon. I smell politics and politicians, and it ain't a fresh aroma."

"Tangled webs, lad. Tread carefully so they don't snare your feet. Word is, this Naaman might be involved with someone on our side. Someone with access they shouldn't have."

"Someone on what level?" I asked, my gaze flicking to Billee. "I'll explain later."

"Not about which level they're on in the order of angels, but that they're *outside* those levels," Pher answered with all the darkness the message deserved.

My breath caught. "You're kidding?"

"Wish I was."

"Dammit, Pher."

"I know."

"Will one of you explain what's going on since I'm in this car, on my way to Seattle, to find a demon who Heaven is demanding I help find?" Billee said with a major dose of merited attitude.

Damn, I liked her spunk.

Pher apparently did too. After he finished chuckling, he said, "I'll let you take care of that, Rev. You two, be careful. I'm serious. I don't know what you're walking into, but I know I don't like it. Don't enjoy asking you to. But it's got to be done, and there's no one better. So, get to the task and let us know what you find out about this demon and his connection to the misbehaving angel. Rev, the Order will want details on the angel. Who they are. What they're up to. Whatever is going on, it's way above my pay grade. You know when something starts that high, it's going to get a lot of eyeballs. Be careful. Be smart. But get information."

"You got it, boss."

We hung up. In the time we'd chatted with Pher, I think we moved a quarter of a mile. Like I said, I-5 is a mess. You haven't lived until you've tried it.

"Start talking, Revelation Carver," Billee said with a wide grin.

"Don't you start," I replied, and then briefed my partner on the mess the Upperworld had just involved her in.

By the time we'd reached Seattle, Billee was as educated on the ten orders of angels as I could make her, at least for now. All the way from the lamely named rank of angels, the lowest of them all, to the seraphim. The idea of the Upper-world structuring its society on classism is a nuanced discussion, but very much a reality. Trust me when I say angels are just as broken as demons, just as broken as mortals. Angels and demons have just had longer to learn how to cover it all up and present a false image.

When I finished, Billee was at it with her first question. "So Nephilim aren't angels?"

"They are."

"But you didn't include them in the order of angels."

"They are angels, just not included in our order."

"Why?"

I shrugged. "Hell if I know. There are the ten classes of angels I told you about, and then there are the Nephilim. Ugly bastards too, in their true form. Not a pleasant thing to see, trust me. But the fuckers are beautiful when they take mortal form."

"So they *don't* look like you?"

I noted Billee's chuckle with a squint and fired back. "Hey, I can't be too bad. I've been married. Can you say that?"

One eyebrow raised while the other remained flat.

"Too soon?"

Billee slugged me in the arm. "You're an ass."

"All's fair in love and war."

"Are we at war?"

"Never." I tapped the steering wheel as we pulled off the exit and onto Seattle's surface streets. "But seriously, Nephilim scare the shit out of me when they take their true form. God's hit squad, if you will. Called on to do the nastiest of the nasty work. Secret stuff. Like Heaven's CIA. End of times-type stuff. My job is to not only get information out of this demon but to keep you away from any Nephilim who might be associated with him."

"Why? Don't think I can handle myself?"

We were at a red light, so I could face Billee and let her know, in no uncertain terms, that I could be playful, but right now was not one of those times. "You're mortal, and a medical provider."

"Clinical social worker. And part-time at that, thanks to this gig."

"Fine. But what you're *not* is ready to take on a Nephilim. Fuck, few Reapers are. I can, but I've graduated from the school of ass-kicking, and I still have to be careful."

Her soft brown eyes widened. "You've fought one?"

"Even Nephilim need a spanking from time to time," I said as the light changed and we made it an entire city block before another light stopped us. At this rate, Billee's grand-kids would have grandkids before we reached Pike Place Market. "Promise me, Billee. If shit goes down in the market, you'll stay out of the way. If, and that's a big one, this Naaman is in cahoots with a Nephilim, I don't want you getting caught in the crossfire. Angelfire is no joke. Nephilim's magic is potent."

She didn't respond, but her throat bobbed as she swallowed. Good, I had her appropriately scared. I would have been too if I gave a shit about dying.

We parked up Pike Street and made our way downhill toward Elliott Bay and the market. Crowded with people, like always, this was going to be interesting. Confronting a demon with so many mortals around wasn't one of the Pro Tips in the handbook of demon wrangling. Being a weekday in January, it wasn't as crowded as it would have been during the summer. Good. I wasn't about to add a collection of mortal victims to this job. Being a Reaper and having to escort any casualties across the divide to the Veil Gate would be enough of a deterrent if I wasn't already a good guy who abhorred the thought of taking innocent lives.

We needed to buy time and let the market clear out until it

closed. So I suggested an activity literally everyone who visits the market partakes in. "Let's hit Starbucks."

"Coffee? In the afternoon?"

"Yeah, but it's the *original store*."

"Ooohhh." Billee threw her hands up, waving them in the jazz hands style of being a smartass. "The original. It's still coffee in the afternoon. I'm never going to get to sleep."

"Good. Then I can get more work out of you." Without waiting for an answer, I rounded the corner and started off on the two-block trek to the smallest coffeehouse I imagined the chain operated. The line was long, because the line is always long, but I made it up to Billee after we got our coffees. We stopped next door, and I bought her a handmade bacon cheeseburger piroshki. I think she finished hers before I had my napkins sorted.

We ate in the public park overlooking the water for as long as our expensive coffee could fool us into thinking we were warm. We rushed into the market to avoid a sudden drizzle threatening to become fat rain.

"Ah, can always rely on this place to stink," I said with a fake inhale.

"The flowers almost mask the smell of the fish," Billee said as she inspected one of about four thousand bouquets along what felt like fifteen vendors' tables. I'm being dramatic, but I swear, Pike's always feels like it has more flowers than all the fields in Holland combined.

I accidentally sniffed. My nose sucked in the distinct smell of Alaskan halibut and salmon. Big mistake. I hate fish. I hate anything that comes out of the sea. The sea is gross. With seven billion mortals flushing, literally, their crap into its waters, why in the world would I ever eat anything that spends its life swimming in mortal piss and shit?

"Come on, let's stroll by this demon's shop and get a lay of the land," I said, and we headed downstairs.

Pike Place is huge. Somewhere on the top side of five

hundred shops and stalls of various sizes and offerings have turned the market into a multi-storied maze. I'm not much of a shopper, but if you need it, the market probably has it. Odd shops. Hip shops. Unique shops. A smorgasbord of capitalism for any eye, discerning or not. Naaman's shop was none of the above. He sold sports memorabilia, all Seattle teams, of course.

We passed, moving on to the shop across the aisle that sold incense. The tight confines wreaked with a combination of pungent aromas I was sure smelled pleasant and light on their own, but when combined with the other four thousand in the store, did a number on my olfactory receptors.

Billee seemed to enjoy the combo of incense as much as I enjoyed songs about Alabama.

"What time is it?"

She checked. "Almost six."

"Good. He's got to be closing up soon."

The back of her hand was at her nose. "Can we wait in another shop? I'd take fish over this."

"You would." I nodded toward the exit. "Let's head to the left. That'll force him to the right, just in case he picks up on our presence. That way, I can corner him out of eyesight. The other way, and we might run into problems."

"Got it."

Once we were back into fresh air, we both breathed deeply.

"I'd forgotten how much of an experience this place can be," Billee said, wiggling her nose.

Lights started blinking out as shops without customers got an early start to their evening. That worked to our advantage.

Naaman kept his shop open until the last minute. The crowd had evaporated. Tired incense, fish, and trinket sellers said goodnight to each other or simply ignored the people they spent nine or ten hours around each day. As quiet settled over the market, the thin demon stepped out. Naaman locked the door to his shop, giving tight smiles to those who wished him well, but not verbally responding to any of them.

"Friendly," Billee said as we drifted toward a corner we could use as a shield.

"Looks pretentious."

She pulled his arms, angling them like she was trying to scratch her sides. Her lips pushed out. "Oh, strong fighter knows big word."

I hoped she hadn't noticed, but I put myself between her and the demon while she was picking on me. If anything went down without warning, Billee was going to get a shoulder shove from me that would send her into the corner. A bruise might become her new accouterment, but she'd be alive to complain about it afterward.

Naaman didn't seem to notice us in the ever-thinning trickle of people emptying from the market. His back to us, he made his way out into the night. He turned left at the corner.

I bolted forward, shooting the loudest message I dared to my partner. "Stay behind. Not too close. I'm going to pinch him in the sky bridge."

From ahead, Naaman yelped.

The chase was on.

Naaman glanced over his shoulder. A thin demon, he parted his short hair to the side, combing it over in that style that shouted to the world, 'hi, I work in a bank.' He wore black-rimmed glasses to complement his hair color. In that fraction of a second, I noticed his nose was almost as wide as his mouth. Don't ask me why I picked up on that; just accept that I've got a weird attention to detail.

Naaman spirited away. The corner only hid him for a second.

I chased, my boots slapping against the cool tile. Whoever Naaman really was, he either was comparatively inexperienced, or he wasn't smart. The slick shoes he wore probably cost as much as my rent, but they wouldn't help him outrace me unless he had a super secret Ability that blessed him with lightning speed.

Twenty yards proved that wasn't the case.

Naaman was halfway across the sky bridge when I tackled him.

We tumbled to the floor and rolled against the wall. The Plexiglas window rattled.

"Billee, make sure no one comes down here from the market," I shouted as I tried to wrap Naaman in a chokehold. He might have been thin, but he was wiry.

"What about the parking garage?"

"Don't worry," I groaned. "More eyes in the market."

Naaman threw an elbow. All of about a hundred and forty pounds, the demon was gifted with a lot of bone, and he knew how to use it. It connected, hard and sharp, and I suddenly found that my heavy breaths had been a blessing. Easy to be enlightened when you can't breathe at all.

The demon was on his feet and dashing down the sky bridge toward the parking garage. Billee zipped past me.

I tried to cry out a warning, but a few things stopped me. One, I couldn't breathe. Two, even if I could, who was I fooling? Billee wouldn't listen, anyway.

By the time I was on my feet, both Billee and Naaman wrapped around the corner and disappeared. Their echoes were absent of squealing car tires.

The sky bridge was isolated at this time of night, but I had the unnerving suspicion someone was watching this chase. I pushed the worry from my mind. Snatching Naaman was the priority. Creepers could be dealt with later.

When I caught up, they were approaching the edge of the garage. Without a pause, Naaman jumped over the lip of the wall, disappearing as he fell twenty feet to the ground.

Billee skidded up against the concrete barrier, bending

over to look down before spinning in my direction and giving me a helpless shrug.

Leaping atop the wall, I looked for the demon. He'd obviously hit a branch of the neighboring tree on his way down, because it, freshly broken, lay next to him on the ground.

Before I could worry about getting the answers the Thirteen needed, the demon rolled onto his back. I knew I was in trouble when I saw his hands. His palms were the color of the sun, just about a billion times dimmer. Bright enough to blind me, I fell back off the wall and into Billee. It turned out to be a good thing.

I fell and knocked her down. The two feet of concrete wall I'd been standing on had stopped Naaman's Fire spell. Well, most of it. Chunks of concrete were blown into the sky and rained down. Thankfully, the angle of his spell carried the carnage of broken wall over us. Not so fortunate for the very expensive electric car three parking spots away, but the person who could afford that could probably afford another. Right now, I had bigger worries.

"Stay here," I said to my partner and pulled Maggie, my trusty Ruger, from my duster. There's a neat slip pocket I had custom-made for the liner so the gun doesn't jostle or jiggle during my many escapades. I hate holsters. People who wear guns on their hips look like douches. As I get older, my resolve to never be a douche grows firmer.

As a Reaper, I prefer using contemporary weapons to tap into my Angelfire. I've found it keeps things from getting dull, and trust me, this pistol makes me far more nimble than the old days when I'd use a rifle or spear to direct my fire. Sure beats the crossbow I used during the mortal medieval period. And I don't even need bullets. Angelfire fed this puppy.

On my feet, I dashed to the wall that now featured a new asymmetrical design of jagged concrete in the form of a lopsided 'W.'

Naaman was trying to get to his feet, which kept slipping out underneath him. I raised the pistol.

Across the street, on the rooftop of an apartment, something shifted in the dying light. I couldn't get a glimpse but hoped I hadn't just put myself on the 'Most Wanted' list. Distracted, I rushed my shot before Naaman could escape and do more damage.

Aim.

Squeeze.

Boom.

The beam of Angelfire that left the muzzle was not pretty, but once set in motion, there wasn't anything I could do to control or stop it. The beam expanded as it bore down on the demon.

My aim is excellent.

I didn't even have time to curse when my white bolt of pure angelic magic tore through Naaman's leg, ripping it off and sending it spinning across the street. A semi ran over it just before it reached the other side, splattering it against the guardrail.

"Fuck."

Leaping over the wall to the ground, I landed hard. The ground was hard this time of year. Pain shot through my knees to my hips. I'd pay for that later.

Naaman was trying to shuffle back along the grass. What remained of his leg was a mess. I had to pull my eyes away, or I'd throw up all over him.

"Shouldn't have run."

Naaman cough-snorted. I think it was supposed to sound cocky and rebellious, but it came off sounding sad. "Fucking angels, man. I swear."

"Didn't have to end this way." I kneeled in the grass next to him, looking up and down the street for anyone who might cause trouble for two immortal creatures having a small, very significant chit-chat.

Naaman spit. A glob of bloody saliva landed on my duster.

I grabbed the demon by his collared shirt and pulled him close enough to tell he'd eaten a bag of chips during his shift. "Why is the Upperworld interested in you?"

"I don't know, man. Ask them yourself. I don't make a habit of talking to your kind."

His teeth were becoming pinker by the second. He wasn't long for this world or the Underworld. The mortal realm is the only place angels and demons can be killed, and right now, this demon was about to slip out of my grasp.

In my periphery along the rooftop of the apartments, a blotch of the sky, about the size of an adult, shifted. I missed spotting them again. We had to get out of here.

"Listen, it's really shitty that your last few minutes are going to be spent bleeding out on this stretch of grass. I feel bad. But my bosses think you're a big shot who's working with an angel, and that's got everyone scared. You know what our kinds do when they scare each other. Let's not kick off something neither one of us could stop on our best day, okay?"

"I'm not telling you anything, angel," he said, coughing up a few specks of blood.

I lowered him back to the grass and straightened his collar. "My bosses know your name. What do you think happens when I return without information? We've got spies in the Underworld. They'll make a little visit to your family and, *voila*, no more family. This doesn't end here. You got yourself on the wrong side of us. Give me something to satiate those who pay me so they'll leave your family alone, okay? Sound fair?"

Naaman's mouth opened, forming a circle that quivered. When he spoke, his voice was noticeably weaker. "Wasn't working with an angel, asshole. I was..." He took a big breath. "Was spying."

"Why?"

Naaman pinched his eyes closed and inhaled sharply.

"Come on, man. I need to know or I can't help."

Loud, hurried steps announced Billee's approach. How did someone so small make so much noise? I didn't want her to see the end of this demon's life for more than a few reasons. Might as well get it over with.

Another smirk exposing teeth becoming pinker with blood. Another wince. The demon didn't have long.

"Come on, spill it. Why were you spying on an angel? Who?"

Cough. "You angels, man. So busy worrying about us you don't even realize your house is a mess. One of yours is here. Was spying..." Wheeze. "Be... because we suspect they stole one of your Bowls."

In that second, Seattle disappeared. If the demon was telling the truth, the world had just changed. The shit storms of shit storms had just been kicked up. "How sure are your kind about that?"

"Enough to have me spying on angels in Seattle for the past two months." A round of coughing and blood spitting followed.

"Give me a name. A description."

"No. Name. Don't even have a description."

Billee was over him, turning away as soon as she looked at his leg.

"How do you spy on someone without a name or description? Don't be a dumba—"

"No description because... they don't... come in their true form."

He couldn't mean—. But he could, and it would make sense. It also may explain the sense I had that we were being watched.

"This one... took the form of... a Penumbra Man."

Son of a biscuit. He meant it.

"Better... sort... yourselves... *angel*..." The last word came out in a raspy death exhale.

Pressing a fist into the ground, I pushed myself to a standing position. "Might want to back away, Billee."

"Why?"

Naaman started convulsing.

"Back up, Billee."

A white haze formed about the demon's corpse, swelling to engulf him. Brighter lines arced across the surface of the energy swell. They zipped and arced, arced and raced over and back again.

"I hate this part," I said, just as the lines of energy coalesced at the center mass of Naaman. I could no longer see the demon, which was a good thing because the violent shaking of a corpse is a tad bit unsettling. The energy brightened until his body could no longer hold his immortal spirit. The bolt took me in the chest, as it always does. I felt myself arc. The bolt of immortal life energy flowing from Naaman into me was stronger than I expected.

Who knew he could pack such a wallop? In my younger days, he might have knocked me clean off my feet and into the street. I was much stronger—and jaded—now. Another benefit of thousands of years of consuming immortal energy against my will.

When it was over, I fell forward into the grass beside Naaman. Rolling onto my back, I held up my hand to let Billee know I was okay. She didn't listen.

Falling to her knees, she took my hand in her tiny one.

"Firm grip," I said through a wheeze. "Mind letting up?"

To my side, faint wisps of ash-sized flakes of what remained of Naaman's body whipped through the air. Sure enough, I rolled to my side to be greeted by the sight of thousands of swirling white specks. Atop the apartments, the night no longer shifted. Whoever or whatever I'd caught up there was gone now.

"Wha—what's that? What happened?" Billee asked, opening her palms at the white specks.

"What's left of the demon."

"Wha—how?"

How could I tell her about the eternal exchange of energy between all life forms? Not just flora and fauna, but mortals and immortals. How could I tell this kind, sweet, caustically funny twenty-eight—or twenty-nine-year-old that when she died, her energy would go back into the All after she crossed through the Veil Gate? How could I possibly tell her what really happens when angel assassins like me absorb the energy of immortals we kill?

I couldn't.

So, instead, I just said, "Looks like you're stuck with me even longer." I squeezed her hand. "Now, help me up."

3

COFFEE, BAGELS, AND THE END OF THE WORLD

"I'M WAY OVER MY HEAD, REV."

Billee wasn't wrong. Her head was under troubled waters. Way down. If what Naaman said was even half true, forget just Houston. We all had a problem. A Nephilim shifting into the form of a Penumbra Man, skulking about the Overworld, among mortals, and possibly stealing one of Yahweh's seven sacred Bowls?

The next time I saw the Order of Thirteen, I was asking for a pay raise.

Billee flicked her hand. It shook. "And… that thing that… happened." She stopped, looking around to see if anyone in the diner set in a 1950s motif was listening. "What *was* that?"

I placed my hand over her coffee. Probably not hygienic, but I cared. "Might want to lay off the caffeine. At least until we get through today."

Billee dropped her hand in her lap.

"Reaper assassins absorb the energy of other immortals we kill. Even if they're demons. An immortal is an immortal. We don't get a choice. When we do, their energy adds to our own. Which means, lucky me, I get to live even longer now."

"Y—you don't want to live longer?" Billee cast her head down, almost speaking into her chest. "Why not?"

"You're young. You'll understand one day. When the aches and pains come. When it takes longer to get out of bed for your coffee than to grind the beans by hand and slow-drip them, you'll understand. When you've seen countless mortal civilizations come and go, witnessed the destruction they wreak upon one another so they can claim a plot of land or some resource that won't matter in a few decades, you'll understand. When you escort those who killed in wars and humanitarian conflicts to—" I almost slipped and told her the truth—"to what waits on the other side, you'll understand. More of this isn't just more of the same. It's, well, for lack of a better way to say it, soul-sucking. After doing it as long as I have, I'm comfortable with my perspective." I shook my head. "I'm at peace with it. They say you only have one life to live, and that's true. But a never-ending life is hell, Billee."

"I… I didn't know. I'm sorry."

"Don't be. You aren't responsible for the expectations put on us." My hand went from protectively hovering over her coffee to her hand she'd left resting on the black-and-white checkered table top. "And you're more than capable of handling the duties you've been unfairly assigned."

Billee's eyes flickered like someone had just poked her in the ribs a little too hard. I let her be. After a moment, she broke the silence. "I don't understand."

"Understand what?"

"Why me? Why was I chosen as your familiar?"

I sat back. The very uncomfortable chair creaked as my weight shifted. A slight sound, but a reminder that everything in creation has a terminal point. "Politics."

A man drifted by, carefully balancing a small laptop, tall coffee, and a bagel piled with meat and cheese. Before I could shut it down, my third eye confirmed his end was near. By next summer, his name would be entered in the Book of

Planes, the eternal list of names of all, mortal and immortal, who had ever lived across all planes of existence. What a shame. In terrible shape? Sure. Still, he looked so young.

Billee had pulled the corner of her bottom lip into her mouth, biting down hard enough to lighten the skin. "That's not an answer."

"It is. Just a shitty one."

That pale pink lip popped out and twitched in a sad smile. "You're going to have to clean up your language before you meet my mother. She'll pin you down if she has to so she can wash your mouth out with soap. She's old-school like that."

"Don't wait around for me to learn new behaviors." I snapped my head away from the walking heart attack as he set his laptop down on an empty table. His bagel and coffee threatened to spill out of his other hand. The man at the next table stopped tapping his foot to the Elvis Presley song played at a respectful volume to lean over and offer help should either the food or drink topple. Though at least two decades older than heart attack man, the kind bystander would live three decades longer. I just off my third eye before it picked up on anyone else's story. "Wait, are we to the point of meeting each other's parents? I didn't realize I meant that much to you. You'll have to earn your wings to meet mine. Sadly, that's not a thing that happens, but I'm sure I can sneak you in."

She swatted my arm playfully. "Is that what it is? Was I selected because…" Her swatting hand lifted from my arm, a single finger extended, which she wagged between herself and me.

I laughed. "Because we're supposed to be something?"

Billee sat up straight. "Well, now I feel like a fool. I didn't think it was such an odd question. Plus, you're the one winning in that exchange. A nice, intelligent, young, healthy woman to help you feel younger. I'm the one who has to settle for the sugar daddy, just…" Her gaze slowly traveled up and down the parts of my upper torso that weren't blocked by the table between us "...without the sugar."

"I paid for your coffee."

"Whoa, big spender," she said with a wink and a wave of hands. "I'll reserve my comments until I see my Jaguar."

"Oh, I've got bad news for you, then."

"Hmmm, that's what I figured." She shifted in the chair, scooting closer. "So what was it that got me stuck with you, taken away from my full-time job and my clients, to sit around bars and coffee shops and watch for supernatural creatures?"

"Fu—hell if I know," I answered with a shrug. "The Order of Thirteen makes the matches. We're not involved. We used to be, but that changed a while ago."

"Why? Favoritism? Or did you pervy old men always match yourselves up with hot young mortals?"

"Guilty."

"Gross."

A kid on a skateboard flew across the front of the store, forcing an older couple to dart out of his way. The husband shouted something I couldn't hear on this side of the glass and shook his fist at the twat. He needn't worry; in five minutes the kid was going to take a rail, slip and tumble down a set of stairs, and dislocate his elbow. Sometimes karma wasn't a bitch.

"I'm kidding. Reapers used to make their own matches. It fell under one office. A council, of sorts, I guess. They were called The Ministry, and they handled administrative stuff."

"What happened? Why did they give it up? It seems Reapers would want to keep the responsibility of assigning familiars to their personnel, or whatever you call each other."

"Usually, asshole. Jackass. Asswad. Take your pick."

Billee scrunched her eyes. "Hilarious."

"That's my fault. I disbanded The Ministry about... hell, I

can't remember anymore. Maybe four hundred years ago now."

"Wait. What? You?"

"I'm sort of a big deal."

"More than in your own head?"

"Ha, ha. No, in the Upperworld too. I'm the most senior Reaper. The Minister."

Billee's eyebrows raised, the corners of her mouth turning down as her bottom lip punched up over her top. "Impressive."

"Not really. Just means an angel or rogue demon hasn't killed me yet. But yeah, I disbanded them when the politics of it got to be too much. The Order said they'd take care of the familiar assignments until I could get a better handle on the Reapers."

"And you never did?"

"Never bothered." I raised the cup to my lips, steamy heat brushing up my cheeks as I savored the sweet taste of what was really nothing more than liquid sugar.

"Whoa, I cannot believe I'm sitting here, the property of the head honcho Reaper."

My head tipped toward my steaming mug. I stopped mid-sip and shot her a look.

"What? Am I wrong?" Billee asked. Her question held a slight laugh, but there was a billboard-sized bit of seriousness in her tone.

"You're not property, Billee." I set my coffee down, feeling the conversation turning more serious than we could settle over a single cup. This was a conversation that required one of my master-chef meals.

"Maybe not, but what am I? We're together half the time I'm not in my office. I'm with you more than I am my own girlfriends and boyfriends."

"You don't have significant others."

"Because I'm with you all the time," she said with a smirk.

"We do these stakeouts, or whatever you call them. You have me running down to city hall to see how far into people's lives I can pry. I'm your free pass to live in this realm."

"Pretty much sums it up, but that doesn't mean I don't value you and what you do for my bosses. What you do for me. But you're not property. Please don't think that. If I could break that contract today, I would. Especially now."

"Why? Because of what happened in Seattle?"

I nodded. How many more centuries had I added to my life by absorbing Naaman's energy? "This is serious business."

"Which is exactly why I don't feel like I'm ready, or capable of doing this job." Billee's mouth hung open as she looked out the window that reached from floor to ceiling. Outside, a gray day stared back, not providing answers. "You know, when you met me, I thought this was a joke."

"Most do."

The levity of the conversation was gone faster than the heart-attack man's bagel. "I honestly thought you were an old creep hitting on me." She put her elbow on the checkered table and dangled her arm. Her eyes fell on the bracelet, hanging from her thin wrist. My throat swelled. "I mean, who gives a woman a gift like this the first time they meet unless they want to sell something I'm not buying?"

"Someone with a disgusting job to do and no choice."

"Making sure I also didn't have a choice."

There was no response, no defense, I could give. My partner had brought up an ugly aspect of being a Reaper. When a mortal is assigned as our familiar, we make first contact and give them a gift. Gifts that, once given, cannot be ungiven. They are as much a part of the mortal as their own skin. One, until they or the Reaper die. Some Reapers sneak the gift into the mortal's home or their desk or use even worse ways to ensure the mortal contacts the trinket. Once, I fired a Reaper after discovering she had used someone's child to 'bring daddy a new watch.' The kid couldn't have been five years old. I'm not sure where she was working now, but I hoped it was spending eternity cleaning toilets.

"I remember that day," I mumbled, not afraid to let my shame show. An eternal life as a slave to the Upperworld's management team helped me feel comfortable feeling like shit about the things I'd done. I shook my head. "When I handed you the box, there was a fraction of a second I wanted to shout and slap it out of your hands before it connected with you. Ageist. Sexist. I don't know. But you opened your door and looked so… you had, *have*, a lot going for you, Billee. I didn't want to ruin that."

"But you let the bracelet bond us, anyway." Ice was warmer than her comment.

"I have a job to do. *We* have a job to do. An important one."

"Reapers are just supposed to escort the dying to Heaven. They're not supposed to chase demonic spies through the damn market. Right?"

Her expression twisted. A thick vein in her neck bulged like a blocked waterline.

"Reapers do more than escort duty," I said in a low voice, calmly and slowly. I had warned her before that a time would come when she might have to help with dangerous jobs. A warning I should have repeated more often.

"You don't say," she said, that vein still thick, still swelling. "Not only are we chasing a demon who can jump off garages without getting hurt, but we're spying on another demon who—" she caught herself, lowering her voice—"who might be the next Lucifer. Now, a Penumbra Man and something to do with one of God's Bowls. I'm not exactly brushed up on my biblical studies, but that doesn't sound like a good thing. For anyone." She sat back against her chair hard enough that she wobbled slightly. Crossing her arms, she said, "I'm not made for this."

I wanted to get up, cross the table to her side, wrap my

shoulder around her and quietly support her while she processed everything. But that felt too 1412, so I just said, "You're exactly what you need to be. Look at it this way. Before long, my bosses will put us in some morally ambiguous situation where you'll feel you lose no matter which way we decide to go."

"Oh, joy."

"And there's no 'get out' clause. You're a familiar for life. Fun stuff, huh? Could be worse. You could be stuck doing something you hate for tens of thousands of years."

She flared her nose and sat a little straighter. "So, how deep is the shit with this Bowl?"

"Oh, swearing now, are we?" I asked with a wink.

She gave me a deadpan look.

Elvis Presley gave way to The Pretenders singing about a great pretender.

I cleared my throat. "Well, it's bad. If it's true. That's key. We don't know for sure. That could have been the ravings of a demon struggling to face his own demise. I reported to the Order. They're doing what they always do, and we keep our ears to the ground and eyes open. A rogue angel is bad. It being a Nephilim is really bad."

"That's what I don't get," she said, leaning on her elbow and tipping a finger in my direction as if I had something to do with this. "What does a rogue angel have to do with a Penumbra Man or these Bowls."

"Nephilim do what the hell they want, and that includes shifting when they come to the Overworld. They get away with a lot." I felt so, so tired of explaining the order of Nephilim. Not at Billee's need to know, but at Billee being yet another familiar—my three hundred and fifteenth—I needed to have this discussion with. "They were the first of the angels created at the forming of the Upperworld from the All. A select few administrators, I guess you'd call them, were created at the inception of what we understand to be our universe, but that was before there were Upper and Under-worlds. That's when it got fun. Being the oldest, they're far different from the rest of us. And, honestly, they're assholes."

"So they get benefits the rest of you don't? Like being able to come to Earth whenever they want, doing whatever they want? Like this traitor with the Bowl?"

I shook my head. "No. Well, they're not supposed to, but that falls back to my opinion of what they are."

"Assholes."

"You're catching on. In theory, they're supposed to abide by all the rules of the Upperworld. They're not supposed to come here without permission. Even when they get it, the rules are clear about them not wandering around all willy-nilly. That would break some minds, I promise."

"Which is why they shift?"

"They certainly can't blend in like the rest of us."

"I've noticed. That Ezekial is a little hottie."

"He's way too old for you, and he's a demon." She didn't need the reminder, but I wouldn't pass up the opportunity to take a dig at a demon, either. "So, yeah, Nephilim shift to fit in."

"Into what? I mean, I've heard stories about Penumbra Man, but I thought that was just an urban legend."

"Penumbra Man. Bigfoot. Werewolves. Vampires. Bogman. Shadow people. Boogieman. You name it. If there's an urban legend or folklore, you know, I'll bet a Nephilim is involved."

With each famous creature I named, Billee's eyes widened. Now, they were about the size of the coffee spoon's head.

Did I mention I hate this job? Having to rock someone's world is never fun.

Since I was on a roll shattering Billee's worldview, I continued, "The Bowl is the worst part."

"Worse than a recalcitrant angel walking freely around the world in monster form?"

"Way worse."

"Like, how worse?"

I clicked my tongue. "You need to be a better Christian and learn your Bible."

"You need to mind your own business and answer the question."

Dishes clinked from the kitchen just under the racket of cooks shouting "order up" every ten seconds. Bacon grease hung in the air.

"Short version," I said, regrettably watching my coffee get colder, "there are seven Bowls of Yahweh's wrath. Each contains a plague. If you believe the Bible's Book of Revelation, seven angels protect the seven Bowls. But that's not true. They're kept in the Safe in the Upperworld. Imagine something the size of a large city, filled with magic beyond your comprehension, that mutates and reacts to any illegal entrant's mind, confusing them and, usually, leading to their death. The Bowls are heavily protected because they're that important. Yahweh has the power to use the Bowls as He or She sees fit to reset the Balance in the Overworld." Her mouth opened. Another question was coming. I waved it away. "We'll get to that another time. Not important right now. The missing Bowl is. *If* a Nephilim got their grubby paws on a Bowl, that means the Upperworld has a shit-ton of problems. The Safe isn't so safe, meaning the other six Bowls could also be vulnerable. Bad enough someone might have one Bowl, but if they could also get to the other six… Yikes."

"This reset? Can only God use the Bowl to reset this Balance or whatever?"

"I don't know."

Billee whistled quietly. It wasn't a cheerful sound. "Heaven has their hands full."

I picked up my coffee and took a long swig now that it was room temperature. I set it down a little too hard, and it *thunked* on the table. "Something tells me we will too. Be ready."

"Demons. Secreted angels. Nephilim. Penumbra Man and Bigfoot. Every day with you feels like a revelation... Rev." She paused, her lips twitching. "See what I did there?"

"Not funny."

"What other joyful monsters does this book of yours in the Bible talk about? I want to be prepared to do the best job I can if I have to deal with them." Her twitching lips now spread into a smirking behind her coffee mug.

"Careful what you ask for. You just might get it."

4

MANAGEMENT 101

My Overworld home isn't much to gawk over. It's a townhouse apartment in downtown Olympia. Top-floor, baby. Pet and partner-free, though I honestly miss having a dog to come home to. They have a tendency to make you feel important in a way that doesn't feel slimy. So different from how those in life who need something make me feel.

Olympia may be the state capital, but it's not an impressive city. It's a tiny place populated by big dreamers. My building only has five stories above the parking garage, and yet I can still look out over all of downtown. The apartment is big, thanks to hefty Upperworld paydays and a sweet deal that allowed me to lock in a lease for longer than my management company will be in business, according to my third eye. I also rented the neighboring units on each side because I like my privacy, and I need the space for things such as Rifts and practicing cool assassination moves.

The Upperworld is connected to the mortal realm. Anywhere, any time, someone who knows how and has the ability, can open a Rift and step into Heaven from this realm or vice versa. Us angels are privileged. Most of the world would fall over themselves in joy if they knew how many of us were neighbors or the guy seated at the next table in a restaurant. Mortals think they know what angels are about. Trust me, they're wrong. If they knew about Reaper angels… best to leave that book closed.

Angels do things like rent three apartments when we barely use the one we live in, so we can hold meetings, do reconnaissance on targets, and open Rifts to cross over into the Upperworld. Which I was about to do because, even when you're the Reaper Minister, there's always another staff meeting to conduct.

Snapping my fingers at the bare, open room in my second apartment, the air itself rippled like small shimmers in a jostled bowl of water. Same, just shinier.

The ripple stretched horizontally until it was five feet across. As slow as time passes when you're broke and waiting for payday, the Rift spread toward the ceiling and floor. Once formed, a blazing white border framed the Rift, connecting from the bottom, up along the sides, to the top. The border sizzled. Behind the shimmering air, a familiar place came into view, distorted but recognizable.

"Here we go," I groaned to no one in particular, and stepped through into the realm of angels.

Reaperworld, as I affectionately call this meeting room shoved off into the corner of the Eighth Level of the Upperworld, is sparse and dark. An oak table, thirty feet long and obnoxiously wide, ran along the center of the room. Painted portraits of historically significant Ministers interrupted the wood paneling, dark enough to match my feelings over yet another staff meeting, every ten feet. Small mahogany tables, complete with deeply carved cherubim faces, were spaced along the walls. A coffee pot, and far too many cups too small to enjoy a rich brew, topped one. Tea dominated another. Finger foods at a third. The last, reserved for fruits. It was the least-attended table of the bunch. Get it, bunch? Fruit? Nevermind.

"Rev, nice to see you," Anapheil Icogto, a politician on the rise who was one of the Upperworld's best Reapers, said when I stepped through the Rift.

"Hey." I gave her a smile I hoped disarmed her suspicions. She always made me feel like I'd done something wrong. "Where is everyone?"

Currently, six Reapers milled around the long room between picking at the spread of food. Inian and Herchel sat at the meeting table. Inian was rolling her fingertips on the wood, making a very rhythmic *dum-dum-dum-dum* beat. Herchel's head was connected to his crossed forearms. In between his snores, I swore he stopped breathing.

"They'll be here soon," Anapheil said, snapping off the corner of a white cracker with her perfectly aligned teeth, pushing up her glasses with the back of her hand. "You're a little early. Which is a surprise."

"I was bored."

"Not enough to do? I can share a portion of my assignments with you."

Her comment stopped me in mid-stride. "I told them to not load on you. Are they?"

She tipped her head, but it snapped right back into a vertical position. Always careful to present the correct image, this one. The cracker stayed near her mouth. "I've had less dull times. What about you?"

"Same." I nodded to the tea table. "I'm going to get a drink before the meeting. Seems we might have more to discuss than I thought."

She moved off to her spot. I patted Inian on the shoulder as I passed and flicked Herchel on the earlobe. He shot straight up and looked at Inian with a mixture of confusion and irritation.

She rolled her eyes and smiled. "Hi, Grim. How's it hanging?"

The Reapers had taken to calling me "Grim" a century or

two ago when the toils of the job really started getting to me. I didn't have the energy or inclination to live up to the moniker, then or now. 'Fake it 'til you make it' was the principle to live by in Reaperworld. At least everyone pulled back on the unwanted nickname over the past decade.

If I didn't know the freckled redhead, I would have checked with Herchel to make sure I heard correctly. But I knew the grief she enjoyed giving to the older Reapers, especially the men. I appreciated Inian.

By the time I'd made a cup of tea, stolen a handful of crackers, and taken my seat, the room was filling with arrivals as another fifty Reapers joined.

"Take your seats," I said as I stood at the head of the table. "We've got a lot to get to, and I don't feel like being here all day. I'm sure you don't either."

Muted agreement that sounded a lot like grumbling greeted the comment. When you've attended thousands of staff meetings, it's hard to not feel that way. I wanted to get to the bottom of a few things quickly because none of us had time to waste. As the Minister, it was my responsibility to make their jobs as smooth as possible.

"None," Diniel Amok said over his shoulder while piling grapes onto his silver plate. Somehow, he managed to not spill the coffee pinned between his ribs and elbow. A straight-shooter, Diniel was a wonderful vector whenever I worried about how well I was performing. As soft and cuddling as a netted bag of razors. "Too many assignments."

"You too?" I asked him but watched the faces of the fifty-plus around the table. Judging by their reactions, they were all being heavily taxed by the Order. "How many?"

"Right now?" he said as he shuffled to his seat, his head cast down at each careful step his load required. "Got my fiftieth just before coming to the meeting."

"I got five cases this morning," Yesil Gnobr said from the

end corner of the table. "I've done three... four hundred escorts this week."

More heads bobbed.

Around the room, they gave me a quick run-down of what they were balancing. Being a Reaper is not an easy job. No one ever said it was, but things were getting out of hand.

On average, just shy of a hundred and eighty thousand people die every day around the Overworld. That's a lot of work, and you might wonder how Reapers handle escorting so many mortals to what awaits them after death. That's where The Interlude comes into play. It's a nifty love child of the All, the everything. In the same family as matter and anti-matter, life and death, cells, photons, neutrinos, quarks, and everything else in existence. Detectable and undetectable. Everywhere. I could explain further, but even I don't under-stand the All, and I've been around the block. The Interlude is the complete and utter stoppage of time that allows us to escort mortals to the Veil Gate. When it's activated, nothing outside the reality of the Reaper and the newly deceased mortal changes, moves, alters state, or breathes. Less the blink of an eye for everyone else. When you look into the—usually —frightened eyes of a mortal who doesn't understand what happened or what is about to come, the last thing Reapers need is to be rushed because there's another scroll with yet another name waiting. The Interlude is, if you'll forgive me for the insensitive term, a lifesaver.

"The scrolls never stop coming," Jenniseler Handido said, raising her hand. Always polite, that one.

"We need help, Rev," Anapheil said, obviously deciding now was a good time to jump in.

I raised my hand, trying to tally the number of escort duties this room was going to accomplish just today. It was too high, and I'm not that good at math. Finally, I repeated the same message I'd delivered to these poor bastards for the past few hundred years as mortals kept spitting out offspring like free t-shirts from an air gun at sporting events. "I know."

"It has to stop. I want to have a life. At least something that passes as a social life," Inian said. "Do you know how many dates I've lost out on because of this job? A girl's got to get laid."

That received the loudest agreement of anything to come out of a staff meeting in ages. I empathized. The last woman I touched divorced me a while ago.

"It doesn't help that the mortals' Technology Abilities keep getting stronger," Tanlis Jolt said with a flick of his hand. "Less believe in us each day. Those stupid smartphones, I tell you. They'll be the downfall of our kind."

Tanlis is a little old-school. The problem? He wasn't wrong. As mortal Technology Ability improved and propagated, belief dwindled. As it did, so did the level of fear mortals had about seeing 'the Reaper.' Not that long ago, the mere mention of the word Reaper would have grandmas clutching their pearls. We had stories, man. Now, we're lucky if some jack-wagon in his mother's basement isn't drawing comical cartoons with us as the punchline. Being the butt of jokes and an interesting side-note of lore wasn't exactly my proudest accomplishment as Minister, but there were only so many fires I could put out before my bucket of holy water ran dry.

That's the irony, isn't it? If I had more time, I'd be able to work with the Order to devise a way to increase our numbers again—not that I was looking to send mortals back to Stone Age-level fear and understanding of their world, to be clear. But the assignments never stopped coming, mortals never stopped dying, I never got more time, and the number of Reapers kept diminishing. The result was more and more work and less time to do the things to alleviate the demands.

This was my mess to manage, and I had to fake it until I made it.

"We'll figure out a way to deal with everything, but right now, I need to know what everyone is seeing out there. We've got a few things I'm worried about."

"The Order is taxing us," Tanlis started.

My hand shot up, cutting him off. "*Besides* the Order. Listen, they're not looking to do us any favors. They've got their priorities and they need us to perform. Worry about performing, and I'll worry about the Order."

The problem with having fifty Reapers around a ridiculously long table is that when someone grumbles something smartass under their breath, drawing snickers from other smartasses, it's hard to tell who started the smartassery. I did my best to ignore the latest example.

"Again, what are we seeing?" I took my seat.

The same tried-and-true problems our crew had seen for millennia were tossed around.

"Lots of disappearances," Jenniseler said. "Up and down the west coast."

"East coast too," Diniel said.

Yesil nodded. "We're seeing it in the Far East as well, I'm afraid."

In fact, everyone at the table did.

"Try to get numbers together for the next meeting," I said after it became obvious the disappearances were a concerning trend. "I'll need to know exactly what's going on before I talk to Cascade. I'm sure the Guardian Angels Minister has better things to do with her time. To the best of our abilities, let's gauge the extent of the disappearances. No stone unturned, folks. What else?"

Anapheil was the one to hit the target. "Tacoma has an outbreak. I have concerns it might be a new virus." She tapped her finger on the table, her steady gaze rotating around the room to ensure she had everyone's attention. "From what I'm seeing, remember, this is my opinion based on initial observations, it's not widespread. At least not yet."

"What sort of disease?" Inian asked.

"Skin irritations."

"Well, that doesn't sound bad at all," Herchel said.

"That don't go away," Anapheil said forcefully at being interrupted. "It starts as a slight irritation that spreads. Topically. Usually on mortals' cheeks and necks. But then the irritation worsens, usually after forty-eight to seventy-two hours, and becomes these..." She finally released everyone from the steely gaze and flicked her hand over and over, her mouth turning down. "Into unsightly sores."

The room stilled.

The crew might not understand what she had just revealed, but I sure did, and I'm not the type of leader—and I use that term loosely—to keep information from anyone I feel needs it.

I cupped my hands, staring into my palms. "We might have a big problem."

"What kind of problem?" Anapheil asked.

"A Bowl might be in play," I said, not enjoying having to deliver the news, and knowing no better way to do it. This kind of shit isn't in the Management 101 handbooks, folks.

"What?" Herchel said, suddenly sounding awake.

Anapheil's voice held an icy tone. "Rev, that can't be. The Bowls are in the Safe."

"Maybe," I said, returning my gaze to my palms. "Maybe not. Either way, it's not a risk I'm willing to take. We need to keep our eyes and ears open. We all know what this could mean."

Inian's mouth bobbed up and sound, yet not a snarky word of hers flopped out. Not even inappropriate jokes about needing sexy time.

I gave the crew a shortened version of what Naaman told me. You could have heard a fairy's wings flap when I finished.

"Nephilim," Herchel said as if he had a foul taste on his tongue. "That's a huge problem."

"That could mean a showdown," a faint voice said from the far end of the table.

"Risking the Balance," Yesil said, bringing up the point none of us wanted to recognize.

The Balance was *the* primary reason for angels and demons to exist. Maintaining it was our highest calling. The Upperworld needed to put all effort to ensuring mortals were kind and unselfish, that they thought of others first in their actions. Yes, problematic if taken to the extreme. That's where the Underworld comes in. Demons helped guide mortals to more self-centered thoughts and actions. Note, I didn't say selfish. Demons get a bad rap for that, if I'm honest. If it weren't for them, the Overworld would be full of people trying to do things for others at their own expense, essentially killing off the species. Outwardly directed and inwardly directed thoughts and actions. A balance. *The* Balance. The mechanism to sustain a species. Without the Balance, there was no need for angels or demons.

"How could someone get in the Safe without approval?" Anapheil said, sounding like she was completely out of breath.

My jaw twitched. "Hell if I know."

"If someone has poured the First Bowl, it would mean this disease Anapheil saw was…" Diniel couldn't bring himself to complete the sentence.

The First Bowl of Yahweh's wrath. The one that caused painful sores to break out on people's bodies. Don't believe the hype. Stories are stories. The truth is far worse and has nothing to do with only affecting those having the mark of the beast. No, this very real consequence had the potential to touch everyone.

If that happened, that explained the outbreak Anapheil noticed.

If that happened, a traitor had breached the Upperworld's Safe.

And if all that happened, we were all royally fucked.

Looking around the table at the fifty-plus sets of eyes seeking answers in their Minister, I groaned. "Okay, this is what we're going to do."

5

SIGHTS UNSEEN

"I'll be there in about…" I pulled my phone away from my ear and checked the time as if doing so would impact my arrival. Don't worry, sometimes I don't get me either. Bringing the phone back, I answered Billee. "Give me fifteen."

"Twenty, you mean?"

"You're not nice, Sparky."

"And you're always late."

That was not a lie. Thanks to the Order, time was a luxury I couldn't swath myself in like a rapper in pass-off gold chains. Though, I'd bet my demands hung just as heavy.

"Twenty-five," I answered honestly.

Billee sniffed. "See you in thirty."

Thirty-eight minutes later, I pulled up to the parking lot. I was to meet a mortal who had something my partner thought might interest me. Billee was sitting at a green metal table, one of those with the seats welded so any unscrupulous city park-goer couldn't walk off with a token of their visit. Says something about a society when a city is concerned someone would steal a butt bench that's seen more ass than a rock star, doesn't it?

The lady across from Billee was someone I didn't know.

From her seated position, I couldn't tell how tall she was, but I could hazard a guess by the way her feet fell short of the ground. An assassin observes these types of things.

The woman was Hispanic. Her short, brown hair, too vibrant for her age, was cut in one length and failed to reach her shoulders. She'd tucked a healthy segment behind her ears, ostensibly to keep it out of her narrow eyes. She smiled as I approached. A warm, grandmotherly smile. But it flickered like she was unsure or nervous. Or a little of both.

"Rev, this is Delores," Billee said without getting up. "Delores, this is Rev."

I took a seat between the pair. "Nice to meet you, Delores."

I offered my hand. She took it, wrapping it in her gloved hands, and squeezed. Decent strength for such a tiny, older woman. I'll bet she used to kick ass back in her day.

"Hello, Mr. Carver." Her voice shook slightly, even as she tilted her chin up, her chest swelling under her silver down parka.

"Just Rev, please. What can I do to help?" I said as I glanced between the women.

Delores looked at Billee. My partner said nothing as the women communicated almost telepathically—a truth as old as time, I swear, it's a secret superpower all mortal women have.

Billee cranked her head in my direction while still keeping her eyes on Delores. Something was about to drop in my lap.

"What is it?"

"Delores volunteers with CFC."

"CFC?"

"Center For Caring," the older woman said, her cheeks shining with pride. "It's an advocacy group for the homeless in our city."

I nodded. "Very kind of you."

"Thank you. It's important work. To serve. You understand?"

I did. What I didn't understand was what this had to do with me, especially when Billee knew how busy I was. "Not enough is done for them, so it's nice to see when others step up and get involved."

"But that's not why I wanted you to meet," Billee said, redirecting the conversation. She focused fully on Delores. "Do you want me to tell him?"

Delores' lips pinched, and she subtly lowered her head.

Billee said, "Okay. Delores called me because she's worried about the local camp over on the west side of the city."

"What about it? Something I can help with?" I definitely didn't want to be rude, but I wanted to keep this conversation targeted on things I could influence. Billee was still fresh enough of a familiar that she wouldn't yet grasp the full responsibilities I held, no matter how insightful she was. That was my fault. Not hers. Mortals tend to see immortals as all-powerful creatures. At least for the first few years.

"Possibly," Billee said, her eyes boring into me in the way people do when they're sharing apprehensively while in front of others. "That's why I wanted to talk to you, with Delores. In case you can."

"Shoot."

"Delores, there are how many people in the camp?"

"Now? Roughly seventy-five. It varies. The nature of their lives, of course. But that's our latest figure."

"Big camp," I said.

"That's the problem," Billee said. "It used to be bigger, but there have been disappearances."

My hand involuntarily clenched at the news. I covered the action by rubbing it with the other as if I was cold. I hoped neither woman noticed. Billee couldn't have. She fixed her gaze on me, worried. After everything I'd educated her on lately, that was understandable.

"How many?"

"Over twenty in the last week and a half," Delores answered.

"Any idea what happened? Could they have up and left?"

She shook her head, blinking rapidly.

Billee reached over and it wasn't until that moment that I realized the older woman was on the verge of crying.

Way to go, Rev.

"They're scared," Billee said. "Delores. The other volunteers. The people in the camp."

"Those people would never leave," Delores said. "Not of their own free will."

"The police? The state? Are they clearing out the camp? Encouraging everyone to move on? Not like the cops haven't done that before." Harsh though it may have sounded, I needed to rule out very corporeal possibilities before entertaining what I feared I'd have to entertain.

Delores was shaking her head even before I finished asking. "No. CFC works with the local authorities to ensure the camp and the surrounding blocks work together to keep the area clean and safe for everyone. Olympia is a sanctuary city, not one that our people flee for other cities. For so many to vanish…"

Billee squeezed her hand. "These people wouldn't have just left. One or two? Maybe. But even that's rare. Definitely not within the same week. Over twenty isn't right. Not with what the residents are going through."

"Which is?"

"Something is wrong at the camp," Delores said, her hand wagging near her cheek, her fingers spread. "A… I… I don't know what to call it. But I'm worried about them. They're breaking out into these… these rashes."

Shit. Here comes the hammer. "Rashes?"

She bit her lip. "Their skin… a strange rash. One that's *getting* worse. I haven't been by today. Not yet. I planned to go after we talked. Billee wanted to make sure I shared what I was seeing. Not all of them, but a good portion, are breaking out in rashes that are turning into pus-filled sores. I don't know. I don't have a medical background. They're running fevers. Too many volunteers refuse to go there now. They're worried about an outbreak."

Billee leaned closer. "That's not the worst of it. The residents are scared."

"I have a feeling they're scared about more than whatever is running through the camp?"

"Delores?" Billee prodded.

The older woman dropped her gaze to the table and shook her head.

"I want to help if I can, Delores. But I need to know everything. Whatever is happening, whatever the residents are going through, I've got to know everything if you want my help."

"It sounds crazy."

"Not to Rev," Billee said. "Tell him."

Delores took a moment. I gave it to her. Billee and I glanced at each other and she nodded slowly as if to tell me to hang in there. The finishing move was coming. So we waited and gave Delores the time she needed to share.

She straightened, now seeming taller. Though she lifted her chin again, her eyes remained cast down. "I thought it was crazy the first time I heard it. But you have to be careful when you're working with this population. They have so many challenges as it is. Society has shunned them. Most people make them feel subhuman. I never, *never* want them to feel that from me. So I listen. Even when what they have to say sounds crazy." Her lips formed a small O-shape, and the air whistled as she slowly inhaled. Her bottom lip shook when she exhaled. "A couple of days ago, one of them came to me with a story. The next day, three more said something similar. Yesterday, ten of them. And they told me others in the camp could testify to what they saw."

"Saw? What did they see?"

Billee patted Delores' hand lightly. "It's okay. He's safe. I swear it."

Delores chewed her lip for a moment before looking up at the sky. "Lord, forgive me." She never made eye contact, even when she looked away from where she thought Yahweh was listening. "A horrible thing to say, I know, but I thought they were delusional. I can't remember where. South America or something. But I remember hearing a story about how hundreds of people thought they saw the sun disappear one day. Everyone, at the same time. Mass delusion. I always wondered how that could happen. So many people seeing something that isn't true." Her head snapped up. "I trust these people, Mr. Carver. They wouldn't lie. They're not like that."

Delores wasn't being hostile or targeting me. She was frightened. With good reason. Regardless of what Billee told the woman, she saw me as someone who could provide grounding, at least. Maybe even have a few answers on a good day. "I'm sure they are. What did they tell you?"

"Many think those who disappeared ran away," Delores said. "But that doesn't make sense. We have all the services they need here. Leaving the city would mean that they would go without many things they need to survive. Those who stayed said the others didn't run away. They claimed people were… abducted. By…"

"By what?" Shit and double shit.

Delores shook her head, her short hair swaying. "I—I don't know, Mr. Carver. Rev. I'm sorry. It doesn't make sense. This— this wasn't a person. They said." She stopped, putting a gloved hand to her mouth as her eyes filled with tears.

"They said they saw a shadowy creature, same shape as a human? That they only seemed to see it out of the corner of their eyes, never directly?" I said, trying to build a bridge to get her to tell me the residents of the camp had seen a Penumbra Man. "Long arms, with fingers that extend from mid-thigh, past the knees, to mid-shin? Spikes of what look like long hair shooting away from its body. All over. Shoulders. Head. Chest. Legs. Every time they tried to look at it, the creature would shift to the corners of their vision again, always flickering away when they tried to catch it?"

Delores shivered now, and I doubted it was from the cold. Billee stood and was around the table in a flash, cradling the older woman in her arms. I leaned closer and rested my hand on Delores's arm.

This woman cared deeply about the residents of the camp. Their fear was her pain. A burden she'd been carrying. One she didn't understand and couldn't solve. My description had painted a very real picture of everything that probably had her mind buzzing since the first signs of trouble.

Billee watched me from above Delores's head. Her face was drawn and haggard. My heart ached. For Billee, this was becoming very real, very fast.

"I'm—I'm sorry. I'm acting like a fool," Delores said.

"No. No, you're not. Listen, I'm going to ask you to do something you're probably not going to want to do, but I need you to hear me out."

She squeezed her eyes, bit her lip, and nodded.

"Stay away from that camp," I said, and continued even as she shook her head. "Those sores? If I'm right, they're highly contagious. I'm not sure how severe the symptoms will become and I won't insult you by guessing. If you don't stay away, you'll likely contract the virus soon. Then, you won't be much help to those you want to serve."

"Th—that's not fair t—to them."

"I know. It's not."

"They're s—so scared, Mr.—Rev," she said. Her arm shook under my hand. "They can't sleep. Some of them can't eat. One—oh, blessed God." She drew and blew out a slow, shaking breath. "One of them committed suicide last night. Jumped off the Friendship Bridge."

Billee rubbed her shoulder, her lips pressed against the top of Delores's head.

"His friends... th—they told me he'd encountered this... this creature the night before. Said it *told* him to ju—jump. Will you help, Mr. Carver? Please? Whatever is happening, they don't deserve this. Please help them. Will you?"

There was only one answer I would ever give someone like Delores.

"Yes."

6

PAIRS NICELY WITH WINE

HAVE YOU EVER TRIED TO RUN WITH BAGS OF GROCERIES? NOT easy, let me tell you.

Tonight, I was hosting Pher. Because that's what I wanted to do after a miserable day of staff meetings and strategy sessions.

Alas, the grim Reaper's job is never done.

Arms burdened with two sacks of spaghetti sauce, noodles, artisan bread, cheeses, and everything else I include in my secret spaghetti recipe, I was weighed down. Normally, not a problem. I'm an assassin, meaning I've got a hyper-awareness of my surroundings at all times.

This time was no different. I heard the stiff January wind coming before it blew through the intersection. I smelled the Korean barbecue a block away. The woman arguing with what sounded like her lover inside the Tesla across the way didn't escape notice either. Seems the lover forgot an important appointment.

Those weren't the only aspects of life around downtown Olympia that didn't escape me.

The shifting, unseen, unseeable presence of what I suspected was a Penumbra Man was as evident as the sun hanging in the sky behind the thick blanket of Pacific northwest clouds—which is as good as it usually gets with Penumbra Men.

The downtown bank is a two-story, nondescript structure straight out of the weird period in mortal history between clean-cut living and the days of embracing anti-establishment interests. The bland facade of gray makes the concrete building an easy oversight during a usual trek from the local market back to my apartment. Not today.

Behind a slab of square concrete, I think the engineers meant to add to the bank as a feature, the air fizzled. A semi-transparent shimmering black. Almost unnoticeable.

I covered my brief unsteady step at the surprise, instantly recognizing the likely threat, and stayed true to my course.

I needed to get closer.

Keeping my steps steady, I watched the bank pillar while shifting the bag in my right hand to my left. The heavy load did no favors for my aching knees, but it freed my hand to keep at the ready. My trusty pistol was in its familiar location inside my leather duster. My hand twitched. I just needed to be sure what I was dealing with was exactly what I thought it was.

Picking on mortals was bad enough. Targeting the homeless was disgusting. If this Nephilim dressed up as a Penumbra Man wanted to tussle with me, I'd have my wrestling gear on before it could figure out which side of the jock strap to put in the front.

Parallel to the pillar and separated by the street, I groaned at seeing the gray, dull concrete wall. No supernatural monster.

I pretended that one of the bags slipped in my grip, giving me a chance to catch the blasted thing in my periphery without it knowing I was onto it. With this type of creature, even angel assassins needed every advantage.

Stooping to adjust the non-problematic grocery bag, I

swiftly swept my surroundings. Cars. Delivery trucks. Innocent mortals. No Penumbra Man.

I was about to stand up when something told me to hit the pavement. I did. Probably saved my own skin too.

The Penumbra Man flashed above me, swiping with the long, sharp tendrils of his hand. Long, black blades designed to rend flesh and bone.

As soon as it was beyond me, the Penumbra Man dodged the trash can, blinking into the smear of ambiguity of my periphery. I was back on my feet, pulling the Ruger free and keeping it hidden from the onlookers who were wondering what this crazy dude with long hair and wearing a leather duster in the middle of January was doing.

"Shit." Between keeping hold of as much discretion as I could manage and scanning for the next attack, I was doing a piss-poor job.

One man pulled his cell phone out. Damn creatures of Satan if there ever was anything He could create. Back in the old days, I could have fought the Penumbra Man right here and only the eyewitnesses could capture the essence of the fight and the fact that angels and these creatures of lore existed. Nowadays, these blasted manifestations of mortal Technology Ability could record every action and spread it worldwide before I'd kicked the Nephilim's ass and checked that my tomatoes hadn't busted open.

Without an obvious threat to the mortals by the Nephilim, my next greatest threat was the guy and his phone. If I ran, he'd record me, so I did the only thing I could to protect myself and my secret life as an angel among mortals.

Lifting the pistol, I fed a small dose of Angelfire into the chamber and squeezed the trigger. Less of a beam and more of a sliver of bright light, the Angelfire shot pierced the poor sucker's phone. A small tendril of smoke swirled into the January day from the now useless rectangle of plastic, glass, copper, and whatever else those devices were weaved out of.

Checking my surroundings and seeing nothing but stunned bystanders, I snagged the bags and raced in the direction the Penumbra Man had fled. Rounding the corner, the sidewalk dimmer than the street I'd just left thanks to a four-story building and a low winter sun behind thick clouds, I pulled out of my sprint. Doing so probably saved my grocery bags, but it also gave me time to glance at shadows and corners.

The Penumbra Man was tucked in a corner or long gone. Either way, he wouldn't provide any answers, and I had a hungry boss waiting on dinner. Now, I was going to have to add a side order of paranoia to the dinner. This meal was going to require more wine than I planned.

NOTHING GOES WITH TRAUMA LIKE SPAGHETTI.

I don't mean to be flippant, I really don't. Blame thousands of years of demon hunting, target assassinations, escorting mortals to their eternal fate, and just the general malaise of doing it repeatedly, with no end in sight. Or today's run-in with the Nephilim. The warning shot across my bow. Just don't blame me. It's my way of coping with too many things I can't control and lacking the resources to change any of it.

A rich aroma of pasta sauce, a special recipe I picked up in Italy sometime in the seventeenth century, filled my apartment. I've evolved it as trends and food production evolved, but it's pretty close to the Sicilian secrets I learned back then. Staying true to its fresh roots, there was nothing like it in any store. Not here in Olympia. Not in the entire state of Washington. Not even smack-dab in the middle of Rome.

Which was why Christopher "Pher" Montjoy sat on the other side of my bar, swirling a glass of red wine like he was a highly paid sommelier. We'd just finished my brief on my earlier run-in and my boss seemed more interested in the wine than the supernatural attack.

"Where did you get this?" he asked as he watched the red.

I'm sure there was a reason to watch wine swish and swirl, just as there was to sip it annoyingly, or to smack your lips after said annoying sips, but I didn't get it. Alcohol existed to be drunk. Mouth open. Alcohol inserted. Joy swallowed. Rinse and repeat. Simple.

Food, though? Food was another matter altogether. Hey, it's not called a culinary art just to make it sound relevant or to appreciate the thousands of generations of cooks who brought billions of beings together around a meal. If one thing helped with the business of being a Reaper, it was cooking. I. Love. It.

Tonight's meal was che buono chicken spaghetti. I was mincing the garlic and dicing grape tomatoes when Pher opened the Rift in my apartment. He'd been here often enough to open one in the entry's corner so he didn't knock over a lamp or split my sofa in two. I'm a big fan of my sofa. A lot of my non-work time is spent on it, watching sports or porn, and I would have been pissed if anyone destroyed it with a careless Rift.

I was onto concocting a cream sauce base when Pher was on his third glass of wine. We'd moved on from the Nephilim, for now, because when you've had countless run-ins with them, they're hardly a conversational centerpiece. Plus, I was busy.

Do you think he helped? Nope. Probably better, though, if I'm being honest. No one cooks like me.

"I've got to say, you sure know what you're doing," Pher said. Even with my back turned, his sniff was clear. "That smells wonderful."

I turned away from my meal preparations, doing a double-take. "Clean your beard. You spilled wine in it." As he grabbed a white napkin—white napkin plus red wine equals annoyed Rev—and dabbed the most groomed beard in mortal or immortal history. I sighed and went back to the cream base. "And be careful with that wine. That bottle cost me a week's wages."

"You need a pay raise, then."

"You can say that again," I said, nodding at the cream. "Especially with everything the Order keeps sending me."

"Definitely busy," Pher said so nonchalantly I stopped stirring, risking burning the cream, to stare at him. "What?"

"I love you, Pher."

"I love you too, Rev. You're a good friend. A confidant. One amazing Minister."

"Platitudes will get you nowhere... unless they're about my cooking."

Pher sat back on the stool, pushing the wine away and crossing his arms. The warm light reflected off his glasses and his shaved dome of a head. His dark skin seemed to suck in most of it, but I still played it up. Because he's bald and I've got enough hair to donate to a gorilla in need. I shielded my eyes. "Put your dome away before you take someone's eye out with it."

"The Minister of the Reapers acting like an eight-hundred-year-old," Pher said, then *tsk*'ed me. He actually *tsk*'ed. "I would have thought better of you, Revelation Carver."

"And I would have thought that one of the most senior members of the Order Of Thirteen, basically the only member I trust, would know better than to use my full name. He's been told not to for about ten thousand years."

Pher squinted one eye as if I was making him think. "Sorry, my friend, but it's been more like a little over eight thousand. But point taken. Which is a real shame when you think about it. Revelation is such a wonderful name. Flows off the tongue. Holds great importance. An angel whose adventures have inspired a book."

I snorted above the cream. "One of the most fucked up books in the damn Bible."

"I hope you don't talk like that to the mortals you're escorting or to your familiar. An angel with a mouth like a barbarian wouldn't please the Upperworld's marketing department."

"I'll worry about them when I'm not working eighty-hour weeks. Until then, I've got bigger issues on my mind."

"I figured you hadn't invited me just for the wonderful dinner and a story about running away from a fight today."

"Nope."

"How long has it been since we just sat down and had social time? Without work coming up?"

"Forever."

The sound of glass sliding over marble indicated Pher was going back to the wine. Not a bad idea. Mine was just to the side of the stove. I lifted my glass in salute. "To you, boss."

"To you, Rev."

We sipped, allowing the silence to guide the next thing that had to be brought up. Pher was a dear friend. He was most definitely the only Order member I fully trusted. But he was also here, about to be served a delicious meal, because I had to get stuff off my chest and he needed to listen.

"I'm pretty sure that was a Penumbra Man," I said after a moment, hating to have to go through this again.

Pher pinched the wine glass stem between two fingers and his thumb. He had been spinning it. He wasn't now. Dipping his head to peer at me over the black rim of his glasses, he said, "Are you sure?"

I briefly covered what Delores Garcia said about her volunteer experiences with the homeless camp. Almost forgetting the cream, I slid the pan off the burner and leaned against the counter, crossing my arms and facing the angel I considered my mentor.

"And that's not even the full picture." Pulling a hand free

from the protective armpit, I held up my thumb. "Disappearances." Pointer finger. "Rashes turning into sores." My favorite finger, the middle. "Sightings of a shadowy creature that hangs in the periphery of eyesight. What's that sound like?"

"A mess."

I aimed my finger at him and clicked my thumb down against it, mimicking a gun action. "Bingo."

He tipped to the side to look around me. "Is dinner almost done?"

"Close. Why?"

"Because business is going to spoil it. Especially this business."

"Promise me we'll discuss this tonight before you leave, and I'll finish it up now."

He sniffed deeply, his wide nose expanding. "The way this meal smells, that's a deal I'll take every day."

So I did the right thing, again, because I trust Pher, and actually like him. The meal came out as I'd hoped, pleasing me. That's harder than it sounds. I can be hard on myself with my cooking.

We ate at the table in front of the sliding balcony doors. With it being the dead of winter, only black sky and the faint glow of the street lights below penetrated the glass. It was raining, because in the Pacific Northwest, it always is. The light *dunk* of raindrops against the glass was soothing.

We chatted about what each of us had going on. We caught up on each other's opinions of the best and worst movies of the past few weeks. We did what all the cool guys do—we talked about books. Pher was getting into podcasts lately. He said they worked better for his workouts than music. I disagreed, mostly because he was in better shape than me, even with an extra twenty millennia of living. I didn't enjoy thinking about how much gym time I'd missed.

With dinner finished, it was time to address the herd of unicorns in the room—and I don't mean *that* kind of unicorn.

"The guy in Seattle, the demon, he was a spy. Assigned to watch for a Penumbra Man up there. But that was Seattle. The volunteer was talking about seeing a Nephilim in the camp on the west side of Olympia."

"Could be the same one. Wouldn't be the first time the Nephilim used the Penumbra Man cover in multiple cities to rile folks up."

"This is more than riling, Pher. The disappearances? The guy leaping to his death because he supposedly interacted with it? For all we know, the Penumbra Man is the same Nephilim who might have stolen the First Bowl."

"If you connect those dots, you'd be saying it also poured the Bowl."

"Could it not have been?"

"Sure." Pher's fat bottom lip pulled his upper lip down. Behind his glasses, he winked rapidly. "We don't know for sure. We don't have confirmation."

"Any names? Any suspects?"

"You know the Nephilim don't share that information. And they most definitely do not hand over the names of their order."

"Yeah, well, when their top-secret bullshit dribbles out into the world, that's a problem. When it creates more work for me and the Reapers, that's a bigger problem. If what they're doing is unsanctioned? Well, someone needs to step up."

"Be careful where you step, lad. The Order is digging around, but we have to be careful."

"Why?"

Pher shrugged. "Politics."

"Fuck politics."

Pher sighed. But what would a dinner chat with the two of us be if I didn't frustrate him a little? "You'll never get a promotion out of the Reapers with a perspective like that."

"I don't want a promotion," I said in a clever counter. "I just want *out* of the Reapers. We've discussed this."

He nodded. "We have. But it isn't happening. You know that. Now, if you'd just accept it."

I let my head bob. The few seconds of visual isolation from Pher would help temper my irritation. "Pher, I'm tired. No, I'm exhausted. Eight-thousand-plus years of demon hunting, being a political hitman, and supporting mortals is long enough."

"Plenty of Reapers have served longer. Not all acted as grim as you."

"True, there have been longer-serving Reapers." I held up a finger because I had a good point coming. "But they didn't do it when seven-plus billion mortals polluted the earth. They didn't do it with such a small crew of Reapers. The vast majority of them only performed one duty. They didn't have to be the Order's personal clean-up hitter. They were either assassins, demon and monster hunters, *or* escorts. You have had me doing all three for thousands of years."

"Because you're good."

"Great. Now let me go out while I'm on top of my game."

Pher had joined me at the sink to help clean dishes. It was one of his more redeeming qualities. Because we were busy with the dishes, we didn't have to make eye contact. That was usually a beneficial aspect whenever men talked about something significant. I blame testosterone.

He sniffed again, deep and slow. "Rev, that's not going to happen. You know that. We've talked about this. You're too valuable to the Order and its priorities."

"Like they even know what those are. I've never seen a group of supposedly smart angels or people struggle to define a priority like the Order. To them, everything is."

"Many things are happening. Not all of which you have insight into or knowledge of. I know it may seem chaotic, but I hope you trust me enough to know I would never mislead you. If we could take some of the burden, we would."

"I trust you, Pher. *You.* I don't trust jack-wagons like Jericho."

Pher snickered.

"But it's not just me I'm asking for either." Though my hands were wet, I placed one on Pher's shoulder. It was slimmer than I remembered. "All the Reapers are exhausted. Interlude or not, they're struggling to keep up and the demands are wearing them down."

"We know that, you understand? It's not like the Order is unaware."

"Then help."

"How?"

"Send in the cavalry." I flung the dishtowel up when I said that. The end whipped into the air and then promptly landed in the soapy water. Recognizing my error, I flicked it up out of instinct. What resulted was exactly what you might think would happen. A wonderful arc of soapy dishwater curved through the air, spraying the hanging lights, the ceiling, my face, and Pher's silk shirt. It was funny. Trust me.

After we finished laughing like two guys who were far younger than we actually were, I turned serious. "No, really. We need bodies. A lot of them."

"I'll see what I can do," he said after a moment. "But I'm not promising anything. I don't have the first idea where we could draw reserves from."

"I've worked for the Order long enough. I know not to expect much."

Pher squinted, like the comment stung. "You don't work *for* us. You work with us."

"Doesn't feel like it."

"When?"

"Most times." I drew a deep breath. "The problem with you guys is that none of you have ever been Reapers, so you have no clue what this is like. No idea how taxing it is."

"With a singular exception, Reapers perform escort duty."

My skin itched with irritation. "That's my point, Pher. Escort duty is probably the toughest thing we have to do."

"Tougher than assassinating demons? Than investigating Nephilim? Saving the world from Armageddon?"

"Way tougher." Putting my slightly drier hand on his shoulder again, I squeezed. "Until you've looked into the eyes of a mortal who is crossing over, with no idea what they're facing, you cannot understand. Having lived one of their lives thinking there might be more after death, but clueless to the true nature of what that 'more' is? Even someone as kind as you will never understand what it takes to be a Reaper, Pher. No one in the Order can. The greatest problem with you guys."

Pher bobbed his head in agreement. His dish towel pressed harder against the plate like he wanted to scrub the paint off. After a moment, he said in a tone that held more rust than usual, "We have shortcomings. That much is true. I'll be honest, Rev. I fear that we, too, have too much to tackle, and it's blinding us. We can't see that we may be simply pushing the problems downstream."

"Thank you for saying that. Seriously."

"Besides looking into how to build a reserve force, what else can I do for you so you can focus on this potential problem with the Nephilim?"

That one was easy. "Put this kid on hold."

Pher's face scrunched. "Which kid?"

"Ezekial Sunstone."

Pher pinched his lips. "Not sure that one will fly. He's important to the Underworld."

"Yeah, yeah," I said, pulling the plug in the sink to empty the water. "I know. Possibly the next Lucifer. But here's the thing. He's not. Not now, anyway. And even if he will be? So what? He's a kid. It'll take millennia for him to figure out his balls from ball bearings, even if they put the damn crown on his head tomorrow."

"Demons don't wear crowns."

"Does Yahweh?"

Two shoulders rose and fell in a shrug. "No idea. Do you honestly think the Order sets eyes on Him?"

"Thought rank had its privileges?"

"It does."

"Just not that kind?"

"Bingo." Pher snagged the wine bottle by its neck like a ruffian. Gross. "Now, if I promise to get approval to delay Sunstone's assassination, can we please finish this wine?"

I smiled. "I thought you'd never ask."

7

PUT ME IN, COACH

When you live in an apartment, sometimes you just have to get out. Yes, I know I'm lucky to afford three spaces when so many have so little. Call it a work necessity rather than any desire to live a playboy lifestyle. But even with three of them and the nearly two-thousand square feet of space they provided, the walls occasionally feel like they're closing in. Especially during the winter.

With too much to do and no time to do it, I used my mental reprieve to call Billee and ask if she'd like to join me for a stroll around downtown—you can't just flippantly mention a search for supernatural beings over the phone. She lives in a house that's bigger than my three apartments put together, and she was going stir-crazy from the endless gray days typical of this part of the world at this time of year, so I think she was happy for the work.

"Let me grab my jacket," I said after opening the door for her.

She stepped in, dressed in a black parka that reached her knees. I whistled, not in a creepy way, but in a way that said she impressed me.

She snorted. "Just tell me you're not wearing the duster."

"I always wear the duster."

"I know. But it's been raining on and off, Rev."

"And it always is," I shouted from the bedroom. "If I waited for a dry day to wear it, I'd never get a chance to look kick-ass."

Now it was her turn to whistle. She did. Loudly. "Wow."

"Don't hate me because I'm trendy and you're… is it appropriate to call counselors names?" I slid my arms into the duster, walked to my safe where I kept my .327, and slid it into the duster's custom pocket.

"Not if you're older than five," she taunted back.

"Billee, that was so long ago."

She was smiling when I emerged, duster donned like a badass. She looked at it like I was wearing someone's skin. "That thing is going to stink by the end of this walk."

I pulled the lapel to my nose and inhaled deeply. "Mmm. Like a wet dog."

Billee grimaced, but couldn't hold it. "Let's go. I need fresh air. Especially this close to you."

We headed downstairs and out into the day. For January, it wasn't cold. Maybe low-fifties. Almost as a treat from Yahweh, it wasn't even sprinkling at the moment.

"Where too?" Billee asked.

"I was thinking of strolling down by the farmer's market."

"It's closed. Wrong time of year."

"I know. But it's by the water and we're not getting blasted in the face with rain, so I thought it'd make for a pleasant stroll that'll take us near the homeless camp. Maybe pick up gyros at that food truck while we're down there?"

She wrapped her arm around mine. "I like your thinking."

Two miles of city blocks separate my place from the market. I love the area, but don't need to be too close to the water. Rent goes up and the size of apartments goes down the closer you venture toward Budd Inlet. I might have a nice salary that allows me to focus on things other than my next meal, but that didn't mean I was going to splurge. Spend money on quality, not quantity, I say. Thus, the awesome duster and the long walk toward the market.

That ended up being a problem.

The thing about having a third eye sense is that you get a lot of noise in your head. By my best guess, I can sense the past and future of everything around me for a half-mile. Think about that for a moment. A half-mile around you, in every direction, knowing the past, present, and future of every mortal occupying the space. That's a lot of head noise. Terrible when you can't block it all out. Usually, I can do that without thinking. Sort of like breathing. But I had the Nephilim on my mind and that unconscious barrier slipped and my third eye opened. Pretty crappy for a middle-aged angel beaten down by the unforgiving march of existence.

When I stiffened, Billee asked, "What's wrong?"

We unlocked our arms.

"Shit."

A block away, I picked up on trouble.

"Rev?" Billee's voice sounded dreamy.

I scanned the buildings partially blocking the signal. "A fight. Bunch of people ganging up on someone."

Scan. Scan. Scan. *There!*

I tugged Billee. "This way. Come on!"

Down the side street just south of a hotel too large for this small city, the signal became clearer. I took a hard left. Billee easily kept pace at my side. If I had the time and oxygen to think about it, I'm pretty sure she could have pulled away, stopped the fight, and placed her gyro order before I arrived. But she's good people and stayed by my side to protect my fragile male ego.

Percival Landing Park is on the eastern edge of the West Bay. It's a small park with not much going on and no privacy. At least, definitely not enough for a gang fight.

Herein lies the dichotomy of my secret. As the Minister

Reaper, my job is to manage every Reaper responsible for escorting mortals after they die to the Veil Gate, on top of my super secret assassin work. The last thing I need is more work. But I also have a third eye sense no one else knows about. No one else, as far as I know, possesses an equal ability. If my third eye picks up on a crime, I don my crime-fighting cape because I'm compelled to act. Why? Because I'm a nice guy, if you can look past the whole 'assassin' thing. Is it any wonder why I'm overworked?

We raced down State Avenue, past new apartments totally out of my price range, and slowed only when the buildings gave way to a clear view of the park. The fight was going down right in the middle of the green.

Fifteen-on-one. Not cool.

"Oh my God," Billee said without breathing hard.

"He won't help. We are."

We dashed through the packed parking lot and into the park. The tussle was moving toward the side where large playground equipment sitting unloved by children during the cold winter months. Just beyond that was two feet of concrete separating the victim and assailants from the dry ground and the waters of the inlet. I didn't feel like jumping into the water to save the victim or even the group terrorizing him, so the fight was going to end now, right in the middle of the soft—and probably wet—grass.

At my side, Billee pumped her arms, easily keeping up. "Look at them."

I was, and I also noticed. The gang was attacking their victim not only in superior numbers but with a disturbingly crazed approach. Wild kicks. Uncultured strikes. Roundhouse punches. Most of them missed because they were directed so forcefully. More concerning? Even from fifty yards away, I could make out the reddish sores on the faces and necks of the ruffians. More evidence of the First Bowl being poured. I'd deal with that after saving this guy from getting his ass introduced to his face.

The victim, a thin man whose brown hair was disheveled in the fighting, dodged, leaped, spun, and somersaulted away from most of the attacks, but he was wearing down. His energized attackers showed no signs of slowing. Even with Billee and me adding to the target's numbers, I wasn't confident someone wouldn't get hurt.

"Be careful," I said to my partner as I scanned for the biggest threat in the group, wary of what we were racing into.

"Same to you."

I flicked my arm out, pointing at the lone car parked in a parallel spot alongside the street. "Stay wide. Let me draw their attention. Strike from the periphery." She started away, but I snagged her wrist. "Only if you have a definite advantage. Otherwise, stay out of it."

Billee nodded without argument and angled off, relieving me of the pressure of having to worry about her in this scrap. We hadn't had enough time together for me to see how she performed on a test of this magnitude. Yes, I trusted her. She'd given me no reason not to. But this was different. And I wouldn't know just what it was until I enjoyed a distraction-free jump into the foray.

As Billee peeled away, I closed on the first man. He was overweight and slower than the rest. But boy, was he solid.

I hit him from behind with a shoulder. Right in the middle of his back. He stumbled forward while the impact flung me in the opposite direction. I regained my balance first. After that, he didn't stand a chance.

I jumped on his back, putting him in a choke lock, and rode him to the ground, throwing an elbow to the back of his head and knocking him unconscious.

Fourteen more to go.

I stood, straddling the unconscious man and sneering at the grotesque sore that was larger than a quarter and smack dab in the middle of the back of his neck. I was so distracted by it, I almost didn't see the punch coming at my face.

Instead of getting clobbered, I pulled my head back just in time for the fist to miss. Close enough to blow my black locks across my chin. A few strands caught in the corner of my mouth. I used the guy's momentum against him, giving him a two-handed shove that sent him sprawling. He tripped over the unconscious guy and went down. A quick kick to the ribs made him curl. A second one broke bone.

Someone tackled me and we fell to the wet grass, rolling. He had me by the throat, so I returned the favor. A kick made me see stars. I let go of my assailant's throat to catch the foot before it struck again. That gave the guy giving my throat the once-over an advantage. He squeezed.

I sent a knee to his groin, and that got him to loosen up. Using his distraction, I tried to free myself of his weight. I kicked up again, watching him sail over my head.

I swung my legs out in a scissoring movement, gaining momentum with the second leg and sweeping the second assailant's legs out from underneath him. When he went down, I pounced on him, about to choke him out. Sores covered his neck, so I changed tactics and punched him instead. He'd have a nice shiner by the evening.

The fight wasn't going as well as I'd hoped when I got a lay of the land. The poor guy they were targeting at the outset was under a two-attacker pile-on. A man and a woman. So nice when couples can bond over extra-curricular activities. Others had been helping subdue him until they noticed I was faring far better than their victim, otherwise the poor bastard would have had all of them on him.

A redhead with eyes too wide for his face pointed at me. "Let's get him."

Six people broke off from their original target to charge. Depending on their skill and durability, I could handle a six-on-one without outside help. But if they thought to add to those numbers, I was going to have to do something I didn't want to do.

I patted my duster, just below my breast. I'd only pull Maggie out if necessary. The last thing I needed was collateral damage to the thin man, Billee, any passersby, or buildings if I unleashed my Angelfire. I also didn't need witnesses or another good samaritan with a cell phone.

One of them must have caught sight of Billee because they broke off in her direction.

"Hey!"

The grimace he gave in return was just downright evil.

I was busy watching the approach of the other five while also trying to monitor the guy running toward Billee.

She'd have to hold her own for a minute or two while I dealt with this large partition of the gang.

The five didn't have a particular strategy besides bum-rushing me. That worked to my advantage.

I sidestepped the first attack. Ducked a punch. Swiped away a pathetic kick. Punched a rib, a face, a chest. Got way too close to about twenty-five sores and rashes that would inevitably develop into sores. But I came out unscathed. Even the punches they landed would do nothing but leave bruises and welts I'd have to tend to. I can take an ass-kicking and keep fighting, and I think that discouraged them. The more punches and kicks they landed, the longer I remained on my feet, taking the fight to them, the less forti-tude they showed.

Panting over top the last to fall, I tried to spot Billee, ready to help.

Turns out, Billee didn't need my help. She had the greedy jerk pinned to the car and was pummeling his stomach with fists and elbows. Not the fastest punches I'd ever seen, but I'd been around the block and had seen more scraps than stars in the sky, and Billee showed real promise.

Whipping around, the last seven stood around their prone

victim, taking turns kicking him. He was unconscious and in real danger.

Sprinting at the ones with their backs turned, I closed in. They were too focused on what was frighteningly turning into attempted murder. My third eye telling me not to worry about that; this guy wouldn't die today.

The two closest turned when, from the other side of the assault circle, heads snapped up. I caught the pair with a solid clothesline. They flipped head over heels, and not in a romantic way.

I spun, swinging a fist into the cheekbone of the man to the left, while I kicked out at the woman on the right.

"You broke my leg!" she screamed from her new position on the ground.

The guy I'd punched didn't make a sound. Just collapsed like an inflatable Christmas decoration when the power is cut to the blower motor.

"The rest of you would be smart to leave," I said, scanning the group for the next clearest threat or idiot. None of them moved. No one flinched. "Now!"

Four did exactly what I needed them to do, but one remained. There's one in every crowd.

A burly sucker, with a broad nose and a thick beard comprised of tight, orange curls. He looked more like a bear than a grown man. In a voice so deep it, too, could have belonged to one of those large animals, he said, "We have to."

His comment stopped me. "You have to? What the hell does that mean?"

I was looking into the eyes of a madman. I saw that now.

A shade over six feet tall, this guy cut an intimidating figure. He could have done real damage to the thin, unconscious man. The way he teetered, that vacant look in his eyes, and the subtle fidgeting with his hands told me something else was going on here.

"I'm calling 911," Billee said behind me.

Without taking my eyes off this bear, I backed toward her. 911 meant emergency vehicles. That meant authorities. Questions would be asked. Packing a magical .327, using souped-up senses, and the general supernatural undertones of the situation might mean nothing but headaches if I was around when they got here.

Wishing I had the time and privacy to use my soul stone on the guy to get the absolute truth out of him, I stabbed my hand down toward the victim. "In what world did you need to do that? Why? You could have killed him. You would have if we didn't interrupt. Give me one good reason to not snap your neck. Make it a good one. I'm in the mood."

Flicker.

What was that? Confusion? Clarity? Guilt? Actual fucking human decency?

My third eye picked up on something changing. A vacancy?

"We… were told to," the bear of a man said, shifting his weight again. Foot to foot. Rocking faster now.

"By who?"

Flicker.

The blotches on the man's face and neck seemed to deepen. Darkness pulling back, revealing truth like how a slow sunrise warmed a black sky.

"*By who?*"

Two swift jerks of his head, once to each side as if he suddenly found himself in a crowd, and the man found me again. "Wh—where?" He stopped, his eyes finding the thin victim and going wide. "What happened to him? Is he okay?"

With surprising speed, the bear man shuffled forward. I moved to step in between him and the guy he'd just accosted, but Bear was quick. He was sliding to his knees, grunting. "Can I help?"

Billee had moved to hover over the victim. She shot her

arm out toward the man while holding her phone to her ear with the other. "No. He's going to be okay. Just stay back."

Her voice was so firm, so authoritative, even I didn't dare to crowd out the unconscious man.

Bear shuffled back, still on his knees, his hands raised. "S —sorry. I—I didn't mean. If he needs help. I c—can. Prior military. I have a First Aid training."

I side-stepped closer. "Do as the lady says. Back up. You've done enough."

Flicker.

What was this man's past was becoming clearer to my third eye, but something still blocked it. What could do that besides Yahweh or Lucifer?

Bear shocked me. Starting at his shoulders and moving down his arms and to his hands planted on his knees, he jerked with a cry. Clear trails of tears ran down his cheeks, leaving his sores to shimmer. "I—I just want to h—help."

"You've done enough," I said icily.

His cheeks jiggling, he looked up at me. "Wh—wha—what did I do?"

"Are you serious?" I pointed at the man lying out in the grass while trying to push my third eye onto the instigator's past. "This, man. You did this."

Bear's head fell. "I—I did? How?"

"This is a bad joke, right? You're doing this to piss me off? Trust me, I can kick your ass before the cops get here and not feel the slightest bit guilty about it." To drive my point home, I grabbed him by the collar and struggled to pull him to his feet. I think he played along nicely because he was a big boy, and even though I can take an ass-kicking, I can't deadlift bears.

When he was on his feet again, I shoved him backward toward the multi-colored roundabout that sat empty of kids.

"If I did something, I'm sorry," Bear said, his hands still in the air even as I roughly jabbed him back. "I—I didn't mean to. I just. I don't remember anything. I swear."

He grunted as he fell on the roundabout. This was one of those new-style ones. Long gone were the panels of corrugated metal with their diamond-shaped ridges. No more bars of this steel. This one was all kid-friendly plastics and soft rubber, complete in a sailing ship motif. The cargo netting accoutrement really completed the entire package. I had shoved Bear so roughly that his hand got tangled in the netting. He didn't fight. Instead, he laid back, holding his free hand out as if to plead with me to not hurt him.

The urge had gone out of me. Damn my conscience.

I squatted in front, my arms resting on my bent knees, hands relaxed. My right was close enough to slip into my duster if I needed the gun. "What the fuck was that about? Who are you? Is this some bullshit gang initiation? Who is the victim? Why him? Start talking, or I'm going to shove my hand so far up your ass you'll think I'm a ventriloquist."

With each threat, Bear flinched. "Mind if I untangle myself? I swear, I—I don't know what happened. But... I've got back problems and I can't focus like this."

"Sit up." I stayed where I was, right hand ready.

Bear shook out his wrist and winced. He leaned down, planting his forehead into his palm. "I... I don't feel good."

"I don't care," I said, and meant it. "I'm sure that guy you beat the hell out of won't when he comes around again, and I'm sure his last few minutes of consciousness weren't exactly a party, either. So start talking, asshole. I've given you enough time."

Forehead still planted in his palm, he shook his head. "I'm serious, man. I—I don't remember—oh, fuck." He said that last, delectable word with a gasp.

Curiosity killed my aggression. "What?"

Bear's hand pressed against his temple. "It's still—still

foggy. But… we were just hanging out in the park. Playing… well, you wouldn't get it."

"Try me."

Flicker.

Damn the film over this guy's past. What was blocking me?

Sirens '*waaaah*ed' in the background. Still a few blocks away. Billee now sat next to the thin man. The unconscious and injured in Bear's beat-down party went ignored. She rested her hand on the victim's chest.

"We do this thing. LARPing. We play—"

I rolled my hand in a circular motion, telling him to speed it up. One of the last things I'll do is talk about LARPing. Even as an immortal, I don't have that kind of time.

"It's spotty," Bear continued. "One minute, we were playing. I was about to conquer—oh, sorry. Anyway, that's when I started to not feel good. Like… dreamy!" He snapped his fingers as if a brilliant idea had just come to him. "Everything started feeling like a dream."

"I heard LARPers can get into it a little too much."

As if he didn't hear me, Bear went on. "That's when some of us started vomiting. I did a few seconds after Becky. I almost fell off the net tower."

I squinted. "You climbed up on the net?"

"Yes. Why?"

I eyeballed his frame.

Bear pulled his shirt more tightly around himself. "I almost fell."

"Remind me to feel sorry for you when I care. Keep going. What got everyone sick? Too much patchouli? Home-grown Mary Jane gone bad?"

"You're a jerk."

"I've been told." I rolled my hand again. "But you're about to be a felon, so I'll worry about your opinion when it matters. Story. Now."

He rubbed his face. "A group of people don't get sick all at once. Not like that. And, no, we weren't doing drugs or anything. We are straight edge. No drugs. No alcohol." He sat up, patting his stomach. It made a thick sounding *thunk*. "Looks may deceive, but I also try to watch what I eat."

Flicker. More of his past was coming into view, but only right here, right now. The rest was blocked. I'd never come across this before, and it was disturbing on a deep level. As much as I don't enjoy being bombarded with everyone's secrets, I rely on my third eye in moments like this. Without it, I felt handicapped.

"Fair enough. And so the story goes? Out with it."

Sirens. Coming closer.

"You'll think I'm nuts."

"Don't care. I'm on a time crunch." I slid my hand inside the duster and exposed my trusty .327 just enough so the grip was visible. A gross, trite tactic mostly inspired by terrible Hollywood tough guys, I admit. But it was effective. "Talk."

His eyes flicked to the gun and back up at mine so instantly I had to question his sanity. Or his comfort with handguns. "A couple of us kept saying weird things."

"Like?"

"Like we were seeing things. No, not things. Like we were seeing someone."

"Is this someone the same person who told you to gang up on that poor bastard?"

Bear nodded.

Rashes. Sores. Crazed behavior. Coming out of a stupor in a sudden moment of clarity. The puzzle was framed, and each testimony filled it in. The blockage into this man's past was a worry for another time.

"Let me guess," I said slowly, carefully, each word measured and carrying the right amount of import. "You don't want to tell me who made you beat the shit out of this guy because it doesn't make sense. Too scary to think about a shadowy figure you can't seem to put your eyes on. Always lingering just out of clear eyesight?"

Bear's jaw shook.

"Maybe your skin itched. Maybe it didn't. But you knew you were in danger. Not from the shadowy man, but this poor sucker my partner is taking care of?"

Bear nodded.

"You probably don't even know who he is?"

Again, a side-to-side shake.

"You just knew that you and your LARPing buds had to beat him to a pulp."

More silent agreement.

I secured Maggie in her secret pocket and pushed myself to my feet. The sirens were becoming annoying now. "Do the right thing. Wait for the ambulance."

"I—I wouldn't leave my—my friends," Bear said, his eyes falling on the man whose day they'd ruined. "I w—w— wouldn't leave him either. Doesn't matter that I remember nothing. He looks bad off." The tears started again. "I'm s —sorry!"

Billee was watching us. I gave her a flick of my head that said it was time to leave. She took a last look at the man she'd been protecting and joined me in walking as far away from this scene as we could get, as fast as we could.

"You're l—leaving?" Bear called out after us.

"Do the right thing. I'll know if you don't," I reminded him over my shoulder before breaking out into a slow jog.

I don't think Billee breathed until we were south of the Kissing Statue on Fourth Avenue. "What the hell was all that?"

"The fucking Nephilim," I growled in frustration.

"This won't be the last we see of stuff like this, will it?"

I jammed my hands into my very useful duster pockets. "Not at all. I'm convinced the First Bowl has been poured. That explains everything we're seeing. That whole 'I'm too stupid to act this stupid' wasn't an act. It's a very real symptom of getting uncomfortably close to a Penumbra Man. Called the Penumbra sickness. Nasty shit. Spreads like fire in California in the summer." I shook my head. "Hope you're ready for the big leagues, Sparky, 'cuz you're in the starting lineup."

8

BE ALL, END ALL

I LIKE COMPANY. WHEN YOU'VE LIVED AS LONG AS I HAVE, THERE is a certain level of aloneness that is comforting. But sometimes, the quiet gets too quiet.

During those times, I enjoy warm bodies in my apartment. Not a lot. Too many people, say, like three, becomes exhausting. I keep my get-togethers smaller. Like when Pher comes over to mooch off me and eats a wonderful dinner he neither paid for nor prepared. I love Pher. He's the man. But I can't have him over all the time. One can only have so many boys' nights.

Today was Billee's turn. Her presence helped dispel the silence in the apartment and the turbulence in my head. Her company was enjoyable. She definitely looked better and smelled nicer than my boss.

And we had unfinished business after the gang-jump on the innocent man in the park.

Turns out, he was a local pastor. Without confirmation that the induced fight was the work of the Nephilim, I knew in the deepest, darkest corner of my gut that it was. What other explanation could there be when every piece fit nicely together? No hand-jamming required.

All of this supernatural business of the immortal realm had Billee underground for a few days. Even when I remind her of her duties as a familiar, she didn't get the intended humor. We'd done some recon around the city, searching for clues to a Nephilim presence, and found nothing. Each time we'd finished a recon, Billee was back home, quiet and reflective.

I really was joking about reminding her of her duties, I swear. I told her I'd make it up by cooking dinner. When I said it was barbeque pineapple flatbread, she was less-than-impressed with my culinary peace offering. Right until the moment she sat at my bar, a glass of water in front of her.

"Mmm. That smells amazing," she said with a big sniff and a bigger smile.

I grunted in agreement. I'm cocky like that when someone digs my cooking. "Thank you. Are you sure you don't want something besides water? I've got whites and reds. There's a huge beer fridge in the other apartment."

Billee lifted her glass. "I'll stick with this, thanks. Too much alcohol is bad for your brain."

"Mmm, I'm not sure that's scientifically valid."

She cocked her head. Loose curls of dark and tan hair fell to her side. "Mmm, pretty sure I'm the smart one in this partnership. Long-term use of alcohol can have lasting effects on neurotransmitters, decreasing their effectiveness. Sometimes, these effects mimic your neurotransmitters. *That's* what science says."

I spun, holding the knife up to ward her off. "Whoa, whoa, dork. I yield. I yield. No booze for you." I turned back to my cutting. "That means there's just more for me."

"Does booze help you find solutions to your problems?"

"Nope. But it sure as hell makes food taste better." I turned just enough that she could witness my wink. "Speaking of problems? What's on your mind?"

She sighed. "This is scary, Rev. No lie. I'm supposed to be

sitting in an office, listening to other people's problems. Not having them for myself."

"Everyone has problems," I said. "The smart ones go see counselors. The idiots are the ones who keep trying to fight through, failing constantly because they won't talk to someone. Then they wonder why their problems continue. All the while, they're over-eating, over-spending, over-fighting because they're not taking care of shit."

"Is that what we're doing?"

"I'd like to think so."

"By cooking pineapple pizza?"

I wagged the knife in the air. "Call it pizza again and I'll cut you. It's barbeque pineapple flatbread."

She chuckled. "Oh, *excuse me*."

The faint sound of glass being rotated over marble drew my attention back to her. I brought the cutting board to the bar, pushing a small pile of unsorted mail away. "Probably less rude to face you while we chat."

"Definitely less rude."

"You have questions. Ask them. It's unfair to put you in this situation. I've never been a fan of forcing mortals to serve as familiars, but I can't do anything to change that. Though I may be powerless in that respect, I do have the power to educate you on what this all is. At least, to the best of my abilities. Put it out there. What are you thinking?"

"That's a big question."

"This is a massive responsibility."

She blew out a big breath. Her lips fluttered. "As crazy as it sounds, I get this whole thing about these people believing they've seen a Penumbra Man. Too many testify to it. Too many similarities. Plus, I trust Delores. No questions asked."

"Known her for a while?"

"About ten years," Billee said, rocking her head. "She's a wonderful soul."

"Seems it."

"As long as I've known her, she's given to others. I don't remember a time she wasn't volunteering somewhere, for someone. She always has. And I know her heart, Rev."

"You don't have to convince me. Even from that one conversation, I could tell what kind of person she is."

"That's why we have to help. I just don't know how."

"We are," I said, slicing through the red onion with sharp cuts, a manifestation of my frustration with the Order. After the events in the park, I made a brief trip to the Upperworld and reported in to my trusted friend and boss. Pher had little to offer but said what he always said when handcuffed by the lackadaisical pace of bureaucracy. "And while we wait on the Order to figure out whatever it needs to do next, we prepare here. Because, trust me, while those politicians do what they do in the Upperworld, the Nephilim will still do what they do. They won't stop. If it ends up that the First Bowl actually was stolen, it's because someone has aims we can't see yet. My goal is to figure out what those aims are."

I rubbed my face with the back of my hand, careful to not do that over top of the food preparations.

"You okay?" Billee asked softly.

"Just tired," I said as honestly as I could.

Cooking always brings out the peace in my soul. Whatever I feel throughout the day, put a knife in my hand and fill my nose with the scent of onion or garlic, or just about any spice ever created, and Rev is a happy assassin.

"Can I help?"

I stopped cutting, smacking the knife on the cutting board, and smiling. "Are you on the clock, counselor?"

"Touché."

"Have you ever had a job, maybe you've even felt it with the counseling gig, where no matter what you do, the outcome is still the same?"

"All the time."

"That's what this is like. Just on a longer timeline." I waved the knife around in the air like I was trying to stab a fly. "I've been putting up with Nephilim shit for eons. It's always the same with them. The privilege of their rank, I guess. Doesn't mean it doesn't get old. Back in the day, we used to be even. Back when mortals were less skeptical. But now? Talk about a challenge."

"Why's that?"

"You all have gotten too smart for your own good," I said, resuming my work on the onions. "The less your kind believes in the spiritual, the less power us Reapers have. We're like the great peacekeeping force in the Upperworld."

"Isn't that God's job?"

"I'm not really sure what He does. Him. His Council. Shit, most centuries, I don't even know what the Order is doing. Sure doesn't seem like a lot."

"I'll have to ask when I get there."

"Where?"

"Heaven," Billee said bluntly, then cocked her head. "What? Why are you looking at me like that? What do you know? Am I—am I not going to Heaven?"

I wanted to chuckle at her tender understanding of her place in the big picture of existence. Were the consequences of doing so not so harsh, I might have. I mean, this wouldn't be the first time I entertained a mortal's whims about the after-life. But this was serious shit.

Once before, with my eightieth or so familiar, I told the truth. By the time I finished, I'd broken his mind. Not metaphorically. The guy was no good afterward. To me. To his family and loved ones. His friends were no help. He spent the last few decades of his life under constant care. My third eye hadn't seen that outcome—I told you it's not a perfect science. I never forgave myself. His name was Dagobert. Poor bastard.

I found a sudden, serious interest in my onions.

After a moment, Billee said, "Rev?"

She sounded scared.

Tired. Oh, so tired of this.

I stopped chopping. "You want the actual truth?"

"Holy shit," Billee said, shifting on the barstool. "I—I'm going to Hell?"

"No," I said with a heavy sigh.

Her eyebrows drew down. "So... I'm not going to Heaven. I'm not going to Hell. Where *am* I going?"

"Neither."

"Wait. What? How can that be? How do you know? Tell me."

"Because almost everything you think you know is a lie," I said, not meaning to bite. "I'm sorry. That was an asshole move."

"Yes, but I'm used to you being an asshole. It's how you show you care. How about you hook a girl up and tell her exactly what you're talking about concerning her afterlife?"

"You're a person who understands reality. Understands science. Verifiable information."

"Yes." She drew the word out, sounding like she was leaking air from an orifice.

"Okay, do you want the hard facts? The actual truth?"

"Rev," she said, sitting up a little straighter. "I don't have time for anything but truth."

"Promise not to stab me with my knife when I tell you?"

A humored quirk of her lips. Good. "I promise."

"Heaven isn't for the dead, it's for the living. There is no afterlife, Billee. Not in the way you know it."

"No Heaven? No Hell?"

She was so matter-of-fact about the topic, I couldn't help but relax. Maybe I'd tensed up for nothing.

"Nope."

"Then what happens to those people who believe in having a soul and the afterlife? Do they just..."

"Rot in the ground?" I said with a chuckle.

"Yeah."

"No."

She held up her hands, dropping her head and shaking it. She grabbed a slender finger with one from the opposite hand, ticking off her points. "One, you say there's no Heaven. No Hell. Two." Another finger was added to the mix. "You say, what? We don't have souls or we don't just rot in the ground? Color me confused, Rev. I'd like to know what I'm fighting for here."

"Everything."

"Everything?" she repeated, sounding like she was pronouncing an unfamiliar word.

"The importance of what we're doing isn't reduced because there's no afterlife, not in the sense that mortals would understand."

"But something exists, and that's what we're fighting for?"

"Imagine this. On one hand, you have all the physical stuff you know about, even if it's too small to see or too large to comprehend. Think cells and the universe."

"Okay."

"Then there's the non-physical stuff. Things you can't put your hands on. Love. Compassion. Hate. Not just those, but forces, too. Like gravity. All the physical and non-physical, the energy of existence, if you will. Everything is made up of it. It is everything."

"This is getting a little woo-woo for me."

"Trust me, the longer you deal with it, the more *woo* it becomes," I said with a smile as I moved on to the poblano pepper. "So all of this energy, if you will, is what we see as existence. Doesn't matter if you're an ameba or a god."

"A matter of perspective?"

"Exactly." I tipped the knife at her. Told you she caught on quickly.

"Okay, so what does this have to do with mortals, the

afterlife, energy, and whatever else I don't have the first clue about?"

"The All encompasses everything." I snickered. "I know. Not a very engaging name. But it captures the spirit of it." I swirled my hands in the air. Billee flinched. I think she was worried I might take a finger off. "It's this beautiful symbiotic relationship. Everything made up of the stuff that is everything."

"You sound like you're smoking good stuff."

"Wish I was." Scraping the ingredients into a bowl, I moved on to dicing the mozzarella. "Might be tacky, but I like it."

"So that's what becomes of us after..." Now she whirled her hand in the air. "After everything. Our bodies decompose. There is no spirit, so what 'we' are no longer exists. But the energy that was us returns to the universe?"

"The All," I corrected. "Not the universe. The All is bigger than the universe."

Her mouth fell open. "How much bigger?"

"No idea. A lot. Full of universes. Maybe even structures that are bigger than a box of universes."

"Rev," she said, slapping the bar only half-playfully, "what's bigger than the universe?"

"*A* universe," I said and couldn't *not* smile. "Remember, we don't know how many there are."

"Why not? You're an angel."

"Pretty sure even Yahweh doesn't have the answer."

She whistled. "I need a minute or ten years to wrap my head around this, but I'm okay with thinking our energy returns to the very thing that birthed it. Does that happen to you? Angels? Demons? Gods? Does your energy return to this All when you die?"

"In a way. When we die, our energy is put back into the All as a morning star. It's an ego thing for angels. Gross, I know. Beyond that, it depends. If we die a natural death, yes. If we die in the Overworld, by accident. Yes."

"By accident?"

"Yeah, if we are killed by another supernatural being, an angel, demon, god, then they absorb our energy."

She snapped her fingers. "That's what happened with the demon in Seattle we chased out of Pike Place? You absorbed his energy. That's why he gave off that… What would you call it? A light display? You basically took on his life force."

"That's one way of saying it, yes."

"Wow. As an assassin, you must have done that often."

"I have," I said to the small white cubes of cheese. "Too often."

"How old are you?"

I stopped chopping the cheese, laying the blade flat on the cutting block. "Do you really want to know?"

The question hung there. Finally, she shook her head.

"It's exhausting," I said as I resumed my cheese duties, feeling like I owed her more of an answer. "Each time I have to do it, I'm filled with regret in the seconds before I absorb their energy. I know I have to. What choice do I have? Then, I do my damn job and my existence is extended so I can do it for an even longer time."

Billee said nothing. Sometimes, that's all you can say.

Behind me on the counter by my toaster, I heard the chimes even as Billee cocked her body to the side to see the delivery of a new scroll.

I slapped the knife down on the cutting block and sighed.

"Want me to get it?"

"I got it. Plus, you can't touch them until I open them, anyway."

"Not even to pick it up?"

"Nope." I picked up the scroll. "Yeah, more work." I tried to smile as I wagged it at Billee. Unrolling it, my smile fell. "You've *got* to be shitting me?"

"What's wrong?"

I re-scanned the scroll to make sure I hadn't misread it. Another escort job. Like the Reaper Minister didn't have enough on his plate. The next Lucifer. A meddlesome Nephilim acting like a Penumbra Man. Possibly one of the Seven Bowls of Wrath poured onto the world to kick off Armageddon.

"Another escort," I finally said, hoping she wasn't in the inquiring mood to know whose name was on the scroll.

"Oh, I'm sorry. Hopefully, for someone who has lived a long, fulfilling life?"

"Yeah, something like that," was all I could muster to say.

Had Delores Garcia's work with the Center For Caring, looking out for Olympia's homeless, been fulfilling? Had it provided her with the sense of peace and joy she deserved? I hoped so because according to my new assignment, she wouldn't be doing it for much longer.

9

SICK AT SEASIDE

PHER MONTJOY DOESN'T SPEND A LOT OF TIME IN THE Upperworld. He claims it's because when he's there, he doesn't feel he can relax. Too many things to get done. Too much politics. A place where even a simple stroll to the corner market turns into a drawn-out debate over some voting issue or other type of power positioning. According to Pher, the Overworld provides a sense of peace he can't find in the immortal realm.

I get it. One of the last things that brings a smile to my face is being around other angels.

It's not their fault, of course. Well, not most of them. They have regular lives, filled with regular worries. Kids to drop off at school. Who forgot to pull something out of the freezer to cook for dinner? The dog tore up the carpet... again. A leaky faucet. A dickhead for a boss. Too much to do and not enough time to do it. Yes, immortal life is full of the same crap as yours.

So, Pher is less than excited when he has to go to the Upperworld. Imagine how I feel. I spend a sixteenth of the time he does there and hold an equal dislike for it. I'm also less than excited to have to be there. So, guess where I was meeting my boss?

"As much as I dislike being here, I've got to say, you did well for yourself by picking the Fifth Level," I said as we strolled down the cobblestone street.

Unlike the Overworld, there are no cars or vehicles of any type in this Level. The Fifth is a tranquil place. A very calming slice of Heaven, if you will, even for an angel assassin. White stucco homes, narrow cobblestone streets, and quaint parks overlooking an ocean of blue blanketing the rest of the Level.

"Why do you think I chose it?" Pher said as we walked, his hands clasped behind his back and his head cast down.

I'd seen him walk like that for thousands of years, and to this day, I still didn't understand why. It had to be misery on his lower back. He said it helped him think. I wondered about that. I was half his age, fitter, and didn't walk like my jaw was chained to my feet.

"Might have to think about moving here," I said, staring down the slope of the street leading to the open market. On the horizon, the ocean stretched away. The smell of salt water was in the air, clean, with just a hint of musk.

"When were you home last?"

My lips flapped as I exhaled in thought. "No idea."

"Years."

"For more than a day or two? Definitely. At least five."

"Your house is probably falling apart."

"I do some housekeeping when I'm there. But," I said with a chuckle, "if it did, it'd take one more thing off my plate."

"Would be a shame."

"Not really."

I'm from the Third Level. Whereas Pher got to enjoy quiet streets, bright colors, serene parks, and communal spaces overlooking the largest ocean in the Upperworld, I have diversity. And I don't mean that in a progressive, humanistic way. I mean, the Third Level has rich and poor. Safety and crime. Extravagant feasts and the perpetually hungry. Hot and cold. The haves and the have-nots. Depending on which neighborhood you're from, you usually live in that same world for your entire existence. Born into poverty? Tough shit. Enjoy the next fifty thousand years of it. Lucky enough to come from an affluent family who owns acres of rolling green? Congratulations! You're one of the lucky ones and will probably tell anyone who listens about how glorious the Upperworld is. I got out because I showed desirable skills. Naming, I can take an ass-kicking and keep on ticking. Becoming a Reaper saved me, as gross as that was to realize. So yes, I was in no hurry to go back.

"Plus, I'm paying a management company to keep eyes on it, do the maintenance, etcetera."

"Hmmm," was all Pher said to that. I thought I had him fooled until he commented again a block later. "As long as you're not avoiding the Upperworld in hopes you can stay in the Overworld long enough to meet a premature demise."

I put my hand to my chest as if his comment offended me. "Well, Pher, I never."

"Cut the crap. Yes, you have."

"A few times."

"This week?"

I pulled up.

Pher drifted a few feet before turning, his hands still clasped behind his back. "Are you coming?"

"Are you going to clarify what you meant?"

Pher's full beard and mustache jolted with his smile. "Come on. I want to get down by the water. We can talk as we walk. After all, I know you didn't come to visit so you could sample my cooking. You're very much a snob in that respect."

Without waiting, Pher puttered down the sidewalk.

"Okay, fess up. What did you mean?" I asked when I caught up.

"About?"

"Don't do that."

"Do what?"

"That? Do you really think I'm staying in the Overworld in hopes I'll decay sooner or get myself killed?"

"On accident or on purpose, the result is the same," Pher said, his head cast down. "And decay is a very real thing. I feel it pull on me when I'm there for even a few weeks. You've been there for years. Nearly non-stop."

"I come back here for meetings."

Almost too subtle to notice, Pher shook his head. "I'd hate to see your talents go to waste because you're too stubborn to recognize your own self-destructiveness."

"I exercise and eat right." After a long pause, I added, "As often as I can. Though I might have a drink now and then, I don't smoke. If you're worried about my health, how about you get the Order to loosen up on those reserve Reapers we talked about? Cutting down on my workload would be an effective way of helping me maintain my health if that's what you're truly concerned about."

"We've had talks about the reserves."

"How's that coming?"

"They don't trust you enough."

"So, no reserves?"

Pher's lip curled. "Maybe. Maybe not. The discussions are still happening."

"Nothing ever moves fast with you all."

"No truer words have been spoken."

"Not so worried about my health, then? If the Order was, they would have done something about this workload imbalance. Would have acquired more angel power for the Reapers. We can't keep up with the duties, Pher. Something has to give. I promise, take care of that, and I'll give thought to popping back into the Upperworld from time to time to slow my decay."

"We're now negotiating to get you to do the right thing?"

I stopped. Flushed in frustration. "Don't talk to me about doing the right thing."

He turned. The street was empty, so we didn't have to concern ourselves with eavesdroppers. "Lad, what are you talking about?"

Everything came back at once, a combination that might become toxic if I allowed it. But hey, tens of thousands of years of living didn't teach you how to balance frustrations. So I let Pher have it.

"I've asked for a release how many times?"

Pher's eyes pinched. "Too many to count."

"How many times has the Order granted it?"

He lifted his hand, connecting his thumb and pointer finger in a loop while the other three remained raised.

"Zero. Exactly."

"We can't afford to not have you run the Reapers," Pher said, not unkindly. "You want out?"

"Yes."

"Then the first thing you have to do is train someone to replace you."

"I don't have time!" My voice echoed off the nearby homes. Drawing a deep breath, I calmed myself before I punched a pristine stucco wall. "Between all these damn assignments and everything I need to do to keep a grip on the Reapers, I barely have time to have a staff meeting and check in. Groom a mentee? Fat chance. How about you come through on getting me those reserves and I'll start focusing on my exit strategy?"

"There's the problem with your logic," Pher said, wagging a finger before turning and heading downhill again.

"Guess I'm following you?" I shouted petulantly.

"If you want to finish this discussion, it would behoove you to do so." I could tell by the way the hands clasped behind his back jumped and bounced that he'd humored himself.

I followed. Naturally.

At his side again, I asked, "What's the problem with my logic?"

"Your aim is to develop an exit strategy. For yourself."

"You told me to train someone."

"For the betterment of the Reapers."

"Wait, so even if I spin someone up to replace me, that doesn't mean I'll be able to leave the Reapers?"

Pher gave me a small shrug. Insignificant. "You're good at what you do. Too good. And, as you have said yourself, clearly and very often; the Reapers need all the help they can get."

"That's a dick move, Pher."

"Did you think anything less from politicians?"

"Fuck politics and politicians. I thought better of *you*," I said as honestly as I'd ever said anything, truly not caring if it stung or not. What he'd just, almost proudly, admitted stung just as much.

Pher stopped, facing me, his aged face, soft. I thought he might want to punch me in the throat, but Pher being Pher, he instead unlocked his hands and grabbed mine. Funny, the way contact between two people who care about each other can override all the ridiculousness of testosterone thrusting emotions into our mush brains, isn't it? "We all have a job to do, Rev. I'm doing mine. Do I like it? No. Do I enjoy this? Definitely not. But I have a responsibility to the greater good. You do as well, and I know you know that. We exist to protect those unselfish motivations. Now, now," he said in a rush as soon as my chest swelled. I think he recognized it before I did. "I'm not saying you're being selfish. Each one of us has to be concerned with self-preservation or we cease to exist. That's just basic evolution. You're not acting selfishly by being all grim and jaded and simply wanting to do something else with your life. I get all of that. But the Reapers need you. There is no one we trust more than you to monitor demons and monsters."

"And do your dirty work."

After a quick squeeze of affirmation, he said, "Do what must be done for the Balance. A new Lucifer might be rising. That's not something we can take lightly or ignore. We can't ignore how effective you are at removing threats. And few have your touch for escorting."

"There's a lot of good Reapers," I said, feeling the need to defend my peers. "You should swing by one of our meetings and see for yourself. All the Order should. Can't remember the last time I saw one of you there."

"Fair point," he said. "We should. It has been a while. Our failings aside, you see what I mean? Were the situation different, I might agree with you. But I don't. I'm sorry. Not likely it's something you wanted to hear, but I won't lie to you. Ever. We need you. The Reapers need you. The Upperworld does, and so does every single mortal you impact."

"Like Delores Garcia," I said now that I had his attention.

"Who?"

"A scroll came through yesterday, signed by you."

"Ah, yes," Pher said, his cheekbones lifting as he smiled at remembering his missive. "I sent a few hundred out. Long day."

"Bet it was."

"I'm sensing you're not happy with the assignment? Can't help you there. We try to keep the escorting away from you, but it's difficult with as thin as your ranks are. I couldn't help but spread the load. Look at it this way, at least it was only one. Most Reapers got hundreds. Your more effective Reapers received a few thousand."

"Thank Yahweh for the Interlude, huh?"

"Yes, sir." Pher grasped his hands with a sharp smack. "So what about this Ms. Garcia bothers you?"

The warm breeze smelled clean. Its light touch on my skin would have been relaxing if I had a life relatively free of worry. Instead of enjoying it, I pressed on with business, because there was always business to press. "She doesn't deserve it. This is the woman who first told me about the Penumbra Man and the sores in the homeless camp in Olympia. She's good people, Pher. Doing good work. And, trust me, she's got plenty more to give."

"If it's her time…"

"It doesn't have to be, though."

"It is written, so it is done."

I rubbed my face with both frustrated hands. "God-dammit, Pher. I don't need you to tow the company line right now. The world is full of shitty, selfish mortals, and she's the one getting called? Come on."

"What do you want me to do, Rev?"

"I don't know, work a trade or something. Switch her name out for a piece of shit child abuser when Jericho isn't looking for all I care. But Delores Garcia is way too good of a person to be called now, especially with everything up in the air."

"It is wr—"

"I swear to God, if you say what I think you're about to say, I'll open a Rift back to the Overworld and step in front of the first oversized truck I see."

"You wouldn't."

"Try me."

"Well, either way, I can't trade her name."

"No one has to know."

"It doesn't work like that."

"Make it."

"I can't, lad. Stop being so stubborn."

Rare were the times when Pher was as firm as he was now. Looking like I was really starting to piss him off, he wasn't budging.

A calmer tone might help me get the resolution I needed. So I switched tactics. "What do I need to do to get your help? Volunteer for another five millennia of Reaper duty? Will that work?"

His head dropped. My boss was done dealing with me. "There's no point doing this, Rev. I wish I could say something. I wish I could do something. But I can't. Her name is in the Book of Planes. One has sent for her because the All requires her energy. Accept it. It'll make the entire thing easier for you." His hands released mine, and he put one on my shoulder. "And, easier on her. You know that's what matters."

He was right. Of course. "I'm tired of seeing good mortals get called too soon. This job is shitty enough."

"I know, my friend."

"Give me hope then, boss."

"How?"

"I want my morning star."

10

RHYMES AND REASONS

Pher didn't give me my morning star on my request. Of course, he can't, but that's irrelevant. At the moment of my asking for it, I was tapped out. Exhausted. Done. Cleats hung on pegs. Board game packed away. Put on ice. Out to pasture. Ready to give Pher both barrels even though I knew it'd be useless and Maggie only has one. Whatever it was called, however it was categorized, that's how I felt leaving Pher's home. What I still felt now.

My morning star, one of the gazillions, real number or not, was out there somewhere. Maybe even viewable from Earth. We're not told these types of things. From time to time, I entertain myself, especially on my darker nights—figuratively and literally—by star-gazing. All those fine, blinking points of light. Each a home to the essence of an angel. Maybe from our universe. Maybe another. An eternal signature against the curtain of black. A way to be remembered. Forever.

After my conversation that ended with a request to my boss, it was obvious I'd need to wait for mine. What couldn't wait was the conversation with Billee.

This was going to suck.

"Sort of cold to be having drinks on the balcony, isn't it?"

Billee said, draped in her parka, her hands wrapped around the blackberry mulled wine. When she pulled the jacket's hood forward over her head, she practically sank into it. "But this is delicious. Is there nothing you can't make?"

"I'm sure there's something, but I'd have to look long and hard to find it." I yanked my head up. My skin prickled at the cold air. I needed fresh air for this. Cold air is clean air, free of the heavy feel of heat, humidity, and guilt of responsibility. Tonight, I was coming clean to my partner and needed all the help I could get. "Plus, I spent way too much on this patio heater to not use it from time to time."

She looked up at the metallic dome of sheet metal that helped spread the heat. The glow of blue flame from the burning propane twinkled in her eyes like the morning stars hiding in the vastness of space much farther above us, behind the cloudy night sky. "It is nice. The heat. The drink. Thank you for this."

"You're welcome." My mind was screaming, *'don't let her thank you for what you're about to do to her, you dumbass,'* but I ignored it.

Billee beat me to the conversation starter. "No, seriously. Thank you for this.." She risked taking one gloved hand off her mug to gesture over downtown Olympia. "The view, too. It really helps."

"Helps with what?"

She faced me. I chuckled.

"What?" she asked.

"You are doing a hell of a job making sure you don't move an inch from beneath direct heat."

She looked up again. Her hood fell back enough that a few strands of curls fell out from its protection. The way her mouth seemed sunken compared to her cheekbones wasn't off-putting. A stunning, intelligent woman without love in her life. And I played a part in that.

Billee caught me. "You okay?"

"Yeah. Just shivered because of the cold."

"You can come under the heater with me. You don't have to stand so far away."

Oh, yes, I do! Instead, I pulled my own mulled wine to my mouth, grimacing behind it. "This is perfect, right here. Don't want to get too hot."

"Why? Then you'd have to take off the duster?"

I tried to sip as I shook my head. "Hating on the duster. Man, not cool."

She patted my arm, laughing lightly. Then her hand was gone. She swallowed and flicked a finger out toward nothing specific. "Okay, before I lose my nerve. I have to tell you something. Don't interrupt. Okay?"

"Okay."

"That's interrupting." She laughed and blew out a long breath. "Whew. Here goes. Rev, I adore you. You're a very sweet guy. And trust me, in social work, you don't meet a lot of nice guys. Makes you appreciate the ones in your life even more."

I started to say 'okay' again but caught myself.

"So I think you'll understand where I'm coming from. Okay, Billee, enough delaying."

Seriously, it was adorable watching a social worker talk themselves through something.

"I don't think I'm cut out for this. In my job, I have to stay balanced and healthy or I'm helping no one. In fact, if I'm not keeping a healthy balance, I can do actual harm to someone. That's my vector, if you will."

"So you feel you're not staying healthy? Is there something I can do?"

"Yes. Stop interrupting."

I put my mug to my big mouth and sipped, promising myself to let her get this out.

"I know when I'm not giving my best," Billee said. "This crazy reality I'm a familiar to an angel is still very weird. Even after all these months. I get the need. I just don't get it, if that makes sense."

I nodded instead of verbalizing that it made sense. I was already running out of nine lives with Billee.

"Even though you've never complained about how I'm doing, I know deep in my heart I'm not doing the best I can for you or those you serve. Now that all this stuff," she said, her gloved hand coming free of her mug again and waving around in the empty air, "is going on, it's only going to get riskier. I've got a problem with that. The other day, we fought a group of people. People who were in trouble. A fist fight. I'm a damn social worker and I'm throwing down in a park like some thug against people who were being influenced by something I frankly don't understand. Yes, what happened was wrong, but I'm smart enough to not cull things down into a false dichotomy. They need to learn from that experience, but they were victims too. If you believe them." She fell silent. I waited. She looked at me. "Aren't you going to say something?"

"And suffer your wrath?" I said with a wink.

"Do you believe what that big guy said?"

"Unequivocally, yes. A Penumbra Man can do that to a person. To a group of people. Part of the power of being a Nephilim."

"So see?"

"They were hurting that guy."

"That's the only reason I'm not shattered by guilt."

This was now, officially, a back-and-forth. Billee wouldn't skin me alive for contributing, so I jumped in. "Don't do that to yourself. I needed you and we did the right thing. Yes, some of them got hurt, but there's always going to be collateral damage in these situations. My primary responsibility as a supernatural being is to limit damage. A few broken bones are something I can live with."

"Except you're not living with them. They are. You're the

one who gave them the broken bones." She shook her head. Curls fell out of the fox-fur-lined hood. "That's not even the issue. If I wasn't your familiar, someone else would be, and they might not be so concerned with everyone's well-being and serving those who need to be served. I—I just don't know if I can do it. My first months with you weren't like this. I don't know if I can be what you need me to be *and* be what I need myself to be for those people and others like them."

"Here's the thing," I said, looking away. Sometimes eye contact makes things too intense when delivering bad news. "You don't get a choice, Billee. Shitty as it is, they selected you to be my familiar for life. Until the end of yours or mine, we're a team. As you can see, I'm not going anywhere, so…"

"Wow, you would really suck as a counselor."

"No argument there."

"So Heaven expects me to do this when I'm eighty? Fat chance."

Oh, boy. "Most familiars don't live that long. It's a dangerous job."

She swallowed. I felt like crap.

"Everyone wants to talk about doing things for the greater good, but no one talks about the cruelty of that mentality," I said. "You're a perfect example. Most familiars are. 'We should all act for the greater good.' That's what people, angels too, say. The good ones do anyway. The catch is, no one wants to be the one doing the sacrificing. So we end up with situations like this, where a mortal is forced into a twisted form of indentured servitude."

Billee cupped her mug, bringing it to her chest as if she was hugging it.

I snorted at a sudden thought. "If you want to blame anyone, blame Pher. He's the one who championed you."

"Oh?"

"Yeah. Asshole."

"Total asshole." She gave a short laugh. "Wonder what he saw in me."

"He likes younger women."

That earned me a swat, and I almost spilled the wine that didn't taste as fruity as I'd hoped when I planned this evening out.

"Gross."

Her conversation had run its course. But I still needed to address the situation with Delores, and holding off on delivering the news wouldn't do her any favors.

"Hey, listen, since we're on the topic of the Upperworld's shittiness, are you okay with me sharing unfortunate news? My gut says it will upset you."

Half of Billee's prominent forehead was covered in the shadow of the parka hood. Her cheeks, smooth with youth and bold with determination, shone in the dim light. She pressed the mug to her mouth as if the drink could keep her warm against the night. Standing close enough to the patio heater to get its phone number, she wasn't ready for the bombshell I was about to drop.

Goddamn, I hate this job.

"That scroll I got the other day when I had you over for dinner?"

"Yeah?"

The words stuck in my throat.

Billee pulled the mug away from her mouth, replacing it with a gloved hand. "Oh, God. It's bad. I—is it me?"

I shook my head, feeling the weight of the strain of delivering the news as I clenched my jaw.

Her hand trembled. "Someone I know?"

I nodded. Then I broke Billee's heart.

"WHY?" BILLEE ASKED AS SOON AS I HAD HER BACK INSIDE MY apartment.

She took the news about Delores as I expected. The balcony was not the place to finish the conversation.

"Here, sit." I threw the couch pillows to the other end, taking her mug, and setting it on a coaster on my coffee table.

"Why Delores?" Billee's eyes were rimmed in red, pools of tears occupying them.

"It's her time," I said, feeling how completely inadequate the platitude was.

Her trembling hand, still gloved, was back at her mouth. Teary eyes stared at something on my floor, but were distant. She hadn't reclined against the back of the couch, but sat slumped. "W—when?"

"I've got some wiggle room."

"When. Tell me."

"Within a month."

Now the tears came in a flood.

Billee leaned forward until her chest was at her knees, crying into her hands. I helplessly watched until I risked reaching over and rubbing her back.

"I'm sorry."

She cried, and I sat with her, wishing I didn't have to be the one to deliver the news, while also being glad it was me who held that responsibility. As my familiar, she had insight into the reasons Delores was dying, instead of spending the next few years, maybe the rest of her life, wondering and questioning. Cruel as it may sound, death is inevitable for everyone and everything. The only way the absence hurts less, the only way it fades, is by dealing with it. As much as this sucked, I could do something good for Billee, and I would do something good for Delores.

After she finished a heart-rending bit of heaving, she sat up, trying to draw deeper breaths. I found a box of tissue and set it at her side, sitting on the couch beside her but cocked to face her. I don't know how long we sat there, but it was as long as Billee needed.

Billee had grabbed a tissue, blown her nose, and got a fresh one. It remained in her hands, where she folded and unfolded it. "You know, she only fully retired a few years ago?" Billee looked up, blinked away tears, and dabbed at her wet cheeks. Her laugh was abrupt and filled with ironic sadness. "She's a lot like you. Hated every minute of her job as a cook. But when she talked about it, you could see her pride in what she accomplished."

"What did she do?"

"She worked in the cafeteria of a local high school. After that, when she was looking for something to fill her days, this was before she started with CFC. Always told me she started questioning where she could serve others like she did for the kids. I don't know how. Maybe she was just estimating, but she kept track of how many kids she fed in the time she worked at the school. A few decades. Tens of thousands of meals. To her, it wasn't just about throwing a dry chicken patty on a piece of bread or slopping corn on a tray. She wasn't lying. You could see it in her face. She knew what some of those kids were going through. In school. Their grades. Being bullied. Broken hearts. Too many preferred being in school than at home because at home they'd have to take care of younger brothers and sisters because their parents were too drunk to uphold their end of parenting. She knew too many went home to be abused. Some had their dreams obliterated even before they could drive. Delores understood that. When she found the CFC, she was thrilled. It gave her something fresh, but also something familiar." Billee's lips rolled, the strain of her pain evident in the lines cutting across the bottom of her eyes. "She'd found her place and wanted to spend the rest of her life serving those people who benefited from CFC."

I rubbed Billee's shoulder.

"At least she got to do it for a time." She sniffed and blew her nose, angrily crumbling the tissue. "But what's a few years against an entire life filled with doing something that doesn't fulfill you? Not finding your own happiness? Someone like her, standing all day, hustling in a hot kitchen for crap pay. Taking part-time jobs to cover the bills the school's paycheck didn't. Only getting to do something that fulfills you for a few years before it all ends, while the greedy wealthy enjoy the best of everything. The best houses. Constant comfort. Great doctors. They never contribute to humankind and they never seem to die." Billee's head dropped. "She'll never see sixty-five. Never see her grandkids graduate from the high school where she spent her entire life in. Not fair."

Billee's voice had softened, but the pain was still there.

"Want coffee?" I asked.

She just nodded, staring at the floor and mindlessly playing with the tissue. I was halfway through piling grounds in the reservoir when she said, "Not too strong, or I'll never get to sleep."

I scooped at least two tablespoons back into the container and re-sealed it.

I stayed by the counter, puttering around, while the coffee brewed. Helping mortals deal with death is a challenge, even on my best days. Spending eight thousand years doing what I do can make you numb to the end of life. Occupational hazard, I guess. It happens to everyone who works in this line. Mortals aren't immune either. Doctors, firefighters, EMTs, police, and mental health providers. Hell, people who work at animal shelters. They all do too, if they stick around long enough. To different degrees, there's something in our brains that shuts off the senses of trauma and loss. Self-preservation. No one could do those sorts of jobs for long if they fully experienced every loss. Well, sociopaths might, but not high-functioning people and angel assassin Reapers.

I didn't want Billee to think of me as calloused. I didn't

want her to think this was 'business as usual' either. This was what it was, and she didn't need to learn that about me. Not yet. We didn't have that kind of history. A decade from now, if she made it that long, I was sure she'd come around and understand, and maybe even develop her own mental safeguards. For now, this was about Delores' date with her ultimate destiny and Billee processing the inevitable.

Coffee finished, I filled the carafe, put two cups, creamer, and sugar on a tray with spoons, and brought it over to the table. I filled her cup while she blew her nose again.

"I don't want to screw up your creamer and sugar combo, so I'll leave that to you."

"Thanks, Rev."

I hated how numb she sounded.

Spoons clinked on glazed ceramic. An occasional sip here and there broke the quiet.

"You're getting really good at not interrupting. I'm proud of you," Billee said, now on her second cup.

"I'm trainable."

"Rev?

"Yeah?"

"Thank you for telling me."

"Of course."

"No, seriously. You could have waited. You could have gone behind my back and taken her without me having a clue of what was going on. But this… I know it couldn't have been easy for you. This was about respect. I just want you to know I appreciate it."

"You're welcome."

"Doesn't make understanding any of this easier."

Finished with my coffee, I refilled my cup and offered to do the same for her. Billee nodded.

"Forget it. I won't be able to sleep tonight, anyway. Might as well enjoy savory coffee and company," she said, and set her cup down for me.

"If there's anything I can do, let me know. I don't have any answers. I can't tell you much. But if I know, I'll share it. Just say the word."

"Thanks," she said, sliding her cup over and dousing it with creamer until it was nearly as pale brown as muddy snow. "I know you can't answer anything. No one can. That's always been the most frustrating thing for me. The lack of answers. I guess that's why religion works for so many people. It provides enough answers to their questions. I just have too many."

"Yeah," I said noncommittally.

"Just… sucks."

"Yeah."

"Makes you question the point of all of this," she said, sitting up straighter. "Why bother with any of it if people like Delores are taken too soon? Does this you have a conscience?"

I spread my hands. "That's a big question I'll never have an answer to. Not even sure if Yahweh Himself could answer that."

"I figured I'd ask. Well, if it does. It, God, Satan, whoever, they can all kiss my ass for taking someone like her. Especially so soon after she found joy. Nothing good would ever do that." Heat returned to her voice. Maybe I should have offered a decaf. "Delores has done nothing wrong. If the All needs her energy, it could rake through corporate America and take those greedy assholes. I'm sure a clean sweep of Wall Street would gather maybe as much good energy as Delores offers."

I chuckled.

She stopped and looked at me. The corners of her mouth flicked upwards in a grin.

"It may not be helpful now, I don't know. It's been a long time since I've been through something like this on a personal level," I said, avoiding the last loss I suffered. My last ten losses were familiars. When you've had over three hundred of them, you stop feeling the deep, lacing pain of loss. Billee definitely didn't need that peek into my personal headspace. "Once you wrap your head around the lack of a rhyme or reason to any of this, that what is just... is, dealing with loss becomes easier." I held up a hand. "I'm not saying that losing Delores is easy. Not at all. This is advice based on my experience. For the future, I guess. The more you recognize the randomness of all this, the easier it is to accept."

Billee set her coffee cup down with a clink. "You're right." She paused, exhaling. The quiver was gone, I noticed. "I'm starting to understand the reason you're so jaded."

I didn't have the courage to tell Billee she was only seeing the tip of the iceberg.

11

TAKING ONE FOR THE TEAM

BILLEE AND I WERE ON OUR WAY TO TACOMA TO MEET UP WITH Pher. He said he was visiting an old friend. He wouldn't say who, but mentioned he'd be in town for a few days. I wanted a face-to-face with him since our last encounter wasn't the best chat we'd had this century, and Billee asked if she could tag along. She needed the company. I didn't mind and knew Pher wouldn't either.

Delores Garcia's scroll was still unfulfilled. The Scroll Eater was going to have to wait—I'll get to that interesting bugger later. Billee was still dealing with the fallout. Maybe she wanted to see Pher so she could punch him in the face and ask him to deliver that message to Yahweh.

On the Interstate, we were just leaving Olympia proper when my third eye sensed trouble.

Yanking the steering wheel hard, I crossed the thick-lined V that separated the exit from the highway, and barely avoided the guardrail.

"What the hell?" Billee shrieked, holding the 'oh shit' handle above her head.

"Sorry." I grimaced and glanced in the rearview mirror, hoping I wouldn't see a highway patrol emerge from the flow of cars behind me to ask exactly what my malfunction was. "Something's going on over there."

I risked flicking a finger at a gated storage facility running parallel to the exit. The aggressive move to get into the farthest-right lane was successful, even though the casual observer wouldn't be able to tell by the way Billee still gripped the handle above her head.

"What kind of something?"

"Punks destroying shit and about to get themselves arrested, from what I can tell."

"How can you te—"

Whipping off the main road, I used a gas station as a cut-through because I didn't have the time or patience to wait at the red light behind the line of cars that weren't in a hurry to get anywhere.

"Watch o—" Billee thrust her hand toward the windshield, warning me about a pedestrian in the right place at the wrong time.

I don't know what she was worried about. I'd already seen the guy and avoided him by at least five feet—a little closer than I would have liked. Still, I'll chalk it up to a mastery of driving. Not bad for a guy who's been an assassin since the invention of the wheel. To satiate my masochistic tendencies, I took a gander in the rearview mirror as we popped back on the street to see him shaking a fist before flipping me off.

"If you get us killed, I'm coming back to haunt you," my passenger threatened.

Around the corner of the block, the trees pulled away to reveal the entrance to a self-storage kingdom. Three yellow concrete poles protected the keyless entry box. A sliding gate, wide enough to allow two vehicles to pass, separated us from the storage buildings. Each building was the type of economical metal I expected from these types of places. The front building had two small windows in one corner. The office. Dark.

"How are we going to get in? We don't know the key entry," Billee said as I whipped the car to the side of the black-top, parked, and shut off the engine. I jumped out without answering my partner.

Ten feet away, Billee's door slammed closed. Fifteen feet away, she was already by my side. Another reminder of how badly I needed to visit the gym.

Now outside, I could hear banging and hooting, accompanied by squeaky-voiced laughter and amateur shit-talking that could only come from teenage boys.

"They're toward the back," I said, gesturing with a thumb at the fence. "Let's go."

"Over?"

"Unless you want to pull apart the bars, Sparky, I don't know another way in." I bent and cupped my hands, offering my palms to her booted foot.

"This is nuts," Billee said but didn't wait. She grabbed the gate, hefted a foot into my hands, and I pushed.

My familiar isn't a large woman by any stretch of the imagination, which really makes her ass-kicking abilities commendable when you think about it. She's nimble, too.

I thrust. Billee went up. In one motion, she landed on the horizontal bar with one foot, while dangling the other over the six-foot drop. Her arm out for balance, she pushed herself off the gate and landed as quietly as a cat.

She glanced around. "There's no gate release."

"Don't worry, I'm coming over." I gripped the horizontal bar at the top of the gate and pulled myself up, kicking a foot onto the bar for added stability. I basically hung like that, one leg swinging wildly for purchase, until I could pull myself up and get enough balance. By the time I dropped to the ground next to Billee, she was smiling, and I was panting.

"That was tougher than it looked," I said.

"Not for me."

"Come on, smartass. Let's find these punks before they ruin their lives."

We ran down the wide, main corridor. The challenge with self-storage places is that, if they're big enough and if the buildings are metal and arranged into neat U-shapes, it can become confusing to pinpoint sound. Any noise loud enough to be carried into the air will carom off the corrugated metal and ripple along the unit's walls until it meets the next building. That will then also carry the sound. If the storage yard is big enough, too much valuable time could be wasted searching for the origin of a simple sound.

The racket in the yard made our task easier. A lot of destruction of personal property was happening, and the culprits didn't seem interested in hiding their criminal enterprising.

I opened my mind to my third eye and came up blank.

"Rev? You okay?"

"Yeah. Sorry." Giving my head a shake, I said, "Let's find these little assholes."

Billee pointed to the left alley.

She seemed confident, so we headed off.

The clamor grew louder. Billee had been right. We were getting close.

I can't say it surprised me when we rounded the next building and saw that my third eye had been correct about the squeaky voices. Teenage boys. Young. Babies, really. Somewhere on the newer-model end of the mortal spectrum, these punks were too young to be punks. Most appeared between fourteen and maybe eighteen. Some of them probably hadn't even sprouted their first ball hair yet. As disappointingly surprising as their youth was, even more disturbing was how many there were.

At least fifty, maybe topping out at around sixty.

I pulled Billee back behind the cover of the building before they spotted us.

"What do we do?"

"No freaking idea," I said.

"There's so many."

"Suburbia creates spoiled punks. They fit the bill."

Billee leaned out again. "Rev, they're destroying other people's property."

I leaned out over her.

The punks were kicking storage unit doors, apparently getting their non-hairy balls off at the property damage each time the metal doors rattled violently. From somewhere, they found baseball bats and crowbars and were taking them to any light or camera within reach, sometimes boosting one another if the job required it. Destruction of other people's stuff knows no bounds.

"Over there," I said, pointing at a unit with its door pulled up.

"One of them has bolt cutters," Billee said, pointing to a kid with long blond locks. His frame was square. Not really athletic, but he might grow into a formidable body one day. As someone who appreciates long hair, I had to admit his was awesome, even putting my shoulder-length black shreds to shame.

The kid was walking from unit to unit with the bolt cutters, snapping locks as he went. A small group of younger boys served as his personal cheer squad, following behind him, hopping on their feet and whipping their fists in the air, rooting him on.

"What are we going to do?"

"Give me a second," I said, watching and trying to pick out details any non-assassin wouldn't notice.

Too many kids with stories. That's the problem with my third eye. In a crowd, it's basically useless when opened fully, especially when that crowd is active and bent on violence. Good stories, bad stories, promise, hope, heartbreak; this group had experienced it all and would live through more in the coming decades. Too many bodies and too much noise, and I had to focus more on protecting life, limb, and safety.

"We can't fight all of them."

Way back in the deepest region of my brain, something tickled. A thought. A memory. Something urgent. I tried to focus on it, but between the overload of third eye information and the damn kids pissing me off with their vagrant behaviors, I couldn't think straight.

The bolt cutter was moving along the row, in our direction. Each *clack* of a cut lock striking the blacktop only seemed to encourage him. And it didn't look like he was slowing down.

"We're going to stop him," I said with final clarity. Now, I just had to get Billee's buy-in. "I'm going to ask you to do something you probably won't like, but they're kids. I don't want to hurt them if I don't have to."

"Okay," she drawled.

"I need a distraction so I can get in position."

Billee stiffened. "What sort? What position?"

Under other circumstances, the skepticism in her voice would have been humorous.

"They're teenage boys."

"Right?" She elongated that too.

"They're easily distracted."

Her forehead furrowed. "Are you asking me to use myself as the distraction? To teens?"

I shrugged as if she was asking which movie I'd like to see. "I'd really appreciate it."

"That's gross."

"But it'll be effective and, if I do my part right, no one gets hurt. Not you. Not me. And, maybe unfortunately, not these punks. All you have to do is bat a few eyes, and laugh at their cocky statements of self-importance. You know?"

"Appeal to their masculine insecurities by acting like that actually charms me?"

"Sort of."

She sighed. "Fine. What do I do?"

I laid out the plan.

"You sure I'll be able to see this sign of yours?"

My back against the wall, I pointed backward with my thumb toward the destructive clamor filling the open-air storage. "Trust me. You'll see a marked change."

"Okay," she said, and was off, racing along the building.

I hated being separated. I had a plan and was pretty confident—*shhh*, don't tell Billee—it would work. But still. Separation introduces risk. Anyone who has ever fought in battle or watched a horror movie knows the truth of that. Truth with a capital 'T'.

At the other end, she stopped before rounding the corner, taking one last look in my direction.

I mustered a confident nod, and she slipped out of sight. I inched toward the corner. Peeking, I saw the long-locked bolt cutter and his crew were still frolicking in their work, constantly moving closer.

"Come on, Billee," I whispered.

Snap. Another lock cut, followed by the clunking racket of another unit's door being rolled up. The boys whooped and hollered. Must have been good stuff in the new unit.

The find might keep the boys distracted, but only for so long. Once the allure of the contents waned, they'd move on, bringing them another step closer to my hiding spot.

I moved back into hiding and waited for Billee's voice. I scanned the two units perpendicular to my position. Fifty feet separated them and they were silent. Even if these kids hadn't scared off any customer looking to retrieve their golf clubs for a mid-January round on the links, there was no sign of anyone coming or going recently. Good thing too. This could get ugly and I didn't need collateral damage.

Something was off, but I couldn't put my finger on it. All I knew was that this didn't feel right, and the same suspicious gut that'd got me through thousands of fights over the millennia was pinging now. A bout of paranoia about the Nephilim in town? Maybe. These kids could be acting like little assholes all on their own, but I wasn't convinced.

The long parallel buildings gave away no sign or clue of the Penumbra Man though. Their roofs were free of shifting shapes. If the Nephilim was here, riling up these punks, he was lying low.

Before I heard the next snap of a bolt, my partner drew the boys' attention.

"What are you guys doing here?" she asked with just the right level of mature assuredness and wonderment to capture their juvenile attention without making them respond aggressively.

A brief conversation ensued. Full of hyper-masculine bragging and posturing. At first, bravado filled their comments and justifications, as if they intended to frighten her away. Before long, Billee switched her tone as if their gumption impressed her.

I could almost hear her tucking her hair behind her ear.

And like all master plans, this one worked. I didn't even have to put my hand near the secret pocket holding Maggie. When I peeked around the corner, the ringleader and his posse of morons had drifted away from the units and moved in Billee's direction.

I slid along the wall, heading to the group of fifty-odd punks who were chatting her up.

Billee didn't appear to feel threatened. In fact, they were showing off their wares as if the punks had earned the property through hard work. Weights. Bikes. An old collection of porno mags. Personal heirlooms that had probably been in families for generations. Golf clubs, which they promptly smashed against metal doors and siding, laughing at the ones that didn't snap in half, obnoxiously bragging when they did.

Billee took it all like a champ; I've got to hand it to her.

Though four dozen doofuses milled closely, flirted, and showed their propensity for awesomeness, she never flinched. Told you I had an epic familiar.

In the distance, something thumped on a nearby roof. Maybe one idiot had tried to get access to a stubborn unit from atop a unit. I didn't need a kid falling and breaking his back. That would undo my well-intentioned efforts at saving them from themselves, after all.

Risking getting caught off-guard by the larger contingent, I focused on where I thought I heard the thump. My third eye gave me nothing and my actual eyes provided little more. I swore I saw one brat for an instant. Rhythmic footfalls on metal convinced me I was correct.

Keeping my back turned on my teammate and the group was not something I dreamed of doing, but I didn't like this. It felt too much like a setup. The noise thumping on the roofs of the unit to my left was somewhat muted by distance, but I know what I heard. Someone was up on the roof.

I slid my hand inside the duster, wrapping my fingers around Maggie's grip and sparking her with a shot of Angelfire.

Though I'm all for coincidences, but the presence of the Penumbra Man in Olympia had me leaning toward that being the cause of the rooftop noise. After all, it had a knack for group manipulation. I knew at least one Nephilim was playing as a Penumbra Man. Maybe more. Regardless if it was a singular or group threat, I'd been attacked by one, so they knew I was aware. I wasn't getting taken down from behind without squeezing off a beam or two of Angelfire into its gut.

I was about to risk a climb up the unit's ladder when Billee grabbed the boys' full attention.

"Shit," I growled, releasing Maggie and reaching into the front pocket of my duster. I wrapped my hand around the small stone, about half the size of a baseball, I kept there for occasions such as this.

The stone is smooth. You could rub this baby on your face and not irritate even the most sensitive skin. A rock of pure white. Stunning and powerful. What's even more impressive is how blinding its radiant brightness is when activated. The outcome isn't so bad either. These kids had no idea what was about to happen.

Time for non-violence, unless the Nephilim was here as the Penumbra Man and wanted to throw fists.

I dropped my head, sending my will into the soul stone. It warmed in my hand. The skin around the stone was the first to glow, but the circle soon spread. By the time I stepped out from hiding, my entire fist glowed.

The group of punks turned.

"Who the fuck are you?" one too young to use language asked.

"Someone who is going to convince you what you're doing is stupid, irresponsible, and disrespectful."

"You a cop?" another, dressed in pants far too large for his thin frame, asked.

What was it with this generation being incapable of forming complete sentences with respectable grammar?

"No." I gestured with my non-glowing hand, looping it in a circle. "But I'm going to make sure you little bastards put back everything. Then my partner is going to get your names."

"Why would we do that, dumbass?" the long-locked kid said. With hair like that, he'd be a romance book cover model one day if he didn't completely fuck up his life beforehand. He twirled the bolt cutters. "All of us against your old ass? Won't be much of a fight."

Chuckles, back slaps, and fist pumps greeted his boast. Imagine his disappointment when neither Billee nor I gave him as much as a tepid blink.

From my periphery, I noticed her slowly moving away, toward the corner of the building. I didn't take it personally. Not that she didn't believe in me, but more the fact that fifty-some-odd jackasses were closing in an ever-tightening circle.

What she didn't know yet was she had nothing to worry about. There may be fifty-plus of them, but there was one of me. Not only was I immortal, and a trained assassin, but I also had a soul stone.

I raised my glowing fist before they got any smart ideas about hurling a golf club or outdated end table lamp through my chest.

"Need you to stop right where you are." The power of the soul stone pulsed in my hand.

The boys moved closer.

The stone wouldn't take effect until they were within the sphere of influence. A radius of twenty feet. With so many troublemakers, I was taking a risk but I didn't see any other way to stop them that didn't include pulling Maggie out, and putting another half dozen Reapers on notice to take out the trash. That's happened before, plenty of times, and it's not fun. Too much damn paperwork. Plus, then there's the whole-spontaneous response of the Upperworld to scribble some-one's name into the Book of Planes, and required internal investigations. Who needs the headache?

A smattering of the group hung back. Even though their crazed eyes told me they wanted to rip me limb from limb, they didn't press closer.

I stepped forward. "You little assholes think you're so cool destroying other people's property? You're not cool; you're losers." Another few feet and I was surrounded, but too many of them lingered on the fringes.

I had lost sight of Billee and hoped she listened when I told her to stay away from the confrontation, no matter how frightening it got. I hoped she held her nerve and didn't whip out her phone to call the cops, or worse, jump into any fray.

This situation didn't need to get screwed up by a gung-ho cop looking to show he's the toughest guy on the block or her getting intentionally or accidentally hurt.

The kids within the sphere of influence weren't paying attention to me any longer. Dozens of faces were upturned, all of them consumed by the soul stone's influence. I was safe with them as long as no one outside the sphere got off a lucky ranged attack.

That was the beauty of this rare device. Few angels possess a soul stone, and those who do are Reapers or have higher levels of responsibility. There are very few of the latter. Extremely powerful in the mortal realm, they're given only to those with an essential need. Even Guardian Angels—yes, it's an actual title—don't have Soul Stones. They're too dangerous in the wrong hands.

"Fuck you, old man!" someone from the back said.

I took another step, still amazed I'd made it this far into their clutches without at least taking one errant golf ball to the noggin.

"Mmm, no. Fuck you," I said to the teen. Hey, I've had thousands of years to use one-liners and ran out of material long before Columbus sailed the ocean blue. I jabbed my hand in the general direction of the voice. "Why don't you come say it to my face? Chicken shit." I added that last part with a cocky smile I knew would irritate any teen boy.

Wouldn't you know, it worked!

The crowd from the back pushed forward. In their eyes, the desire to get at me and dislocate a few things I didn't want dislocated burned. Unfortunately for them, as soon as they stepped into the sphere, they too fell under the influence of the soul stone.

Just like that. Over fifty teenage punks were under my complete control. Good thing too. I wasn't at ease with this situation, unconvinced the Penumbra Man wasn't lurking in hiding.

I waved at the storage units. "Put everything back where you found it. And you better hope to God you put them back exactly how you found them."

"Yes, sir," came the response in full chorus.

As the boys set off to fix as much of the mess as they could, Billee drifted to my side, watching them. Supervising, you could say. "What did you do?"

I had put the soul stone away but pulled it back out for her. It had gone quiet after I set the boys in motion and stopped powering it. They'd be under its influence for the next hour or so, without investment of my energy.

"A rock did that?"

"No," I said with a slight chuckle. "Not a rock. It's called a soul stone."

I shot off bullet points about its nature and power while the boys cleaned up the blacktop yard and wrecked units.

"That's creepy, don't you think?"

"Yep." I nodded at the guys. "But it's necessary. Otherwise, I would have had to throw down with them, and that wouldn't have turned out well. Not for them."

"You'd have been okay? You're not that much of a badass. There are a lot of them."

"Which would have probably necessitated me pulling out my handy dandy gun and firing. Not really a better solution, counselor."

"True." She dipped her head toward the pocket that hid the soul stone. "But that's still gross. What now?"

"We wait for them to finish and then get their names." I raised my chin to shout at the group. "Hurry the fuck up!"

"You were serious?"

"Yep. Got a notebook or something?"

"Do you think all social workers walk around with little scribble pads?"

"How else do you analyze people in line at the grocery store?"

"Ha, ha. I don't have a notepad." Her hand slipped into her purse and she pulled out a tablet. " But I can use this."

"Good."

"Why get their names, if you don't mind me asking?"

"You'll see."

The cleanup took forty minutes longer than I wanted, but the boys had everything packed away and I didn't once catch a hint of the Penumbra Man. Even though Billee and I showed up too late to see the origins of this mess, I have to say that they probably re-stored the items with more care than the actual owners had. Double-bonus points because we were talking about teen boys cleaning up after themselves!

"Line up!" I shouted once all the doors were closed.

The boys did. Single file.

Billee began taking down their names and phone numbers. We had plenty of time to get the information, because they were firing their personal information with zeal. What can I say? Soul Stones are powerful.

As Billee worked to keep up with the deluge of information, I walked up and down the line until I found what I was looking for.

"Shit."

Billee's head shot up.

"Off with your jackets and shirts," I said, running a hand through my hair. "Now!"

She looked at me like I was crazy.

"You'll see."

Less than twenty seconds later, the boys were shirtless.

"Those of you with long hair, hold it up."

"Rev, what are you doing?" Billee asked, sounding like she was quickly losing faith and was seeing herself sitting in a holding cell beside me.

I didn't have time to assure her. "Turn and face me." They did. "Billee, come here."

She swept in beside me, shooting questioning looks at the

shirtless boys. "Have you lost your damn mind? They're children."

My arm swept down the line. "What do you see?"

She looked at me. Looked at them. Glanced back at me, her mouth falling up. But then her head snapped back at the boys.

"They're all marked with... a brand. Who would do that? And to children?"

"That's the Penumbra Man's mark." I pointed at the first few marks. Three asymmetrical circles of various widths, one within another, intersected one another, forming a tilted V. A single, nearly horizontal line, bisected the circles and V. A crap representation of a penumbra and the mark of a Penumbra Man's touch. The Penumbra Man's sickness. "It does that to mortals. Touches them, then infects them. That's how it gains influence and manipulates them to do what they normally wouldn't."

"Like tear up a self-storage business or attack a man, fifteen-on-one?"

"Bingo."

"Jesus, Rev. This is bad."

"Want to hear something worse?"

"Not really. But I'm sure you're going to tell me, anyway."

"In order for this many people to be affected, the Penumbra Man hit them up when they were together. Too much work to do otherwise."

"Then it went into a school?"

"Most likely. Or a sporting event. Concert. Either way, this was deliberate."

"Using kids? For what purpose?"

"No idea yet, but I'm sure it has something to do with the First Bowl." I stopped, still scanning our surroundings for the supernatural threat. I checked the time. We had to go. "Put your shirts and jackets on and run home as fast as you can. Don't stop until you hug your momma. Go!"

The boys dressed like they'd woken to a fire in their bedrooms. They ran for the gate while throwing hoodies or jackets over their heads. Thankfully, no one tripped or ran into any storage buildings. The flood of their collective pasts, presents, and futures hit me like a dump truck. I closed my third eye, wanting to see none of it.

"The worst thing about this is," I said, watching the boys and feeling bad for each one, "they're going to suffer very real consequences for an evening of fun they had no control over. No idea they were doing something wrong. Some of them will probably come out of the soul stone's influence before they get home, and they won't know what they're doing. Tomorrow is going to be a terrible day for them." I cinched my duster closed against the cooling day, scanning the units for any sign of the enemy. Of course, I didn't see it. Sneaky bastard. "We need to be on our toes from now on whenever we come across something like this."

"Why's that?"

"When I was waiting behind the building, I heard something on a roof. I thought it was a kid at first."

"But it was the Penumbra Man? Here?" She pointed her finger at the blacktop, swirling it. "Right. Here?"

"Bingo."

12

STEAKS AND BRAKES

As if Billee wasn't already concerned about her savvy as a Reaper's familiar, coming across the massive group of innocent kids being manipulated by the Penumbra Man apparently validated her opinion. Something I've seen hundreds of times before, the influence of Nephilim in the Overworld is usually a grossly unfortunate event that comes complete with casualties of one sort or another. Billee learned that lesson early in her familiar career.

It took an expensive steak dinner to discuss her fears and to reassure her she wouldn't be a target of the Nephilim disguised as Penumbra Man simply because she worked with me.

Could they discover Billee was my familiar? Sure. Did it matter? Not necessarily. It depends on what the Nephilim saw and heard.

They're not stupid. They wouldn't be among the most powerful of our kind if they were. Dollars to donuts, what I heard on the storage unit rooftop was the Nephilim. The monstrosity made sure it found an excuse to beat it before I broke free to search, which led me to believe it doubted its chances against me.

I patiently and silently listened as Billee ran through scenarios. The worst was when she entertained the possibility of walking right past the Penumbra Man after we split up in the storage yard to execute the initial phase of our plan. Her most legitimate worry was about the Penumbra Man picking her off when we split.

I didn't tell her that was frighteningly possible, then and until I found the damn thing and sent it back to the All in a sprinkle of sparkles. There's no sense in entertaining hypotheticals after the fact, and honestly, even if she nailed the angel by its wings with her guess, it wouldn't solve the problem. A Penumbra Man is a veritable nightmare to deal with, let me tell you. I spent a good portion of my week's salary on wine to go with the steak and her frayed nerves.

Billee made me walk her to her apartment from the car. I didn't mind. Believe it or not, Olympia is a safe city. There isn't too much craziness going on that's not instigated by political crazies invading the state Capitol grounds and demanding the Governor do this or do that.

With Billee tucked safely away, I headed home. I was tired. More than that. The drag of the constant tug of 'shit Rev needs to get done,' from the Order and my sense of duty grew fatter by the minute.

From Billee's place, I would normally take Capitol Way until coming to Fourth, hanging a right, and arriving home before my car warmed up. I like this part of town. One of my common routes, whether I'm heading to pick up something to eat, going to the farmer's market, or planning to pop a squat in one of the gazillion coffee places.

But tonight I didn't take that familiar route. Maybe I should have.

Flashing lights rhythmically reflected off the windows of the corner business on Washington Street a few blocks ahead. The brick building, constructed before big bands were a thing, was framed by windows typically seen in those older buildings. Not very tall, maybe six or seven feet, and sunk into the building's fascia, the glass expanded the reach of the rhythmic flashing light.

I unblocked my third eye to fill in the details. Someone up ahead was dead.

Rolling down the window and getting a stiff swat of cold, wet January air, I yelled at the person taking their time crossing the street to get out of my way because I couldn't stop. It was a lie. My brakes worked just fine, but over the last few decades, mortals have become self-centered twats and don't seem to care to move out of someone's way, even when they're the one impeding. It's like most people get off on being nuisances to those around them. Strolling around this realm, noses in the air or their smartphones, as if they're the center of everything. I wasn't giving this person, wrapped in their rain jacket and gaze cast down, the chance to prove me right again.

The yell did the trick. My car's lack of deceleration probably didn't hurt. The guy high-stepped it to the sidewalk, yelling something incoherent that didn't matter in the big scheme of life. I was turning onto Washington long before he likely got over his butt-hurt.

The lights I'd seen reflecting off the windows were a car's flashers. The driver had left their door open and was standing in the road, looking down. He stood bent in a telltale way that said his spine had given up caring about correct posture well over a decade ago. He held his hands to his cheeks. His tan jacket was split open at the bottom. The wind ruffled one flap.

The old man was alive. The twenty-three-year-old guy he hit wasn't.

To this day, I still remember the first time I saw the floating image of a mortal's energy after death. Like everyone who has ever done or tried something they were inexperienced at, I didn't perform well. It got easier over the millennia, but the sight of someone's energy residue is still a strange one.

As solid as fog, the young man's energy residue lingered near the body, a ghostly hand gripping his shaggy hair.

The Interlude would kick in momentarily, pausing all existence to allow the assigned Reaper to execute their duty. Seven billion people and immortals in the Overworld would be put on hold, unaware of the supernatural work being done on this corner of a small city on the western side of Washington. A slice of time. An occurrence that happens tens of thousands of times a day, and no one notices except those involved.

"Hi," I said to what remained of the young man. "Sorry that happened to you."

He looked at me, his wide eyes blinking once before holding me in their gaze.

A Rift opened a few feet away. I didn't recognize the Reaper who came through Because of my proximity to the incident and the fact I was the Reaper Minister, I could escort the kid, so the Interlude wasn't affecting me. It would if I tried to walk away from the scene, but dammit, I couldn't do that to this kid or the fresh-faced Reaper. He looked more frightened than the mortal's energy residue.

"Hey," the Reaper said, stuttering to a halt just outside the Rift. He was tall, easily a few inches taller than me, maybe six and a half feet, and lanky. Youthful stress lines crisscrossed his face. "I—I'm sorry. I got the scroll with his name. This was my job, I thought. I didn't mean to overstep."

"Who are you?"

"Raphael."

"I haven't seen you around."

"I—I'm being detailed."

"Detailed?"

"Yes, uh, assigned, I guess. Look, I'm new. I was doing security duty for a firm in the Sixth until a few days ago, then

I got pulled for this Reaper duty. I'm still in training." He checked the energy residue as if partially afraid it was going to pounce on his face. "I don't know what I'm doing. I mean, I know they covered this in the training, but this is my first time."

So the Order had listened to Pher and was working to fatten the Reapers' numbers? That would have been nice to know. Who was running this ship, anyway? And sending a barely trained detail on escort duty, unescorted by a mentor? Crappy management. I sighed as I mentally added another item to my to-do list.

"Nice to meet you, Raphael. I'm Rev. The Reaper Minister."

"You're Rev?" The stress lines on his face deepened, and he backed a step closer to the Rift. If he wasn't careful, he'd fall through. "I'm sorry. I didn't know."

"It's okay. How much training have you had?"

"Three days."

Three days and this kid was pulling Reaper duty? Oh, Pher and I were going to have a chat.

I looked around. A car was halfway through the intersection a block away. A couple were in mid-stride walking down the sidewalk hand-in-hand. Shops here and there, mostly the small city mom-and-pop types of businesses Olympia embraces, were as still as if it was closing time and someone oddly placed the mortals inside like mannequins.

We had a job to do, and the night wasn't getting any younger while we waited for the damn Guardian Angel to show up. They didn't always, but in accidents, you could count on them nine and half times out of ten to stand beside the energy residue at the end. Guardian Angels are trained to comfort. Apparently, this kid had a shitty Guardian.

"Do you know what you're supposed to do?" I asked Raphael.

He glanced at the mortal's energy residue. The mortal had moved closer to his corpse and was hovering over it, inspecting it like a child watching a trail of ants carrying food back to their nest.

"All I know is I'm supposed to bring him to the Veil Gate." Raphael dug into his pocket and pulled out a piece of paper.

"What's that?"

He mumbled as if he couldn't read the writing unless he did so out loud. I waited. When he finished, he nodded. "Okay, got it."

"Got what?"

"The location of the Veil Gate."

"I'm assuming that was part of your training, right? They took you there? Or are you bringing the energy back to someone else and they'll escort him?"

"I'm supposed to take him. They showed us once, on the first day."

"Us?"

"The new details."

I scratched my face. "How many were in this training?"

He shrugged. "Think it was like twenty or something."

I wanted to groan, but that would probably unsettle the new Reaper even more than he already appeared to be doubting himself. "Think you can handle it?"

Raphael rubbed the piece of paper with his thumb, watching what remained of the mortal.

Bullshit. Newly assigned Reapers undergo extensive train- ing, and their first few cases are always supervised. Escorting mortals to the Veil Gate is an important duty. Screw it up, and what remains of the mortal stays in this realm. Mortals call them ghosts, but they're not what people typically think of when they hear things go bump in the night. Unbound energy needs somewhere to go, and it's our job to get it to the Veil Gate. If that's not done, that shit will ping around the Overworld for eternity.

One thing I ensured when I managed assignments for the Reapers was that newbies got easier cases. Not to sound crass, but it's better for a new Reaper to deal with a mortal who is elderly and ready to cross. It's difficult for a newbie to deal with a twenty-something killed while crossing the street. Situations like this required a level of tact that came with experience. Someone with a few days of training was not ready.

Raphael's delay gave me the answer I needed. Time to pull rank. "I'm going to escort him."

The other Reaper's shoulders dropped. He exhaled. It might have been the first time he breathed during the entire conversation. "Thank you! I—I would, but—but I don't want to mess it up."

"It's okay," I said, starting toward the energy residue when I heard a voice.

"Shit!"

I looked in the curse's direction to see a woman sprinting down the sidewalk. She was carrying a white cup of coffee from one of those evil 'big coffee' companies, and the hot liquid was squirting from the plastic lid with each of her hurried steps. She tossed the cup in a nearby garbage can without breaking stride. Brown liquid sprayed onto the sidewalk.

When she reached us, she looked down at the corpse before swiveling her gaze at the residue. Sighing, she closed her eyes and held them that way.

"I take it you're the Guardian?"

"I am," she said, her eyes still closed.

"Where were you?"

Her lids snapped open as fast as a prairie dog popping out of a hole. "I was getting coffee."

"You manifested and left him?"

"He—I didn't," she started and then stopped. When she grimaced, her cheeks expanded, making her otherwise pretty face seem distorted. Too wide at the cheeks before narrowing to a tiny chin. Her brown skin paled. Her hair had fallen forward, and she flipped it over her shoulder. "It was only for a minute. I can't be with him at all times."

"You're supposed to be," I said, moving to the mortal kid. "That's your job." Without taking my eyes off the negligent Guardian, I asked Raphael, "When did you get the scroll?"

"I don't know. Like, a few minutes before I opened the Rift."

The Guardian looked ready to pout. One thing I didn't have time for was petulance. "So it wasn't his time. You should have been here. I hope you have learned a lesson tonight. One fuck of an expensive on-the-job-training moment."

In a flash, all her bravado and aloofness vanished. She clasped her hands, bringing them toward her mouth, pressing them against her lips as she moved to the energy residue. "Jarred, I'm so, so sorry. I didn't. I wa—I screwed up. I'll never forgive myself."

"It's okay," Jarred said, looking at his Guardian Angel like she was a loon. "Do I know you?"

She stepped back. A small black trail of mascara seeped down her cheek.

"He never felt your presence," I said in a softer tone. The Guardian knew she'd royally screwed the pooch. It happens. A lot. Every day. There was nothing any of us standing at this intersection could do to change what happened to Jarred, but she could change how she conducted herself in the future. "You'll learn from this. Don't worry. We all mess up. No one is perfect. What's your name?"

She looked at me like I'd asked her to strip naked right there in the street. "Why?"

"Because we're having a conversation, and it helps to connect with others when we have a name. I'm Rev."

"Sachiel," she mumbled. "You're the... you're the one in charge of the Reapers, aren't you?"

"That's me. Nice to meet you, Sachiel." I turned to the

mortal, my heart aching for the kid. Not only did his life end way too soon, but this was an ugly handoff. Usually, these things are much smoother. Nothing like suicides. Those really get angels' panties in a twist. This was bad enough. I've always believed that when you're in the middle of something miserable, it's best to punch through and get it over with.

Sachiel didn't look like she was ready to do or say anything more. Raphael was probably shitting in his pants. This kid was waiting for one of us immortals to do something because he sure as hell was clueless as to what was going on.

"How about you and I take a walk?" I said to Jarred. "I'll explain on the way. Cool?"

He looked down at his corpse one more time before glancing over at the old man, frozen in mid-panic. "Is he the one who hit me?"

"That'd be my bet."

Jarred shook his head. "Man, he's about to have an awful night."

Kudos to this kid for handling this like a champ. "Yes, he will. Want to take that walk?"

"Sure."

With a snap of my fingers, I opened a Rift to the Veil Gate. "Raphael, wish we could have met under better circumstances. Let's catch up at the next meeting and have a chat. That'll be more useful than whatever training you received."

"Okay." He looked relieved to jump back through his Rift, which sucked in on itself as soon as he was out of sight.

Sachiel lingered. As I moved to the Rift with Jarred, she called out, "R—Rev?"

I turned. "Yeah?"

"Am I in trouble? Are you going to tell anyone?"

I could have said a million things. Sachiel wasn't the first derelict Guardian Angel. But, then again, every being is far from perfect except the essence of the All. I could have chastised or berated. I could have read her the riot act. But to what point? Doing so would only sour her opinion of me, and she might carry that back to the other Guardians. Our two organizations already had enough problems and tension. Harsh words are regressive by nature, and I don't believe in taking backward steps. When someone screwed up on the job, it was a way to identify a teaching moment.

"No reason to," I said, putting my hand near the middle of Jarred's back. We can't touch energy residue, but the gesture was a wonderful nonverbal cue, I'd discovered long ago. "We can't change anything, and I'm sure you've learned."

Her head fell, the mass of fine black hair cascading over her slim shoulders. "I have."

"That's what matters. After I escort him, I'm going home. I need a bath. I'm not interested in tattling, Sachiel."

"Thank you," she said to her chest.

"You're welcome." I turned to the Rift, gesturing to Jarred at the shimmering black image outlined by sizzling white magic. Without hesitation, he stepped toward it.

As the blackness absorbed him and before I stepped up to the barrier between dimensions, Sachiel shouted, "I disagree with them."

Her comment halted me. I looked back. "With who?"

"Other Guardians. Actually, a lot of Guardians. They say you're an asshole. But they're wrong. You're not. I think you're pretty cool."

My smirk was timid. The Reapers called me grim. The Guardians think I'm an asshole. Who knew what the Order was going to think when I confronted them on tasking untrained rookies to escort? If the day ever came that I gave a shit, I was going to have to hire the best PR angel in all the Upperworld.

"See you around, Sachiel," I said and turned to escort Jarred to the Veil Gate.

Poor kid.

Damn, I hate this job.

13

STRATEGY SESSION

Turns out, Jarred Bowser was a good kid. Never a high performer in school, he didn't quit on himself many times in his formative years. After he graduated, he moved from Portland and the trouble it held. Seems he ran in tough circles. In Olympia, he found a job and a new circle of friends who weren't more interested in getting high than accomplishing something with their talents. Not long after the move, he even fell in love. Though he never lived a king's life, Jarred lived.

I learned this after we left his Guardian Angel and the only world he knew, and was ever going to know. Before walking him to the Veil Gate and handing his scroll to the Scroll Eater, I opened my third eye to learn about him. I do that for all escorts who prove worth my time. Yes, in the end, it doesn't really matter. What is going to happen will happen. The end, for all things, is inevitable. Everyone and everything. So why not enjoy it while you have it to enjoy? Time. Money. Love. New experiences. Next month, next week, today, five minutes from now, it could all vanish in the next instant. For all anyone knew, they could die on the shitter the next time they took a seat.

A basic, time-tested motto: make the best of things while you can.

In the end, Jarred was a champ. I wish all jobs were as easy.

That thought rang especially true as I tapped a new scroll against my palm. I didn't want to break the seal. It's not like the Order was sending me a 'happy birthday' message. This was another job. The fun never ends.

After stepping out onto the balcony and filling my lung with fresh air, I came in and made black tea. Snagging the scroll, I took it to the reading chair, sipped the tea, and continued bouncing the new task against my knee.

At some point, I became a big boy and broke the seal. Judas Jericho signed the missive. The most obnoxious, pretentious, privileged member of the Order in the Upperworld's history.

Turns out, it wasn't another job. Yeah, for that. Maybe.

Instead of more work, the scroll called me to a meeting in three hours. An encouraging sign, almost every single way I looked at it.

If the Order wanted to meet with the Reaper Minister, that meant this business had to do with me and/or the Reapers. Raphael was detailed to the Reapers, but maybe more were on their way. Reinforcements, finally? Was I going to receive the angel power I'd been asking from them for the better part of four centuries? Maybe they were calling to notify me of my reassignment to another division. Personally, I'd gladly take up a position in Pher's Level as the guy who rents out umbrellas to beachgoers and then spend my eternity soaking in the rays and view of bikini-clad angels. I can think of worse ways to spend the days I had left. Hell, maybe they were firing me and I could spend my time searching for the happiness I'd lost along the way.

Suddenly in a much better mood, I enjoyed the rest of my tea while sitting in the reading chair and soaking in as much of the gray day as possible. Before long, I had showered and opened a Rift to the Eighth Level of the Upperworld. Yahweh's Level. Where all the important shit happens.

"What's up, Rev?" Brock asked as I stepped out into the hall. Almost an eternal fixture around these parts, he's constantly on guard duty outside the Order's meeting room. Brock was as tall as a toppling skyscraper. He had muscles everywhere, clear even under the black suit he wore. How they made jackets that big, I'll never know.

"What's up, my man?" I said with a smile and gave him a hug. It felt like hugging a boulder. The big blond, his hair barely longer than stubble, smiled back even though it was taboo to show emotions while on duty. The door to the meeting room was closed. He was safe from the Order finding out he had a modicum of personality. "How have you been?"

His arm wrapped around his back. "Getting old. Hurt myself in the gym the other day."

"By lifting the gym?"

He chuckled, his face taking a boyish gleam, and slapped me on the shoulder. After three steps sideways, I caught myself. He held his assaulting hand up. "Sorry."

I rubbed my shoulder and winked. "I'd hate to feel your strength if you weren't injured. How about you look out for yourself? You're not thirty thousand anymore. You can't hang with the young 'uns."

One corner of his mouth quirked. "You got that right. Punks still need to be taught lessons by us old guys or they'll think they can take over the Upperworld and turn it into a permanent all-night kegger."

"I've heard of worse ways to spend eternity." I looked at the closed meeting room doors, so thick, no hint of mumbled voices could penetrate them. "Any word what this is about?"

Brock's cheek scrunched as he frowned. "No idea. This one's weird."

"Oh? How so?"

He studied the hall. Analyzing the immediate area for eavesdroppers. Apparently satisfied no one would spring around a corner and tattle that they'd heard us conspiring, he leaned close. "They're being hush-hush about something. Even when they come out of the room, they're different."

"No one has said anything?"

"Not a word." He scowled. "Honest, Rev. I don't like it when it gets like this. Me and my boys are supposed to protect their asses, but we are clueless about what's happening. How are we supposed to analyze threats and prepare for them if we don't know what to look for?"

Maybe this meeting wouldn't be good news after all. I patted him on the broad, round, and way-too-firm shoulder. "Let me see what I can find out. I'll let you know if I can drag something out of them."

Behind the monstrous man, the meeting room door clicked open. Brock shot back to his position at the side.

At least it wasn't Jericho who greeted me. Instead, Dumas Vendetta peeked out of the cracked door, only half his face visible. When he saw me, his half-face crinkled in a duplicitous smile, mostly hidden by his overgrown mustache. "Ah, Rev. You're here. Good. We can begin."

Brock reached over with his left arm which was half as thick as a telephone pole, and pulled the door open, while always keeping watch on the hallway behind me. Good angel, that one.

I stepped into the Order of Thirteen's meeting room.

Dumas shuffled backward, dipping his head in what felt like, but probably wasn't, ten times for every step he took.

"I see you haven't trimmed the 'stache," I said in a jovial tone. Dumas doesn't like humor. For some reason, it offends him. So I enjoy putting on my most jovial persona in his presence, which is a hell of a sacrifice. I do it for other reasons, though. Mostly because Dumas is one of the Order who refuses to understand my offense at the way the Reapers have been treated throughout my time as the Minister. We didn't always have this level of mutual dislike, but thousands of years of head-butting took us in this direction.

"I would never," Dumas said, shaking his head while still dipping it as if a rubber band connected the vertebrae in his neck to his skull.

Pher got up from his spot at the long table and came to me wearing a big grin that brightened his dark face. "Rev, so good to see you again," he said in booming volume.

Uh oh. An over-the-top greeting meant this meeting was going to ruin the rest of my day.

He grasped my hand and forearm in a warm shake, pulling me closer and speaking quietly. "Keep in mind, no matter what's said, we don't have any answers. *Any.*"

Mumbled voices filled the background. None of the other members got up to greet me.

"What's going on?"

"The First Bowl is definitely missing. The rest of it is a mess. Come, sit." When he turned back to the group, he plastered the warm expression on his face again. "We haven't been waiting long, Rev. So thank you for coming so quickly, on such short notice."

Ah, leave it up to my boss to not-so-subtly remind his peers, my bosses, that I wasn't at their beck and call. Well, I was, but not if they wanted me to tackle my primary duties and extra-curriculars like the Penumbra Man.

I pulled out the chair set aside for me at the ass end of the table. A reminder that the members were on one level, any guest on quite another. Politics and power plays.

At the head of the table, Puriel Bliss, President of the Order of Thirteen, sat with a posture so straight I wondered if she could even bend to tie her shoes. A beautiful angel for her age, she still had one of those mouths that never seemed quite capable of smiling, gaping, or frowning. Honestly, sometimes, it was creepy.

"Mr. Carver," she said, beginning the meeting. Her voice was feminine but deep. "Thank you for joining us. As Christopher said, we're glad you could join us on such short notice. We realize you're busy, so it's appreciated."

I ignored the fact that she referred to Pher by his full name. "No worries. I'm hoping this meeting is good news?"

Her dark eyes held mine for a moment before she raised her hand, perfectly vertical, and slowly brushed her gray and black ombre hair out of her face. "I wish that were the case. Instead, we felt it was necessary to bring you in on this matter as soon as we could confirm the rumors to be true. Someone has stolen the First Bowl from the Safe."

Heads dipped as if the news shamed the members. Uziel traced invisible lines on the table with a finger. Sid twirled his thumbs around each other. Pher nodded, his head turned to the President. No one filled in the silence.

Who better than me? "You don't say?"

Just like Dumas, I came to learn that Puriel isn't a big fan of levity. I guess that's how politicians rise to their stations, by taking everyone and everything too seriously. What better way to spin up constituents than to play off their fears and have them see the boogie man around every corner?

"I'm sure you don't see this as a joking matter, Mr. Carver?" she said, more than asked.

"The First Bowl is gone." Pher's chair squeaked as he turned to me. "I've briefed everyone about your reports." Now his attention turned to his peers. "I think we can safely assume the First Bowl of Wrath has been poured based on what we know."

"So my reports do get read? Good."

Throat clearing, muted coughing, and even a groan accompanied that Pher's admission and my poke. Admittedly, this was the first time Yahweh's Bowls of Wrath had been put at risk. Sure, the head honchos had talked about threatening mortals across the ages. Upper management weaponized them when they thought the Underworld was getting too big for their britches and unduly influencing mortals. Hell, they even doubled down by having some yahoo scribble it on parchment to ensure its inclusion in what would later become the Bible. But putting it into play by pouring one, figuratively, on the world was a whole new ballgame for everyone, including the angels in this room.

"Not sure how the Reapers can help," I said. "We're already over-tasked with our current workload and I'm already dealing with a Nephilim who might be behind the missing Bowl."

Heads swiveled back to Puriel at my comment.

"That is one reason we wanted you to join us today," Puriel said. "This is a matter of utmost importance."

"Like everything else?" I said evenly.

"Rev," Pher said, drawing out my name.

"Pher," I returned in a one-for-one swap. "I'm serious. Don't get me wrong; a stolen First Bowl is bad news. The outbreaks of sores we're seeing is a big, ole red flag that it was poured. But if you think the Reapers have the resources to help, you're wrong. I have no one to spare."

"Then recruit," Jerah said, a pure look of confusion on his face.

"From where? When? With what crew?"

"You do it," was his oh-so-narrow-and-unhelpful answer.

"Not going to happen."

"Why not?" Dumas asked, his head dipping.

I placed my hands flat on the table. "Can I be candid?"

"Of course," Turial said at the side of the table. "We hope you always feel you can be with us. The Reapers and Guardians must or we've got problems."

"Good." I tapped the table. "Then we've got problems."

On each side of the room, angels pulled back from the table as if it'd suddenly grown hot with the heat of the Underworld's Hellfire.

"If any of you think I have time to recruit Reapers, you're wrong. For millennia, ever since I stepped down from most of the Minister's administration duties, I've told you that was one area where I needed help. Now, I'm grateful to the Order for using your resources to ensure someone handles the escort assignments, but we agreed on that deal so I could focus on the important tasks you had for me." I lifted my hand, finger pointed at the table, and made a circular motion. "We agreed because it was the only way I could help with escorting while doing the unsavory stuff angels in your position needed someone to handle. Or don't you remember?"

"We remember," Pher said instantly.

I appreciated that. "So unless you're waiting to give me some wonderful news about new recruits or someone taking over my job, I don't know what else to say. I am already dealing with the Nephilim and, probably, the First Bowl. I can't give up any Reapers. They're stretched so thin, they're all about to snap. Plain and simple."

"So disrespectful," Jericho Judas said, but wouldn't meet my gaze. Entitled brat.

"So realistic." Elbows resting on the table, I spread my hands. "Is that all you called me for? If so, I appreciate the heads up, but I won't apologize for not sacrificing me or my crew. You'll have to find someone else unless you have a horde of recruits for me."

Jericho threw his hands in the air. "For Yahweh's sake, Rev. Just give us the criteria for what makes a Reaper so we can set up a draft. We've been over this. Manage your resources and you wouldn't be in this predicament."

All around the table, heads nodded in agreement. Only Pher and Puriel remained stoic.

"No draftees. Volunteers only. I'd bitch about the detailees, but I'm desperate and just—" I really emphasized that word "—learned about them."

"You're frustrating," Jericho said.

"And you've never been a Reaper. Try it for a few hundred years and then we can chat about why the Reapers only need volunteers." I leaned farther over the table, wagging my finger at the middle of it. "Speaking of. What's this crap with detailees? That's nearly as bad as draftees."

Eyes returned to the table. Only the confident and compassionate Order members had the courage to not look away.

"We were testing," Pher said, sounding like he agreed with the tactic.

"With *draftees*?"

"Yes," Puriel answered, tilting her chin slightly. "We understand your position, though it's not one we agree with. So, we tested an alternative. We have to find a solution, Mr. Carver."

"Giving me draftees or detailees only requires more of my time to correct their messes. Trust me, I just went through it with one of your new boys. He didn't have a clue what he was supposed to do. Thank Yahweh for serendipity. Had I not been fortunate to have been in the area, he would have bundled the escort and added yet another ghost to the Overworld."

"All of our detailees can escort the residue to the Veil Gate," Jericho said, rolling his eyes.

"Not compassionately."

"Who cares?" He threw a hand up in the air again. "They're energy. That's all."

I wanted to break off his hand and shove it up his ass. I shook my head. "I need more Reapers. I need angels who, unlike you, Jericho, have the skill set to perform the duties. Want a profile for the perfect candidate? Fine. But someone outside the Reapers is going to have to take care of all that administrative work."

It looked like Jericho was about to say something, but Puriel spoke up first. "We are at an impasse... for now. Let's reconvene to discuss after all of us have had time to think through the best way to do this."

"We're too busy to solve Rev's problems for him," Jericho said.

"I agree." Dumas dipped his head along with his support of the privileged-yet-obnoxious Chief of Security sitting toward the head of the table.

"Yet we will, because we need to," Puriel said forcefully. "Camael, will you please add that to the notes and then circulate three proposed dates and times for us to vote on for the follow-up?"

The Order's Secretary scribbled in his notebook. "Yes, ma'am."

"Then this meeting is adjourned," Puriel announced and stood. "Everyone, be thinking this through. I fear something big is coming. We don't know what, how, or when, but it's only a matter of time. We need to be ready. Go in peace."

"So we're not going to talk about the problem with the Penumbra Man?" I said in a rush.

Puriel's face didn't change from its steady blank slate. "Do you not have it handled?"

"As much as I can."

"Good then. See it through."

"It has something to do with the Bowl, I think. If we want answers, I need to be allowed to focus on it."

The President sat like she was frozen in time. Even though she'd called to adjourn the meeting, no one moved. "We're moving forward, and we trust you. Do what needs to be done."

"That's it?"

"You'll be faster than us, lad," Pher said, almost apologetically.

The other members of the Order stood along when Puriel did. I pushed myself up, glad to be leaving.

They went about their political business while I went about getting away from this political sap. Pher stopped me.

We moved to the doors but didn't leave the meeting room.

He took my hand. "Don't let this get you down."

"It's hard, boss. They just don't get it."

"And we never will."

Interesting that he'd include himself in that group. I mean, Pher made me want to put my head through the walls sometimes. But he cared to see my side of issues. I wasn't sure how many others in the Order could say that.

"I can't do what they want with what I have," I said, being careful to not box him in with my opinion of the rest of the Order. "Something needs to give."

He let go of my hand and rubbed my arm. "And you might have to meet us halfway."

With my free hand, I rubbed my face. "I'm too tired to think about training angels who aren't volunteers, or dealing with the fallout when they realize how miserable they are about being forced into the job. This is sensitive work, Pher. I need the right kind of angels."

"Which is why your squad is so small," Pher said, his round cheeks twitching. "There's the crux. Take Puriel's allowance of time and figure out what you can be at peace with. Either way, we're going to have to move forward together."

"I will." I turned to go.

Pher's hand suddenly gripped my biceps. "One more thing."

"Yeah?" His grip told me more bad news was coming.

"No one has confirmed this yet, but word is that Hellion is wrapped up in this mess somehow."

"Hellion?" I said a little too loudly. I'm sure Pher forgave me since he just threw the Lamb of God's name out there like I should have seen it coming.

Maybe I should have. She has quite a reputation for being

a troublemaker. The crème de la crème of politicians. I'd never had the pleasure of interacting with her, and as God's Lamb, I wasn't in a hurry for that to happen. I mean, as the Reaper Minister, I'm badass. But Hellion was the supervising authority of the Four Horsemen. You just don't mess with someone like that.

"Until I know more, that's all I can say. Keep your eyes open, lad."

"Always."

I stepped out. The thick door thumped closed behind me.

"Good meeting?" Brock asked.

"If you have to ask…"

Brock chuckled.

I snapped my fingers, aiming to open the Rift halfway down the hall out of respect for Brock. Before heading for it, I drifted closer toward him.

Still facing forward, he gave me a sideways glance. "Spill it, Rev. What kind of trouble are we looking at?"

"Not sure they told you about the Nephilim in the Overworld kicking up stuff?"

"No." He grinned, and his crooked lips pulled his eyes to narrow slits. "But I overheard."

"You know about the First Bowl being poured?"

That ruffled his feathers enough to make him look away from his post. "Really?"

"Ninety-nine-point-nine percent sure. Keep it close."

"Sure thing." His massive chest swelled. "Anything else?"

"Oh, and just that Hellion might be up to something," I said with a heaving sigh of my own. "But that's super-super close-hold."

Brock winked, though this wasn't a winking situation. "Never a dull day around here."

"You can say that again."

14

THE BIG PICTURE

"I'M COLD."

"We can sit in the car," I said, looking up at the cloud-covered night.

Even with the blanket of gray hanging low, there was still a bite in the air.

Billee's parka made a swishing sound as she pulled her arms tighter around herself. "Maybe we should? I'm so cold, I can't focus. An elephant could walk by me and I'd miss it."

"Defeats the purpose, doesn't it?" I tapped the hood of my sports coupe, sliding to the gravel parking lot. "Come on. I'll get the car started and crank up the heat."

Billee had been leaning against the hood of the car, wrapped in herself to survive our stakeout. "Won't the noise of the engine keep him away?"

"Chance we have to take, Sparky," I said, pulling my door open and sliding onto the cold leather of the driver's seat. When she popped in, I cranked the car over. "Plus, I didn't expect to catch him moseying around the camp. That's not how Nephilim work, especially in Penumbra Man form."

Billee didn't react. She huddled in her seat, sinking within herself and shivering, her long breaths shaking. "How is one angel supposed to catch this thing? Why aren't they giving you more staff?"

"One of the greatest mysteries of all time," I said. "Hey, what do you say we give Pher a call while we look for this ugly prick to show his head?"

Though her hood was pulled over her head, I could tell by the way it shifted that she'd turned my way. "Who? The Penumbra Man or Pher?"

I chuckled along with her. "Good one! Save your material for our boss, though. He needs the knockdown from time to time." I punched in Pher's number, hoping he was still around like he said he'd be.

A crackling voice answered after the fourth ring. "This better be good."

"Why? It's late, and it's not like you have a social life."

"Exactly why this better be good, lad."

"Don't be so grumpy," Billee said with a shiver. "At least you're in a warm house and not in a car in a parking lot on a freezing night."

"Sunrose," Pher nearly shouted, sounding far less irritated. "How are you? I didn't know you two were out."

"We're working," I said.

"Ah," Pher said with a sigh. "And you called me to make sure I suffer along with you?"

"The Order won't bend to help until they feel my pain," I said unapologetically. Even though Pher was on my side, he was the best shot I had against the Order's lethargy.

I could almost hear Pher slumped on the other end. "Can I help with anything?"

"There's a lot you can help with, Pher. That's why we called while freezing in the car while watching a homeless camp for Nephilim activity."

"Ah, a business discussion at this time of night?"

"We need to discuss business."

"Let me get more wine, then." He exhaled slowly, with all

the energy of an older angel at the end of an endless day. His voice was muffled as glass clanked against glass in the background. I think he had the phone pinched between his head and shoulder. "Okay, let's do this then. I'm tired."

"Grumpy, too," Billee added.

A wine glass tinked on a wood. Pher sighed. "More headaches. But don't let me put them on you two kids. What are we looking at? Any lucky on this stakeout of yours?"

"None," Bille and I said in unison.

"So, what business are we discussing to help you both pass the night?"

I stared at the illuminated panel like I was looking him in the eyes. "The Order and all its glorious bullshit."

"Okay, shoot."

I held up my finger as if he could see it. "Pretend you're talking to a mortal who doesn't understand how the Upperworld works, and an angel who's clueless as to how it could happen that someone got into the Safe and reached a Bowl."

"We don't know."

"No clues? No 'word on the street' or anything like that?"

"Nothing. It's been frighteningly quiet in that respect. Too quiet."

Outside my windshield, the homeless camp was in an equal state. Few of its residents milled outside their tents or temporary structures. The few who braved the night milled around the burn barrels lighting small circles of the camp with their fires.

"That's a problem. No one should be able to get into the Safe without authorization." I waved my hand in the air in frustration. "Hell, I don't even know where that authorization comes from."

"The Council."

"Has the Order asked them then?"

Pher's response sounded as jaded as contemporary pop music. "Who do you think we heard the news from?"

"And," I said, stretching out the word. "What did they have to say?"

"They were just as surprised as us, lad."

"They didn't give anyone permission to enter the Safe, and they don't know who did?"

"Exactly."

"A Nephilim is in the Overworld with the First Bowl and has most likely put it into play. And now these rumors you're hearing about Hellion? What if she's behind it?"

"I wouldn't put it past her. She's used the Horsemen since the dawn of her time for her own reasons. We see it. I think the Council does as well."

"Why don't they fire her? Find a new Lamb of God?"

He shrugged. "Not enough votes. I've seen Council members positioning for ages. Bureaucratic democracies, lad. They're far from efficient."

"So Hellion is going to keep doing what she's doing, and getting away with it, even if she's the one behind the breach of the Safe and the Bowl's disappearance?"

"At least as far as the Council is concerned," Pher said. "You can't see it, but I'm toasting."

I mumbled, "To what?"

"To the fact we're still alive to make a difference, lad. Because someone is going to have to insert themselves into this problem to understand what's really going on."

"Let me guess. That someone happens to have the initials R.C.? Am I right? Tell me I'm right?"

I cranked up the heat now that the car was warm enough. Billee leaned toward the vents on her side, scooting to the edge of the seat. Waiting. Waiting. Nothing. I groaned. "Goddammit."

"The Upperworld needs you. There's something much bigger going on here. That means powerful angels at play. Or worse."

"Demons?"

"Could be. There's that upstart who is supposedly gunning for the seat of Lucifer. What was his name?"

I shook my head. "Ezekial Sunstone, and he's not gunning for anything based on what I saw. He's a kid. Remember? That's yet another task on my list."

"We agreed to put it off for the time being. Doesn't mean he doesn't need to be watched, though. He could be involved."

"Sure, I'll keep a casual eye on him. He's still in town. But I'm telling you, he's young, dumb, and full of... well." There was a lady in my presence, and I'm not a complete boob. "You know. Point is, he's still trying to figure out his own life. He'll be lucky if Lucifer's Council doesn't have him strung up over the gates of Hell before long. Dollars to cents, this is an inside job. An angel. Demons wouldn't work with a Nephilim. This nightmare is one of us."

"Which, again, is why we need you to see what you can uncover."

"Sure, just as soon as the Order tells me which job is my priority," I said and meant every word.

The sound of Pher inhaling deeply filled the car through my four hundred damn speakers. "If we can figure out a solution, then I can take it back to the Order. But you're in charge of the Reapers. You're a leader. None of us can build that Reaper profile. It's up to you if you want us to help."

I waved around at the night. "Hard to concentrate on that when I'm watching every corner of the world so a Penumbra Man doesn't jump me again." My arm shot out toward the homeless camp. "Or kill innocent mortals, if it's not using them to wreak havoc. It takes time to put considered thought into building the profile. I can't sit down with my little notebook and decide on my own, boss. No leader worth their salt would do that. I'll draft it. Hell, I'll do it tonight when I get home. But I won't send that to the Order until I talk with the other Reapers and get their thoughts. Otherwise, I'll end up with ten thousand Rev Carvers."

"That doesn't sound like a bad thing. Imagine how well the Upperworld would eat if that were the case."

"Don't," Billee said. She'd pulled her hood down as the car heated, and I see the mock dread on her face. "If you say things like that, he won't be able to fit his head in the car."

"Oh, I know. Trust me."

"You two stop and focus. Until the Order figures out their priorities, I can't know ours." I dropped any hint of levity from my tone. "You know mine, Pher."

After a moment of nothing, inside or outside the car, he said, "You better be joking?"

"Nope. You say this is the price of being a leader? Well, let's not forget that I've asked you a thousand times in private, and the Order hundreds of times in public, to release me from the duty. Pher, I don't want to be a leader. I want to be me. I want to cook. I want to help mortals where I can. I've served my penance and I'm getting too old to chase demons through parking garages, never mind fighting Nephilim. We both know that's how this situation ends, and I don't see anyone on the Order standing up and volunteering to throw fists with whoever is behind this bullshit."

"Because we're not able to," Pher said. "None of us have the Ability like you, Rev. I've never seen Angelfire like yours. No one has. On top of that, you're the longest-serving Reaper. In fact, you've served so long that no one on the Order can even guess at your pain tolerance now."

"Not even Dumas?"

"Not even Dumas," Pher confirmed. "You've got the chops others lack. You hold an unbelievable power in your Angelfire no one except Yahweh can touch, and maybe not even Him anymore with His current state. How would *you* replace someone like that?"

Dammit. "I don't know."

Pher's voice was soft when he admitted, "Neither do we."

"So I'm stuck?"

"For now."

Billee grumbled something under Pher's response that I couldn't make out.

Pher said, "I love you to death, lad, but sometimes you're soul blind."

I nodded. He wasn't far from the truth. Being soul blind meant not being able to see the truth of things. "Isn't everyone, in one form or fashion?"

"All I can do is ask for your understanding and to trust in me. I'm trying, lad." He went quiet for a moment. "I know what you want, and I'll keep working to get you what I can. Morning star aside. I don't like that talk. That's my promise. But there's a lot going on that needs attention. The greater good over the individual, remember?"

"Mmmm hmmmm," Billee mumbled.

I nodded in the darkness, shifting my tired gaze to pick out a Nephilim disguised as a Penumbra Man hiding in the night.

"I'll tell you something else, but let's just keep this here," Pher said in a tone that made me stop worrying about the Nephilim making an appearance. "The Safe's breach changes everything. Honestly, we're a little scrambled by that. Here's what they didn't tell you at the meeting. Michael and Seraph are up to no good in the Underworld, according to our spies."

This made me want to drive to the nearest bar and have a stiff drink instead of to my warm home for a hot meal. "What do you mean?"

"We don't know for sure," he said. "As if we didn't have enough issues, we've got this news. We can't forget about those who were once our kind who now serve the Underworld."

"I hadn't thought about that pair in forever."

"Nor I. Maybe we should have."

"Don't beat yourself up. They haven't been our problem since long before my time. That exchange between the Upper and Underworlds, two of theirs for two of ours, was supposed to get rid of two problems, wasn't it?"

"What's this about?" Billee asked.

She looked half-perturbed by the diversion in the conversation. "I'll explain later."

"It was supposed to clear up some problems. And it did. But we'd be foolish to lose sight of a pair who know so much about the Upperworld who also serve on Lucifer's Council."

"And this is why we drink, my friend." After a pause, I said, "Also the reason I want my morning star."

Pher answered, but only after I thought the silence had swallowed him. He sounded sad. "I know."

15

NOT A LAUGHING MATTER

IF THE PENUMBRA MAN PROBLEM WAS GOING TO EVER BE FIXED, I was going to have to be the one to turn the wrench.

Pher likes to talk about the typical things intellectuals enjoy thinking and talking about. I'm more of an action-movie kind of angel. Don't let the burning desire to cook and sip wine fool you. I can be pretty low-brow when I want to.

So when Pher gets on a roll about classism and the order of angels and all that stuff, I zone out. Not that it's not important—it is—or needs to be addressed—it does—but because there's nothing anyone can do to change it. Sometimes, most times, the problems of politics have grown far too large for any one angel to solve, no matter their desire, station, or influence. Sometimes, problems remain problems in perpetuity.

I was thinking deep thoughts like that when I was validated. The television was on and the news wasn't good.

Billee gasped at the headline. "Oh my God, it's in Toronto too," she said, with her hand to her mouth.

"Toronto. Tulsa. Paris. Munich. Konya. Seoul." I rubbed my face. "This is out of control. I knew it was going to happen. I knew it."

"Knew what?" Billee turned to me. The fact she was

scratching her hand didn't get by me. She had every right to be nervous.

I flicked my hand at the screen. "This shit. The sores."

"They're calling it a pandemic."

"They can call it whatever they want," I said, more frustrated with the situation than angry. "The local news is focused on the damn breakout at Pike Place. Half of them still think it's airborne. They're going to spin their wheels and use every resource to chase something that doesn't exist."

"A lot of people are going to suffer."

"Billee, a lot of people are going to die." I flicked my hand at the screen again. "This is just the beginning."

"How bad will it get?"

"Who knows? If the Bowl is the cause, this is the first time. No one can give you an accurate prediction."

"I thought there were other plagues? The Bible mentions them. I looked it up."

"Yes, and Yahweh's track record isn't great if you believe stuff written a couple of thousand years ago. Hell, more politicians have translated it over the ages than you'll find one-dollar bills at a titty bar. Don't believe the hype." I pointed at the television, scared for the world. The reporter spoke into her microphone behind a mask, the telling of her frayed nerves already obvious in the way the skin around her eyes crinkled. The HAZMAT and medical crews in the background were dressed in full-body suits, complete with hoods and self-contained respirator units, and they were working. Hard. "This is the real deal. I don't know if it can be stopped."

Billee yipped with a gulp of air.

God's wrath was very much alive and well. Sadly, not only Seattle. Each hour, it seemed, more of the planet's cities were reporting similar outbreaks. The death toll was unnerving, but what the mortals didn't understand was that it was also about to get a lot worse.

My phone vibrated on the coffee table. I snagged it, looking at the screen. Pher. "What's up boss?"

"Are you watching the news?"

Emergency numbers scrolled across the bottom of the screen inside a red banner. Above that, in a blue banner, the channel advised viewers on what signs and symptoms to look for.

"Yeah."

"A real mess."

I sighed. "Pher, we knew it would be. What's the Order doing?"

I swear, what I heard in response could have only been made by pulling the phone away from his ear and grumbling.

"I take it not much?"

"We've been moving things around," he snapped, then grumbled. "Sorry. That was uncalled for."

"Everyone is under pressure. You're going to feel it too. You're not superhuman."

"Have you handled that escort job?"

I glanced at Billee, hoping she wasn't paying attention to my conversation. She was focused on the screen, her foot bouncing across a bent knee.

Pher was asking about Delores. I hadn't bothered delivering her to the Veil Gate yet because I still had time. She still had time and deserved every minute. She was doing good work for others and I had a lot of things on my plate. Giving her as many days as possible would hurt no one, and might help some of them avoid meeting this pandemic face-to-face.

"Not yet," I said. "Don't worry. I know my job and when she has to be delivered. No one outruns the Reaper."

"Correct, lad. But I'm not worried about you not knowing your job."

"Then why are you asking? You've never," I said, stopping myself and lowering my voice so Billee remained focused elsewhere. Standing, I walked down the hall. "You've never asked after one of my escort jobs before. Why now if not because you're worried that I've suddenly forgotten what I was doing?"

"Because…" Another sigh. "Brace yourself. You won't like this."

"Then just deliver the news. Shitty news doesn't smell any less shitty the longer someone holds it in."

"Something you want, but don't want."

Riddles suck, and I told Pher so.

"The Order voted for draftees."

"Goddamnit, Pher. I don't want draftees. I thought I made that abundantly clear."

"You did."

"Then why is it happening, anyway?"

"Remember how I told you something was going to have to give? I urged you to think about a solution we could all work with. Well, they refused to wait. Not with what you're seeing on the news. And that's not even all of it. All around the Overworld, the Bowl is leaving its mark. Places that will never come up in the news. Earlier today, it completely wiped out a small village in Argentina."

"Jesus," I said, flipping my hair out of my face as I dropped onto my bed.

"Leave him out of it. He's a nice guy."

"So am I getting fired, then?"

"No."

My spirit sank.

"We'll work the draftees on our end. The admins are pulling a team together. That's not something you need to worry about."

"The hell it isn't. How many are we talking about?"

"Honestly, we're going to have the team decide that," Pher said. "This is early stages. Too many details are unclear to give you anything close to a suitable answer. Not for a bit. As things clear up, I'll let you know. Even so, you won't have to worry about them."

"If you're not firing me, these unwilling future Reapers will be my problem. Not the thirteen of you. So, yeah, I'm going to worry."

"Anapheil will be assigned as the supervisor," Pher said, dropping an interesting tidbit of news in my lap.

"Anapheil?"

"She's capable, right? You've always spoken highly of her."

"Yes, she's a hell of a Reaper," I said. "A little too interested in career progression, but when she's on a job, she does it right the first time. I can't remember the last time she dropped the ball."

"As you've said before," Pher said. "Which is why I made the recommendation when the Order was ironing this decision out. She'll do fine, and if she has those ambitions as you say, this will serve as her test to show she deserves future consideration. More importantly, this will free you up to focus on what we need you to focus on. This is high level, Rev. Yahweh's Council has been briefed about the mess surrounding the Bowl being your primary mission."

"What about Delores?"

A room and hallway away, I felt for Billee. This was her friend we were talking about. I had made promises. Most I wouldn't be able to deliver on in Delores' lifetime. And I didn't like breaking promises.

"We will just reassign her—"

"No," I said, loudly and firmly. "She's my case. I'm going to handle it."

Pher sighed. Even over the phone, I could picture his face cutting a frustrated father figure. "Rev, we have this covered. You've got to focus on the Nephilim and finding that Bowl."

"I know what I'm doing, and I know what I can handle. If I don't sleep for the next three weeks, then I don't sleep. But I'll tell you this. I'm not letting another Reaper escort this woman."

"Are you sure?"

"Without a doubt," I said, standing again. I was going to have to get to work, and this phone call wasn't helping me wrap things up. "Just keep me in the loop, Pher. About the recruits. About Anapheil. Hopefully, one of you is working with Guardians to ensure they guide the mortals to ways to mitigate the spread of the virus. That should at least slow things down. I need all the help I can get to find this Nephilim… or Hellion… or whoever is behind this."

"You got it, lad."

"Hey," I said, almost forgetting the important part, "one thing?"

"Shoot."

"Good, because that's exactly what I was going to ask," I said, flicking a glance at my duster hanging from a hook on the back of my bedroom door. "Am I authorized to shoot to kill?"

Pher *hmmm*'ed on the other end of the phone. My bedroom felt stuffy. "That's a contentious point with the Order. We prefer you find the culprit and bring them in so we can get answers. Maybe even have a modicum of leverage if there's someone at a higher level who's responsible."

"Hellion?"

"Or someone on the Council."

I whistled. "I'll do my best."

"Rev?"

"Yeah?"

"You know your job better than anyone. Do what you have to do, but be safe. If this turns into a gunfight, I don't want you being the one who falls."

"Funny, neither do I."

Neither one of us laughed.

16

REAPER VS GUARDIAN

BILLEE TOOK IT LIKE A CHAMP WHEN I KICKED HER OUT OF MY apartment. Okay, let's be real. I didn't kick her out, but I told her I had things to get to and that it was going to be a long night. Just because I would suffer didn't mean she needed to.

Like the amazing familiar she is, she offered to stay and help how she could. She also took it like a champ when I told her that what I had to do, she couldn't help with. One day, I'd involve her, but right now I had no guarantees by Pher's word the Order hadn't already sent a missive to another Reaper to call on Delores Garcia. And I was going to make sure the first Reaper on her doorstep was me.

Billee would be there at the end, but we weren't at that point yet and I didn't want her in the middle of a problem between Reapers, should one arise. Not that I expected one. Most Reapers are smart enough to not play 'who's got the biggest balls' with the Reaper Minister. But times, they were a changing. With two hundred on staff now being supplemented by unnamed and unnumbered detailees, I couldn't anticipate every potential problem, and now was not the time to take risks. That would come when I faced the Nephilim and whoever else was behind this mess.

I would have really liked to hop in my car and drive to Delores' place. Driving helps me clear my head. But time was of the essence, so a Gateway would have to do.

I stepped through a door I'd had a contractor install between my living space and the barren apartment I used almost exclusively for my travels. Sure, the building's owner, a corporation, would sue me if the property manager ever found out. But I already knew the manager would quit next year and move to San Diego—she was going to fall in love. The corporation? Meh. I'm not a big fan of uber-wealth and the all-too-real influence big business has on personal liberties. Let them come after me if they wanted. I'd already outlasted every business ever created.

I opened the Gateway. The image of an empty street appeared within the buzzing magical frame. The Gateway provided a narrow perspective of the surroundings. Crossing through always put me at risk of any threat lurking in the shadows, but those threats couldn't expect my arrival. I'd risk stepping into a fight with a Nephilim before I shocked poor Delores by plopping down in the middle of her living room while she was watching shows or walking around her place in the buff. I'm considerate like that. Plus, it wasn't Delores I was here to meet.

When you're a supernatural being, you can pick up on the presence of other supernatural beings. It's not a strong trait in most of us, but some immortals can really hone in on others. A handful, I've heard, can even detect when an immortal is about to use their magical Abilities—though that sounded more like an urban legend.

As long as Delores' Guardian was halfway decent, they would pick up on my presence as long as I hung around long enough.

That's a sore spot for most Reapers. That Guardians can smell us coming a mile away—okay, that's an exaggeration—

but we can't detect them. One of their superpowers, if you will.

Guardian Angels are a special crew. Tasked through Yahweh's archaic agreement with Lucifer, through His Council, through the Order of Thirteen, the Guardians enjoy special privileges every other angel doesn't. Such as being able to mask their presence in the Overworld. In the Upperworld, I'd be able to smell a Guardian before they said 'boo'. But here in the Overworld, one could fart next to me and I wouldn't know until I smelt what they'd dealt.

The reason I could see the errant Guardian Sachiel the night her negligence led to a young man being killed crossing the street was because Jared was already dead and waiting to be escorted. Her coffee run contributed to his untimely death, and once he was no longer part of the mortal plane, her ability to mask her presence in the Overworld from a Reaper was stripped.

Delores was still very much alive, so her Guardian could still mask. He visited before I saw him coming.

I nearly stumbled into the thirty-two-gallon garbage container set out at the street.

Omen grinned when I spun on him.

"One of these days you're going to hurt someone," I said, and lowered my fists, wishing almost any other Guardian was Delores's.

Omen Ash was young by immortal standards. His hairstyle and color, along with his pathetic attempt at a goatee and neck tattoo, marked him as someone too young to have good sense.

"Rev, man," Omen said, stepping back and shoving his hands in his pockets, "so good to see you. How ya' been?"

"Good, you ass. And you?"

"Can't complain. Can't complain." He shifted from foot to foot. My heart picked up a few beats per minute just being near his constant energetic presence. "Whatcha up to?" His eyes went wide, and he pulled his shoulders up toward his ears. "Oh, man. Don't tell me you're here for Delores, man? Seriously?"

I gestured at his white t-shirt. "Ever thought of wearing a jacket? It's January."

He smirked, raising one of his eyebrows, which had looked as weird as his sparse goatee ever since he bleached them an obnoxious color of blonde. "Wasn't expecting company."

"Better me than someone else, though, right?"

"Yeah man, but..." He shifted again, his head repeatedly shooting toward Delores's front door as if someone had snagged him with a fishing line and was tugging over and over. "Man, is it really her time?"

"Afraid so," I said, holding up a finger. "But not quite yet. I want to give her a little more time."

"Oh, cool," he said, hopping from foot to foot still. "Why?"

"Because I know she's doing good stuff," I answered honestly, with as much information as I dared to share. Guardians and Reapers have an interesting relationship. We have to cooperate for all of this to work, but we also have our own lanes to stay in or we'd face conflicts of interest I'd rather not deal with as the Minister. "You know what she's said about the sightings at the camp? You were there when she told me."

He chuckled so fast I thought he might hyperventilate. "I was. You intimidated her."

"I do that to a lot of people."

"And angels."

"Oh?" Now it was my turn to raise an eyebrow. "Do I intimidate the Guardians?"

He shuffled back and forth. "Come on, man. You're the freakin' Minister. Of course, you do. We all know you're a badass. Our supervisors tell us all the time not to screw with you if we end up working with you on a case."

"Smart supervisors."

"They 'aight," he said with another dorky chuckle.

"Just tell them to not step on Reaper toes, and we'll be good."

"We try, man. No one wants to tussle with you."

Nodding in the house's direction, I asked, "How is she doing?"

"She's good. Happy." He tucked his hands further into his pockets and shivered. "Shame she's got to go. She's pretty cool. Watches funny shit on TV. You wouldn't know it by looking at her, but she's got a raunchy sense of humor. I like it. When are you thinking you'll take her?"

"Not sure yet. Wanted to talk to you first and see what she's been seeing when she's out and about, especially at the camp. Especially with this virus going around."

"Yeah, that's nuts, right? Thankfully, she's being careful and listening to my whispers."

Whispers are subliminal messages Guardians send to their mortals. Nothing audible any eavesdropper could pick up on. When a Guardian whispers, the mortal thinks they've come up with the idea themselves. It's an ingenious tactic, really.

"Are you seeing anything strange?"

He looked at me quizzically. "Strange? Like how?"

"Like Penumbra Man strange?"

"Nah, man. She thinks she has, but I haven't. Haven't picked up on anything either. Nothing weird, I mean. If there's a Penumbra Man around, he's damn good."

Horrible grammar aside, I was disturbed to hear that. There was a Nephilim in town, playing as a Penumbra Man. If Omen hadn't spotted him, maybe the Nephilim was spending less time with the homeless than I thought. Maybe I'd been searching up the wrong tree all this time. I pushed the dark thoughts away. "Good. Keep your eyes out. All this stuff you're hearing on the news is not restricted to Olympia or even the Puget Sound. This shit is everywhere."

"Everywhere?"

I nodded. "And the news only knows about some of it. Keep your head low. Be careful. You're just as vulnerable here as she is. I'm ninety-nine percent sure there's a Penumbra Man in the area."

"That's some Nephilim shit right there."

"You can say that again."

"That's some Nephilim—"

"Not literally." I smiled and shook my head. "But I'm serious. She's in as much danger as any mortal, but maybe more so because of her work and the vulnerable population she cares for. She's already in the Book of Planes, but that doesn't mean I want her suffering during her last days. I'm sure you don't either."

"No way, man." Omen shook his head vigorously. The blond V-shaped flop of hair he'd dyed red swayed between his eyes. "I'll stay on watch. Do you know who I'm looking for?"

"Wish I did. If I had a name, you and I wouldn't be having this conversation."

Omen's jaw and weak goatee throbbed forward as he grinned. "You going after them?"

I gave him a friendly shove, the kind men give each other when they're being casually friendly. I'm sure it was as awkward for him as it was for me. Physical connection is not something I like, and I was crap at hiding it.

But Omen played it off well. Shoving his hands deeper into his pockets and bouncing from foot to foot, white clouds rolling from his nose as he exhaled. "Can I tell you something?"

"Of course," I said, watching the front of Delores's house.

"I'm kinda scared. I've never dealt with a Nephilim or a Penumbra Man. This shit has been crazy. The stuff we're hearing. Delores, man, sometimes she just comes home and cries 'cuz she feels so helpless. The people she's been helping down at the camp are scared out of their minds. I hate going down there with her. It's creepy. Always feel like I'm jumping at shadows."

"Good."

"Whatcha mean?"

"If you aren't jumpy now, I'd say you're asking to be Abolished."

"I don't want to die."

"That's my point." I tipped my head at the quiet home sitting on a quiet street that gave warmth and comfort to a kind mortal. I dug a business card out of a pocket. "Here. Call me if you need me, especially if you see something. And stay jumpy. If I hear anything, I'll let you know."

For a second, Omen's youth exuberance slipped from his face as he grimaced. "Sucks that she has to go."

"Yeah."

"You'll be good with her? Patient?"

"Always am."

Omen raised his arm, hand formed into a fist. I raised mine. We bumped.

"Thanks, Rev."

"You got it. Now, get your ass inside before you freeze to death. That would be a hell of a way to be Abolished. I'll see you soon."

Omen nodded a few times. I could almost see the thoughts swirling in his head. He took the stairs two at a time and stepped through the door without having to open it.

Damn Guardians and their cool masking powers.

I hung outside Delores's home for a few moments. Enjoying the cold evening and hoping she was, too. Omen was a good guy, decent at his job from my experience. Young, though. Too young to be creative and guide the caring woman through her last days. Whereas Guardians guide their mortals to take a cruise or travel to a place they've always wanted to see, skydive, or whatever last event of life they could enjoy, I didn't expect Omen to influence Delores that way. His creativity was limited to his choice in hairstyles. Not a knock on the kid, just a fact.

Delores Garcia would remain in Olympia for her last days, serving the homeless during the day and watching television alone at night. As long as the Nephilim left her alone, if Omen did his job, she'd be safe to enjoy what she had left. I sure hoped she would, right until I visited.

Until that time, and every second afterward, the unnamed Nephilim would have my attention and efforts.

A sweet, caring mortal, and a devious, murdering immortal set in my sights.

Because no one outruns the Reapers.

17

THE END OF THE WORLD?

"How do we hunt something we can't see? I mean, you've done it before. What's the secret?" Billee asked.

It was a fair question. I mean, it was January. It was cold. The wind cutting across the inlet sliced through my leather duster and stabbed my legs. Though she donned her parka, Billee looked no more comfortable than me. I just looked cooler. Keeping your mind active by asking critical questions was a good way to stop yourself from freezing to death.

"First, by not thinking you can't see it. You can see it. Anyone can," I said, scanning the camp. "It's just that, as you catch it, the bastard will do this... shift kind of thing. That's what you have to look for."

"Shift?"

"Jumps. Shimmers. Scoobie-Dos away. Hard as hell to get a direct look."

"Hmm." Billee stuffed her hands in her pockets. She rotated her shoulders side to side, making her upper torso rotate as her head moved in concert with them. "So, if we can't look directly at it, or it shifts when we do, how are we supposed to nail it?"

That was the Armageddon-saving question. "You poke the bear."

She swung in my direction, her eyes squinted against the chilly air. "I'm serious."

"So am I."

Something inside her rumbled, and she turned away.

"I know I sound flippant, but it's the truth." A stiff winter wind blew inland off the water, blowing my hair into my face. I held it back and turned into the wind, still scanning. "The only way to get a Penumbra Man to come out and play is to give them a reason to step out. I just have to find that reason."

I stopped my story there. Billee didn't need to know the lengths I'd gone to in the past to corner a Penumbra Man. People and angels have paid stiff prices in the past in the name of exposing a Penumbra Man. To my knowledge, there was no other way except fortunate timing, and I wasn't counting on Lady Luck.

We watched the camp. The residents went about their hard lives. Olympia isn't the coldest place on earth. We're too close to the ocean for wild temperatures, on the high or low end. But it was the middle of winter. The blanket of clouds had been a permanent part of the landscape for two months already and would be for a few more. Not that solar radiation would have changed anyone's conditions in the camp, but it probably made their days slightly better to have staved off the chill for a few minutes.

The camp was quiet. Tired. The malaise, obvious. How could it not be? A vulnerable population—to their plight, the elements, the lack of shelter, food, health care, and the cruelty of the Penumbra Man. Most residents were young adults. The faces I saw belonged to twenty- and thirty-year-olds, broken by a sprinkling of forty-somethings. What worried me most was the fear and trepidation I saw in their sore-marked faces. Wild eyes told the story of the terror they'd been living, both from the supernatural virus they didn't understand and couldn't stop, and from the thing that stalked them. In those faces, I saw some who were already driven mad.

"Okay then," Billee said, interrupting my assessment of the camp's residents, "how in the world can I help you fight it?"

"*You* won't, for one. Plus, my bosses would prefer I capture it and bring whoever is behind the mask of the Penumbra Man back to the Upperworld for questioning."

My phone rang. I snagged it, only after catching my hand on the seam and turning the duster's pocket lining inside out. "What's up, Pher? Kind of busy."

"Confirmed. Someone stole the First Bowl," my boss said. "How's that for getting your attention?"

"What? Hang on. Billee and I are outside at the camp. Let me get back to the car."

Billee watched me carefully. I gestured with my head and we did a slow, careful trot back to my sports coupe. I got in, started it and cranked the heat, and put Pher on Bluetooth.

"Billee's here with me."

"Hi, Sparky," Pher said in his flirty voice that I'm sure he'd swear was his normal conversational tone.

"Hi, Pher." She stared at the phone, waiting.

"What's this about the Bowl?" I asked.

Pher's sigh came through loud and clear. "We just received confirmation. Bureaucracy takes forever, I swear. But Puriel called us into a meeting a few minutes ago and briefed us. I crossed over so I could call you. We're working assignments soon, so I'll head back after this. My first task was to get in touch with you and let you know about the confirmation."

"Finally."

"Agreed."

"Who took it?"

"That, we don't know. Not for sure. But we think a Nephilim named Arakiel is responsible."

"Got a last name," I asked as I made a gesture in the air to Billee like I was holding a pen in one hand and my other served as the piece of paper. Billee always had something to take notes with. She didn't disappoint me this time either, pulling out a small notepad and pen. She's good like that, and even played into the social worker stereotype I staunchly held to.

I mouthed 'gotcha' at her, but still accepted them when she handed the pad and pen over, sticking out her tongue.

"Hale."

"Arakiel Hale," I said, scratching the name down. "Description?"

"Just shy of six-foot. Well-groomed beard."

"A douchey one, like yours?" I said, unable to not get a jibe in.

Pher chuckled. "Actually, yes. Though I wouldn't consider it douchey."

"I'd hope not. It's on your face. Okay. Race? Identifying marks? Anything that will help."

"Brown hair. White guy. Mustache and beard are thick. Well-dressed, too. Unlike you, he doesn't walk around looking like he's ready to go to a rock concert every waking minute of his life. He has taste."

"Sounds like bad taste."

"Solid build, too. So be careful," Pher said. "From the intelligence pictures, he's got a wrestler's form. Not big and bulky, not slim, but solidly athletic. My bet is he'll be a handful to tussle with."

"I'll do my best, boss."

"I know you will. Everyone knows. That's exactly why we've put our trust in you. But listen, this is no joke."

"Never thought it was." I could see that fact for myself outside the windshield of my car that was just now steaming over. I switched the heat to defrost before one of the camp residents thought Billee and I were having a good old romp in the parked car just across the street from their makeshift homes.

"We've got to hurry on this," Pher said, drawing my attention back. "The Council also confirmed whoever has the Bowl, poured it."

"Fuck."

"Exactly."

"What's that mean for our task?" Billee asked.

"Maybe nothing," Pher said. "Maybe everything. The Bowls of Wrath are apocalyptic events. Back in the day, a different angel protected each Bowl. Separation of power measure. Thankfully, before I served in the Order, someone had the insight to see the vulnerability in that, and they got the Council to approach Yahweh to build the Safe. The Bowls have been kept in that realm since. Long before me."

"And he's old," I said.

"Very," Pher agreed. "None of the other Bowls have been compromised, so it's likely this is an isolated incident. Maybe even a lucky break for whoever took it."

"The worldwide spread of a virus that does what I've seen it do is not something I'd consider lucky," Billee said, her face scrunching.

"Nor I," Pher answered. "But it could have been much worse if any of the other Bowls were stolen too. The combined effect of multiple Bowls being poured on the Earth... I don't want to think about that."

"Why?"

"Excuse her, Pher. She still needs to brush up on her Bible studies. I'll give her homework assignments after we're done with this."

Pher snorted. "Because it won't be a lot of fun for the mortals if they are. Look at what's happening now. This isn't the end. The virus will continue to spread and infect millions, maybe tens or hundreds, of millions more. Many will die. Especially those without access to good medical care. It's going to be a scary time. The war on the other side of the world will only exacerbate the problem."

Billee seemed to sink into her seat as Pher ran down the list of his worries.

"We can't do anything about that right now," I said, interrupting the avalanche of dread. "What we need to do is get to the bottom of this First Bowl. Why did this Arakiel guy steal it? *How* did he steal it from the Safe? Is he acting alone or is someone helping him, directing him, more likely? To what aim? When we get those answers, we'll have a better idea of what's going on and how much risk the other Bowls are under. Please tell me the Council is beefing up their security on the Safe?"

"I'd imagine so," Pher said.

Surprising. "You don't know for sure?"

"Outside my purview, lad. That's Council business. They're keeping all their moves hush-hush. Security reasons, you understand. Plus, I'm a little busy with Order business."

"Imagine that. Being over-taxed and not able to manage things effectively because you have too many things requiring your attention."

"Not the time."

"Never is."

I watched the camp, still wary that a Penumbra Man might lurk in the corners, hoping to spread fear, panic, and disease with each interaction. "Pher, are we looking for the good old mark of the beast when I get my hands on Arakiel?"

"Wouldn't doubt it," he answered instantly as if he'd been expecting the question. "When you find him, try not to kill him. Look for the mark, definitely."

"Mark? What mark?" Billee asked.

Almost as a side comment, I said, "They'll have '666' tattooed somewhere on their body."

Her mouth fell open. "That's a real thing? I thought that was made up?"

"Nope." I shook my head and gave her the skinny on how the mark was used back at the beginning of mortal life on the planet. The Upperworld and Underworlds agreed to mark the first humans so angels and demons could tell each other apart and ensure they kept the Balance. A '666' tattoo meant the human would act in the Underworld's interest, their motivations and actions, internally focused. Act for the self, to preserve its place. A mortal without the mark would act in the Upperworld's interest. Their motivations and actions were externally focused. Act for others, even at the cost of the self. The Balance.

"Like 'no man is an island' type of stuff?" Billee asked. "I thought this was all about good versus evil?"

"Nope. Never was. The Balance is what keeps mortals from swaying too far to one side or the other."

Through the phone, Pher added, "It's what keeps your kind alive. We must maintain it at all costs."

"So why all this, then?" Billee asked, swatting the air with a hand. "Why would an angel pour a Bowl and make us suffer? What good does that do if the Balance is thrown out of whack?"

"Power," I said with a shrug. "Even the immortal realms have politics and those who seek power. I can't speak for the Underworld, but the Upperworld is full of them. Isn't that right, boss?"

"Sadly, yes. There are those among our kind who will risk the Balance if it means they gain."

"But if the Balance *is* thrown off, humankind will go extinct?" she asked.

I hated hearing the fear in her voice.

"Most likely," Pher said. "We can't know for sure. None of us have that level of insight into how far off it needs to be before things go bad. But that's the thinking. Without wanting to overload you, Billee, that's our task from the highest levels. To preserve the Balance."

Her words were hot. "So someone in Heaven is willing to rule over a dead planet just to have more power?"

"Well, it wouldn't be dead," Pher said kindly. "All life would continue, except for humankind."

I said, "Listen, as much as I adore you and enjoy our chats about the end of the world, I've got work to do, Pher."

"Yes, so do I. I'll let you know what I know as soon as I come to know something."

"I will too, boss. Talk to you later."

After I hung up, Billee blew out a deep, shaky breath. "What do we do now?"

"I drop you off at home."

"Why?"

"I'm going to see an angel about a Bowl."

The Rift sizzled. I pulled my duster on, checked to ensure my .327 was still in its place, and stepped through.

As I crossed the divide between the mortal and immortal realms, I crossed my fingers and toes that Brock was working.

When I stepped out of the Rift a fraction of a second later, it thrilled me to see him standing next to the double doors to the Order's meeting room.

"Rev," he said with a smile that was antithetical to his imposing physique, "what are you doing here? There's no meeting. They broke a few hours ago. Pulled an all-nighter."

"Why are you here, then?"

He cocked his head at the doors. "Puriel's still working. Pretty sure something big is going down."

I patted him on the shoulder, which felt like tapping a boulder. "Something big *is* going down. That's why I needed to see who's around."

Brock smiled knowingly. "Who are you looking for? Might help you find them."

"Jericho."

He nodded a few times. The corners of his mouth raised in

synchronicity of silent understanding. "He's in his quarters. You know where those are?"

"Yep. Thanks, big man."

"Good luck," he called out as I made my way down the hall. "Let me know if you need any backup."

It was a joke. Brock couldn't leave his station with Puriel working. A joke, but once wrapped in more than a modicum of truth. I sensed Brock sensed my motivations.

"You bet! Just make sure your crew knows I need a little privacy. See you later."

The halls were empty. With everything going on, with Pher admitting the Order had assignments, I imagined Yahweh's headquarters were full of private activity. Everyone working on their angles to uncover what needed to be uncovered. Or covering that which needed to be covered.

Just because the Order gave me the power to handle the situation didn't mean they were exempt from how I handled it. If they didn't like it, they could find themselves another Minister. We'd all win.

At least ten feet across, the hallway was broad. The walls were red oak. The trim was conservative, tasteful, and restricted to large rectangles that dominated the middle of the walls. No fluting. Just bland borders about six feet high and four feet wide. Spaced out every five feet, they were the only decoration except for the slim bar lights casting white light toward the ceiling and down toward the floor.

Each Order member lived in this part of Yahweh's headquarters. This hall housed six of them. Directly behind me was the hall for the other six. Puriel, as President of the Order, enjoyed her own digs near where the Council quartered.

The Order housing was split into separate halls. An added security measure to keep the Order split so a single attack couldn't take them all out. Too many people knew when the Order was in session. It wouldn't be hard for a foe, angelic or demonic, to get to the headquarters and do damage to one of the most important governing bodies in the Upperworld. There wasn't much Yahweh could do for them whenever they traveled back to their home Levels, as Pher was fond of doing, but while they were here, they had the best security He could provide.

Their rent-free residences were stupidly humongous. I'm talking five thousand square feet of lush living. When six angels occupied a single hallway with quarters like that, spreading out wasn't optional.

Ah, to live the good life.

I nodded to the first guard.

She winked.

"Did Brock send word?" I asked her, hoping he had without delay so that none of the four guards in this hall would get involved if things turned ugly.

"He did. The sprite got here a minute before you and is heading down the other hall, making sure everyone has a heads up, just in case," she said. A beautiful angel, even with the thick scar running the length of one cheek, she wasn't someone I'd expect to be dangerous if I saw her out and about on the streets of the Upperworld. "You're good."

"Thanks."

She returned to the stoic posture of a guard.

I knocked on Jericho's door and then rang the doorbell without affording him a pause.

It worked. The lock clicked, and he pulled the door while asking, "Who is it?"

A stupid move brought on by the comfort of a false sense of security.

I thrust my hip into the door as soon as he cracked it, knocking him back.

"Wh—what are you doing?" he asked after catching his balance.

I slid inside and had the door locked behind me by then.

Jericho rubbed his shoulder. "You can't just barge into my quarters."

"Looks like I just did. Since I'm here, let's have a little chat." I jerked my head to the side room, bigger than one of my Olympia apartments. "Let's sit."

"I don't have ti—" he said as he tried to dodge around me to get to the door, and presumably call a guard. They were doing me a favor, and I didn't need him dressing them down.

I shot out a stiff hand, hitting him in the middle of the chest.

He made a sound like that of a young robin waiting for its mother to drop a chewed worm into its mouth, and fell.

The marble floor was pristine. Which made it easy to drag him across to the living room by his collar. His shirt wouldn't fit the same.

I pulled him to his feet and shoved, sending him falling onto an overstuffed couch that was longer than my car. The cushions caught him without a sound. Even when he slapped them with a petulant palm, the expensive material absorbed the smack.

"You cannot do this to me. I'm a member of the Order!"

As if I needed to be reminded. "You're a twat, Jericho." I took a seat across from him. "And I'm busy. So listen and listen carefully. What's your involvement in all of this?"

"All of—" he said, until I twitched, acting like I was going to get out of the chair. This thing was way too comfortable to leave, even to slap the stupid, flat expression off his smug face.

"Who is Arakiel to you? How do you know each other?"

"Wh—ho—what makes you think I know him?"

"His description alone is douchey enough that I wouldn't put it past you to run in the same circles," I said, even though the way Jericho's usual deadpan expression flicked with worry already gave me the clue I needed.

I was guessing. Strong-arming this spoiled brat was a

hazardous, but deliberate, chance to fast-roll my investigation. Time was of the essence. The pouring of the First Bowl meant I no longer had the time to play Mr. Nice Guy.

When Jericho treated me like I was an idiot who didn't know his feet from his wings, I introduced his chest, cheeks, and knees to a few backhands fired by the annoyance of the necessity of getting out of the wonderful chair. That was riskier than it sounds, trust me. Jericho has the emotional range of a slice of bread. I was taking a big chance.

When his cheeks glowed red like he'd just fallen out of a poorly produced kink video, he broke. "W—we went to school together. We—we were fri—friends. Our families knew each other."

Ah, now we were getting somewhere. "How good of friends?"

Behind the hand he held to his face, he glared. "We weren't *that* kind."

"Not what I was implying," I said, inching forward.

Jericho flinched, but it was quick. A lesser assassin wouldn't have noticed. "We were friends for a long time, but we just fell away, Revelation. That happens after school. You'd know that if you ever had friends."

"Call me by my full name again and see how easy it is to hold your cheek with a broken wrist. And the wrong friends can get you in trouble. When did you talk to him last?"

He threw his free hand up in the air and slapped the couch again. Still silent. I was going to have to find out what the furniture cost. I might have to approach the Order for a pay raise if they didn't fire me after this. "I don't know. Centuries."

"Centuries?"

"At least."

"Who in the Order knows you have a personal history with this guy?"

Jericho looked away.

"Ah, no one?"

He was silent.

"Seems they should."

His head snapped in my direction. "Are you stupid? It's too late now. If I brought it up to them, they'd question why I didn't mention it days ago when the idiot's name was first thrown around."

"Not my problem," I said, inching forward again. I had Jericho in full retreat and I wouldn't let up now. "Why would Arakiel want the Bowl and how in the hell could he have gotten into the Safe in the first place?"

"How would I know? I told you I haven't talked to him in centuries."

"Wouldn't be difficult to have planned the theft that long ago."

"If it was, I wasn't involved. Nor did I have knowledge, if that's what you're implying?"

"Then, start digging."

"Wh—what?"

"You're too smart to act this stupid, Jericho," I said. "See what you can find out. Use old connections. Talk to his family. I don't care. Start coming up with something."

"I'm busy with too many other tasks to do your job."

"Yeah, I care about that as much as you cared about my workload or the shit you've dumped on the Reapers for a long, long time. You're going to snoop around and feed me information, or the Order will find out you were once buddies with the angel who somehow stole a fucking Bowl of Wrath."

"You're blackmailing me?" he said in a screech that almost made me slap him again. The only thing stopping me was the fact that I think he had the point by now.

"Do it, or the Order finds out," I said, moving toward the door. "Oh, and the clock is ticking, so you might want to make yourself presentable and get to work."

My hand was on the door handle, pushing it down, when he whined, "You're going to regret this, Revelation."

Over my shoulder, I said, "Tell someone who cares," and then stepped into the hallway, hoping I hadn't made a mistake by not pushing the entitled, yet influential, angel harder.

18

HANGOUTS

"This is the place?" I asked.

Billee, in the passenger seat, used her thumb and finger to zoom in on the map on her phone. She had to do it without gloves. Oh, the sacrifices required of familiars. She nodded. "Yes, this is it."

"You ready?"

Her lips fluttered when she exhaled. "Ready as I'll ever be."

"Let's go then." I got out and slammed the car door closed just in case anyone was watching. Billee furrowed an eyebrow but said nothing. "They might be watching."

Her head shot around. "Re—really?"

"Wouldn't you be if some weird old guy and his old female partner who busted you breaking into a storage yard ordered you to meet up again? The world is full of weirdos."

Her hands were on her hips by the time I was done with my question. "Me? Old?"

I nodded at the old brewery site building, abandoned two decades before. Half the windows were now nothing more than slivers of glass. Black graffiti decorated every reachable part of the building. "They're teens. To them, everyone is old."

"Thanks for the confidence boost," she said and slammed her door. I don't know if that was aimed at me or to intimidate the kids.

We reached the door that had a perfectly circular opening where the knob used to be. I slipped my finger in the hole and checked with her once more. "This is going to be easy, Billee. Remember, we're not only doing this for the investigation, but we're doing it for every single person in Olympia and beyond. The more I learn about what they've experienced, the better armed I'll be to help not only these kids, but everyone."

"I get it, but I don't have to like it," she muttered.

"Let's get this over with then," I said and pulled the door open. We stepped into the old brewery together.

Buildings closed up as long as this one rarely made for enjoyable experiences. Mustiness. Dust. Dampness. Piss and stale shit from years of vagabond residency. Every scent punched me in the nose.

Billee gagged and put her hand to her nose.

"Nice place you've got here," I called out into the empty heights.

Old brewery equipment which hadn't been auctioned off when the company went bankrupt sat under layers of gray dust. The only light was natural and came from the broken windows, which let in slivers of the gray winter day.

"Thanks," a voice echoed from on high.

I looked up toward the railing of a mezzanine, which looked ready to come unhinged from the wall and crash to the filthy floor. The kid with the long blond ropes of hair, the king of the bolt cutters, stood above us like someone who had watched far too many post-apocalyptic movies.

"Can we chat?" I asked, my hands held up at shoulder height, palms facing the kid in the clearest sign of my willingness to take part in the only armistice I was likely to show him.

"Sure," he said, looking at various spots around the wide-open, dingy space. My bet was other kids from the large group at the storage yard were scattered behind stacks of abandoned equipment. "I'll come down."

"Good." I meant it. I would rather face a Penumbra Man with both hands tied behind my back than risk my neck climbing up to and walking on that mezzanine.

Billee and I waited. The vast open room, four stories high, was so quiet I could hear a pigeon *cooing* somewhere in the stale confines.

"I hope you're right about this being safe," Billee said as she craned her head up into the dusty heights. "The Penumbra Man could be anywhere."

"And nowhere," I said. "Remember, these kids are just a means to an end. They're not targets. I doubt the Penumbra Man has been hanging around them. We'll make sure. Just... don't get comfortable. Shout if you see something. I'll need to focus on the kids. Make sure you have my back and yours."

"Will do," Billee said, with a straight face.

Bolt cutter made his way down the ladder, dropping the last five feet to the floor like a cat. Ah, to have youthful knees again. He stuffed his hands in his pockets and walked towards us, constantly casting glances at different spots in the building. His nervousness was etched on his face, in the way the skin under his eyes stretched with the strain.

"Call them all out," I said while he was still thirty feet from us.

His stride hitched. "Wh—what?"

"You heard me," I said, waving an arm at the equipment. "Your boys. I know they're hiding. I told you I wanted everyone here, and I meant it, so don't act like they haven't been here for a bit, passing the time talking shit about guys they dislike and girls their think they can ask out. Now, call them out."

"Don't be too hard on them," Billee whispered. "We need them on our side."

"They will be. Plus, I don't enjoy dancing. The world doesn't have time."

Shuffling, hesitant, and light, flitted out from behind large vats and towering stacks of... something covered by tarps that I was sure were white at a point in their history. Like most teens, they did nothing individually. In batches of twos and threes, the teen boys emerged to join the bolt cutter.

Billee inhaled.

"We'll be fine," I said. "This will be smooth."

Her exhale was slow.

The group of teens formed a U-shaped half-ring around us, three ranks deep.

I waved them in before slipping my hand into the pocket of my duster. No one, not even Billee, noticed. "Don't be shy. Come closer. I'm not shouting."

They cast curious glances. I activated the soul stone. By the time I pulled my glowing hand out of my pocket, the boys were under my influence. Billee would have been pulled under the spell of the soul stone as well if she weren't my familiar.

"Rev? I thought we were just here to talk."

"We are," I said, holding the soul stone up. Fifty-some-odd pairs of eyes followed it. "But I'm not wasting time."

She grumbled something.

"We're going to have a little chat about the other day," I said, skipping the main meal and getting right to dessert. "Give me the name of who told you to attack the storage facility."

"Arakiel," bolt cutter said, staring wide-eyed at the raised soul stone.

Check.

"How did Arakiel come to you?"

"He caught us at a wrestling tournament. We were getting ready. Was before the matches kicked off," a round boy in the second row said, his mouth an oval as he stared at the stone.

"Mostly just us and the coaches and a couple of parents. He made the adults leave. We locked them out. He told us what he wanted."

"Hmmm." I didn't like this. If Arakiel was smart enough to get into the Safe to steal the First Bowl, pour it on the Earth, and conduct mass manipulation of mortals, someone was protecting him. That was the kind of shit that threw the Balance off, and there was no way Yahweh or His Council, or even demons, would sit by and watch, Nephilim or not. "Did he tell you he was going to meet with you again? To follow up? To have you carry out more orders?"

"Yes," bolt cutter answered, then greedily smiled. "He said we were part of his army now."

"We're his proxies," a thin kid with a bad complexion said from the edge of the U, shaking a fist. I couldn't imagine his weight class, but it had to include the word 'feather' in it somewhere. "We're going to burn the world!"

Billee chuntered. "Dear God."

I pushed my Ability into the soul stone. The blinding white pulsated, increasing and decreasing in a steady, mesmerizing rhythm. We stood under the umbrella of white, and I was about to do something dirty, but necessary. Simultaneously, I would cleanse these kids of the influence of Arakiel and then basically do my version of brainwashing them.

"You won't feel the compulsion to work for Arakiel anymore," I said, putting power into my voice, carrying over them as the white light throbbed all around us, washing out the dingy brewery. "Whenever Arakiel comes to visit, you'll act as if you are following his orders, but you'll contact me or Billee immediately." I gave them our phone numbers. "Memorize those."

"Yes, sir," the group said in unison.

"Repeat them back."

They did, in perfect synchronicity.

"He gives orders, and you pretend to follow them until you can call one of us. Then, come directly here, even if you have to walk or steal your little brother's bicycle. Understand?"

"Yes, sir!" Their voices carried up into the dusty realm. The pigeon stopped *cooing*.

"And if Arakiel ever tells you to meet him at a location, you will give me and Billee that meeting place and time before you take your first step. Got it?"

"Yes, sir!"

"When this light fades, you will not remember this conversation," I said. "You won't remember us being here and you won't know why you're in this old factory. You'll go home, do your homework. Kiss your mother. Help your dad. Answer questions your siblings have about homework. Apologize to your girlfriend or boyfriend about whatever stupid thing you did to them lately. And you will feel repulsion any time Arakiel comes around."

With that, I pushed more of my Ability into the soul stone. The light grew even whiter until it washed out the definition of the boys. One second, they were nothing more than outlines of forms, the next, invisible in the blinding light.

Billee yelped and stumbled backward. The sphere pulsed brighter until the world was whitewashed.

Then the light faded, returning color to the world. The boys, stunned, came back into definition. As a Reaper, the light didn't affect me. Even though Billee didn't fall under its mental power, the light blinded her as much as it had the teens, now willing participants in my mission.

I took Billee by the elbow and guided her toward the door. "Come on. We're leaving."

"I can't see," she said, sounding in near panic.

"I'll help you. Your sight will return in a few minutes."

"The boys?"

"They're fine."

"But what if Arakiel finds out?"

"He won't be able to. Not now that I used the soul stone." I stopped her at the car door, opened it, and helped her sit. Once behind the wheel, I got us away from the abandoned brewery. She was uncomfortably quiet. "They're as safe as I can make them, Billee."

"But you might have just put fifty kids in harm's way. You said we were just going to talk to them. You didn't say you were going to do that Jedi mind trick."

Points to her for the pop culture reference. "You would have given me shit if you knew. And right now, the last thing I need to deal with is more shit. This was easier."

"Easier doesn't make right."

I turned onto her street. "What's not right is being put in the position to put fifty kids at risk in order to save hundreds of millions of people." I pulled up in front of her house and got out to help her to the front door. At least now she could open her eyes and keep them open for a few minutes. "I don't enjoy having to do what I did, but I don't get the luxury of taking the moral high ground. I'm a Reaper with a job to do. And that job is to get my hands on Arakiel. No one outruns the Reaper, and I'm going to make sure that includes a Nephilim. Give me your keys so I can get you inside."

It wasn't the best send-off I'd ever have with Billee and probably wouldn't be the worst of our time together, but she was going to have to level up as my familiar. That meant accepting and doing things she didn't like. Unfortunately for her, she was going to learn that Heaven isn't all it's cracked up to be, and life is easier if you accept things as gray more often than black and white. No 'true' good. No 'pure' evil. Life's just life. Better to learn and accept that early.

Damn, I needed a drink.

19

GOING HOME

HOME.

I stepped out of the Rift and into my Upperworld home. The first thing I noticed was the smell of lemon. The company I hired to keep the place clean had recently been through. A nice surprise.

My living room looked like something out of a real estate pamphlet. A staged space. The company had even fanned three magazines on the coffee table as if offering reading material to a guest. If I actually lived in my home, those magazines would be ruffled and folded, and more likely found next to the toilet than anywhere else.

"Ah, good to be home," I said to no one and walked out my front door.

I wasn't home to be home. There was a single destination on my mind, and it wasn't my modest house. This visit would be short and focused solely on making peace, just in case Arakiel proved to be a formidable foe.

The street was quiet. A kid rode by on a bike, instantly reminding me of the fifty or so mortal kids I'd just brain-washed. Even in another realm, I couldn't get too far away from the stain of the job. Which was exactly why I was back in the Third Level of the Upperworld for the first time in ages. Fingers crossed, the kid on the bike was the only reminder of what I'd just done in the Overworld.

"Hey Rev," Jimmy said cheerily as he fluttered by, pulling up a few feet away and hanging in the air in front of me. His lucent wings flapped, he swore, thirty-six times per second. I didn't even want to challenge him on that claim.

Jimmy was a neighbor. A sprite who lived in a community of sprites on the top floor of a tower at the end of the block. I once made the mistake of asking him how many sprites lived in what could only be called a commune, and he spent the next fifty minutes listing each of their names. It was the last time I asked.

"How have you been, my friend?" I said, still walking toward the Abyss, my local drinking hole.

"Great," Jimmy said with a tiny smile. "Estelle and I are official now. I wish you could have been here for it. The ceremony was amazing. We had pipes. An organ... though it took a dozen of our friends to play it. There were hundreds in attendance. Not just sprites either. There were Justine and Jake. They're so cute together. They have a dog now. Oh, Bob was there. Joe. Steve and Sally. Mom and Dad, of course. My uncles, Rex, Tom, Sid—"

I laughed, holding up my hand. "I'm not here long, Jimmy, but I wish I could stay and hear all about it. Sorry I missed it, but congratulations on getting hitched! When can we expect little Jimmys?"

"Well, Estelle and I have been talking," Jimmy started, his chest bulging with the breath to last the litany of factors that went into two sprites deciding to have or not have children. I'd realized my mistake too late. "So many things to think about, Rev. There's cost, of course. The little buggers are expensive. Do you know what higher education costs now? I did a ton of research—"

He went on, continuing his journey off-topic for the next

three blocks. Outside The Abyss, I stopped. "I'm sorry, bud, but I've got to pop in here and get work done."

Jimmy's black orb eyes glanced—I think—at the sign hanging above the door. It's difficult to tell without being able to distinguish iris from sclera from pupil. When the entire eye is monochrome, it's a real challenge to track. "A pub? You've got work at a pub."

I nodded. "Important work, too. So, I'll see you later?"

His disappointment at not being able to spend the next week filling me in on a millennium's worth of plans was wiped away in a flash. "You got it, Rev. It was so nice seeing you. I was just telling Estelle about that time w—"

"Great stuff, Jimmy. Nice seeing you too. Let's catch up the next time I'm in town." I stepped into the Abyss and closed the door behind me, puffing out a breath.

"Well, well," a voice that sounded like living rust said. "Look what the cat-sith dragged in."

"Abaddon, baby," I said in our traditional greeting, spreading my arms and walking to the woman behind the bar.

Abaddon owned The Abyss, the best drinking hole in the entire Level. The most unsettling resident of the Third Level beyond a doubt, she was still a staple of the community, even though she was a little too unique for most of my neighbors. With blood-red hair and heterochromia, she was hard on the eyes for the Third's more conservative residents. She liked to paint her face too. Not just eyeshadow and lipstick. I'm talking full-out white foundation plastered over her face, from hairline to jaw, topped by detailed designs that changed daily. I dug her style, maybe more so because she was often shunned for her appearance. One red and one sky-blue eye took time to get used to, but Abaddon was aware of that. She rarely held eye contact with anyone for more than a few seconds. Once she knew someone was comfortable with her, she had no such problems meeting someone's gaze.

Abaddon was good people. Among the best in the Upper-world. Definitely the best the Third Level offered. And she provided a safe place and friendly ear, which was exactly what I needed.

We were into our third round of drinks and our second cigar before I finished updating her on my latest headaches and moral conundrums.

She snickered, dropping and shaking her head. Ringlets of stringy red hair fell in her face. "I haven't seen you in... what? Three years?"

I puffed out an excellent cloud of smoke, appreciating every minute of the cigar, my favorite brand I could only get here. They were, let's just say, a bootleg brand Abaddon somehow got her hands on. "A little longer."

"And each time you come home, you come back with bigger problems."

"Price I pay for being so goddamn important."

"Still full of yourself, I see," she said with a wink of her red eye before moving down the bar to serve whisky to an elderly man leaning so far over his empty tumbler he looked like he wanted to go for a swim. She slid along the bar until she was face to face with me again. Reaching for my hand, she pried the cigar free and took a long puff. Her long face narrowed and expanded as she inhaled and exhaled rapidly. A white cloud of wonderful aromas hung between us. She took one final, longer puff before handing it back. "Oh, that's good."

"You only get the best."

"You deserve the best. At least the Rev I remembered does. What about the new Rev?"

Her rusty voice held an obvious concern. "I'm good. I swear."

"Are you?"

"Yes."

"You sure?"

"Well, *now* I'm not," I said with a chuckle and another puff of the cigar. "But it's done me a world of good to come home and see you and put this fucking Nephilim out of my mind for an hour."

She snatched a towel from the rack behind her and started wiping down glasses. "And it's good to see you. Doesn't happen as much as I'd like. Would be good to have you around more often."

"Sometimes I feel the same."

"Maybe you should then," she said with a one-shoulder shrug. "You know. To help you stay grounded. To remind you why you're doing all this important work. Sure, it helps the mortals. No doubt." She lifted the glass in her hand, towel still inserted in its mouth, gesturing at the tables. Few were occupied. "But you're working for all of us, Rev. That's a lot of responsibility to carry, and you've been doing it forever. Nothing wrong with feeling you've done your part, but that's not how it works, is it? You're a slave to them until they say you're not or until they have no use for you."

"Or until this Nephilim hands me my ass and I end up at the bottom of Budd Inlet," I said.

"Bud's what?"

I shook my head and laughed, which only caused me to cough. "A place ba—" I almost said 'back home.' "A place back in the Overworld. Sort of like a bay. Mortals have a variety of names for their bodies of water."

"Ah, gotcha," she said, starting on a fresh glass and not sounding compelled to learn more about the ins and outs of Overworld waterways. "So, how does that not happen? How do you not end up at the bottom of a great sea?"

I didn't have the heart to correct her over the nature of the relatively shallow inlet. Instead, we spent the rest of the evening sharing strategies, stories, drinks, and a few cigars as I laid out my thoughts on how I was going to solve my Penumbra Man problem to the safest pair of ears in my life that weren't placed in some obnoxious political position.

By the time I stood to say my farewells, promising this next disappearance back to the Overworld would be shorter, I felt much better about what I'd done, and what I might need to do to understand the circumstances surrounding the stolen Bowl. I'd never feel better about rarely stopping to see good friends like Abaddon. Life was fickle and fleeting, and I needed to remember that.

I'd work on that. Just as soon as I had Arakiel in a head-lock and was dragging him back to the Upperworld to hand off to the Order.

This trip was beneficial, even though it brought me too close to the last angel I wanted to see, and who Abaddon was too kind to mention. Alisha Carver, now Rosi, was better left in my memories—and me in hers if I lost this fight against the Arakiel.

The trip cleansed me. I felt ready for the battle to come.

The next time Arakiel thought to abuse mortals was going to be the last time. He just didn't know that yet.

20

FREE REIN

"They've gained too much momentum," Jericho whined as he paced behind his chair near the far end of the table.

He was irritating, but not incorrect, not from this latest batch of news the Order of Thirteen had called me back to their meeting room to address.

At first, I thought they were calling on me over black-mailing Jericho. Wow, blackmail and brainwashing just in the past two days. I was really racking up the immorality points. Turns out, even if they knew about my strong-arming of one of their own, they had bigger problems.

The Nephilim were rolling forward like an irresistible force.

Across the Overworld, the impact of the First Bowl being poured was becoming clearer with each passing hour. What at first seemed to be a few thousand cases of infected mortals had turned into tens of thousands, turning into hundreds of thousands, seemingly overnight.

"This is bad," Jerah mumbled to his chest. Lots of head-nodding greeted his observation from the rest of the influential angels.

Raphina dropped a tea bag into her cup and filled it with steaming water. "In South America, I hear whispers about overwhelmed healthcare systems. I've put a few angels on it. They'll report back within a few days once they have a better understanding of what we're looking at. But the early suggestions aren't positive. Hospitals are kicking out anyone who is relatively stable, so they have space for emergency cases. Much longer, and no one will get access until they're on their deathbeds."

"Let's calm down," Zephon said, waving her hands towards the table. "We don't know if it'll get that bad, so let's not hype everyone up."

"Screw you," Raphina said, holding the tea bag up by the drip line like a bolas she intended to wrap around Zephon's ankles.

"No," Puriel said, her long-fingered hands pressed firmly on the table. "We will not do this. We will not let the pressure get to us. Our duty is to Yahweh and the Council, to the mortals, to build a strategy. The Council has told us what they expect to see. They want results. We will give them that." She looked—no, she *glared* at everyone—the table as if daring them to challenge her. "Now, this is the biggest challenge we've faced in a long time. We have no idea how mortals will react to the crisis, especially as the virus spreads. But we can't wait until they've given us a clear direction, either. Our duty is to guide them and do our part in helping the Council keep the Balance. And that is exactly what we will do. Pher, can you provide a rundown of what we're facing, please?"

My mentor cleared his throat and scooted closer to the table. Then he listed just how precarious the Overworld situation was. With hundreds of thousands infected in over one hundred and fifty countries, stopping the virus from spreading was far beyond reasonable now. This was about damage limitation. Healthcare systems overwhelmed.

Governments taxed. Economies stagnated. Never mind the individual pain of personal loss. The First Bowl was a runaway train and the entire mortal population was tied to the tracks.

"Every day, the list of names added to the Book of Planes is..." He stopped to rub his forehead. I'd never seen my boss so shaken. "Extensive. Even with the recruits, the Reapers are struggling to keep up."

"Maybe Rev should focus on those important things then," Jericho said, lacking the cojones to look me in the eye.

"Mr. Carver is performing other duties," Puriel said in one of those voices that said 'and you should already know that, dumbass'.

"Plus, if you'll remember," Pher said, "Anapheil is in charge of the draftees, not Rev. And she is doing a smashing job." He gave a nod to Puriel. "The toll on the Reapers isn't the fault of anyone there or the Order. This is a consequence of the First Bowl being poured. Nothing more. What's more deserving of our attention is how quickly this all happened."

"Right under our eyes," Samael, the Vice President, said from the first chair to the side of the head of the table.

Puriel pinched her thin lips.

A hard silence fell over the angels who were supposed to be governing the Reapers and Guardians, arguably, for mortal-kind at least, the two most important organizations in all the Upperworld.

"Maybe I can spread a little sunshine on this matter," I said. Thirteen faces of various skin tones, genders, and ages turned my way. "After a chance run-in with some punks, I influenced a group Arakiel touched." I met Jericho's look, and he glanced away. "Thanks to my handy dandy soul stone, they're going to report to me as soon as he reaches out to them again."

"Nice move," Pher said.

"Yes, that is helpful." Puriel nodded. "We need answers. The spread of this plague is consistent with what we knew about the First Bowl, but a single Penumbra Man didn't do this on his own."

"You think they're walking among the mortals?" Dumas asked, his mustache twitching.

"This is too organized," Puriel said, interlocking her fingers and staring at her palms, "to be a single-angel show. The Council has questioned all of Arakiel's family and friends. As soon as they've compiled their report, we'll know more."

Without turning in his direction, I watched Jericho. He could thank Yahweh for his stunted emotional range, allowing him to cover any reaction he might have otherwise had, not giving away a hint about his history with the troublesome Nephilim.

"Their impression is he isn't capable of something like this. Not on his own," Puriel continued. "Someone helped him get access to the Safe. Or they handed him the Bowl. He probably also had help understanding how to pour it. The Nephilim have always been problematic."

"They have too much sway," Harut, the Treasurer, said from the side table where her fingers drifted over the apples, oranges, and bananas until she found something that suited her tastes. She came back to the table with a single apple on her plate. "They always have. It's only gotten worse."

"That's not something we can control," Puriel said. "We need to stay focused on what we can influence. Now, this might spin well beyond our control, but we can only affect so many aspects. The Council has to deal with the rest."

"They could take other forms," Camael said as he scratched the meeting minutes in his spiral notebook. He lifted a hand to knuckle his round glasses that always seemed to cast deep shadows on his narrow cheekbones. "Can you imagine what that would be like? The Overworld, already dealing with this virus and in a panic, also facing the Nephilim bringing boogiemen out of folklore?"

"That would terrorize those poor creatures," Uziel said. I think she was referring to mortals and not the monsters.

"Exactly what the Nephilim might want," Pher said darkly.

Again, my boss was correct. The order of Nephilim is basically the vampiric order of angels. They literally feed on the energy of mortals who become their victims. Nephilim don't kill mortals to feed. Terrorized mortals give off far more nutrients for these twisted bastards. That works to the Nephilim's advantage. They don't have to kill to survive. If a name isn't in the Book of Planes, killing a mortal causes administrative and disciplinary headaches. But if a name is, the mortal it belongs to will also have a Reaper assigned to them. Nephilim are tough bastards, but us Reapers can hold our own. The vast majority couldn't take on a Nephilim by themselves, but there are a lot more of us than them, even with our Reaper shortage. So why would Nephilim risk a showdown with a Reaper when they could slowly suck the life force of a mortal? No need to stick your neck in the noose you designed. A bigger game was at play here.

"Rev, we need to find out, once and for all, who is behind this," Puriel said, her mouth pinched to a small oval. Using my casual name? She was about to shift the dynamic in our relationship. "Whatever you need from us, just ask. I want everyone in the Order to hear me clearly." She swiveled her head to include her peers. "No one fights Rev if he comes with a requirement or need." Her eyes found me. "If we can provide it, we'll get it. You have my word."

"Thank you."

Pher nodded. His jaw, hidden behind the mass of short curls of black and gray hair, might have clenched so hard was his look.

"This ends," Puriel said, pressing her finger into the

tabletop so hard the tip went white. "During your investigation, it doesn't matter what you discover. I don't care if it's Hellion who is behind this. You will bring them to justice. Whatever it takes. Are we in agreement on that?"

I summoned all the political acumen I could muster. "Abso-fucking-lutely."

21

END OF THE LINE

Buzz.

I rolled over, pulling the couch pillow over my head.

Buzz.

I pinched my eyes closed, trying to ignore my cell phone. Sleep. I needed at least a few hours or I'd be no good to anyone.

Buzz.

Dammit. I'd just returned from the Upperworld and my meeting with the Order. Couldn't I just get a few hours of peace? You think a grim Reaper is bad? Trust me; no one wants a cranky Reaper.

Then my exhausted mind made the connection. I'd told the teens to reach out if Arakiel approached them again. I had given them my number.

"Shit." I rolled over so quickly I almost flung myself off the couch. My hand flailed out, catching the coffee table. That stung.

My phone bounced a few inches away, forcing me to catch it before it toppled over the side of the table to the floor. I snatched it. The screen kicked on at my touch.

Billee.

"Hey," I said, rubbing sleep out of my eyes.

"Rev, please come. It's Delores."

"Is she okay?"

"She's in a panic, but she's physically safe. Now."

"Now?"

"Someone tried to run her over," Billee said. Even over the line, she couldn't mask her rushed breathing.

"Billee, I need you to calm down and tell me what happened," I said, smashing the SPEAKER button on my phone, and tossing it down so I could get ready.

Billee sniffled and exhaled slowly. "Sh—she was at the camp. They're not doing well, she said. A lot of them are getting sick. Since it's cold tonight, she went down there to check on them."

"Was she alone?" I asked. Sometimes Guardian Angels showed themselves to mortals. Stories as old as time tell of intervention by them, so it wouldn't have shocked me. Omen is a good guy, but not the brightest light bulb in the box, so I was curious if he'd unmasked himself.

"Yes, she was," Billee said. "I've talked to her about that and she understands she can't do that."

"Don't share too much with her. Remember our job," I said, hating myself for having to even say it, but Billee was very new at this and Delores Garcia was a friend. I couldn't ignore those factors. A familiar telling a mortal about the upcoming visit of a Reaper was rarely a good thing. That sort of stuff used to cause serious problems back in the days before mortals became more skeptical about our existence.

"I know," she said sternly.

"Okay. Can she get on the line?"

Following a short bit of muted mumbling, I had to pull the phone away from my ear to avoid the scratching on the mouthpiece from the other end. Then Delores was on the phone.

"Hello, Mr. Carver. Thank you for taking my call," she said in a sweet voice as if someone hadn't traumatized her.

"Hi, Delores. I'm sorry to hear about your night. Can you tell me what happened? Don't leave any details out, please. Unless it's too upsetting. I'll understand. Experiences like this can be, but if you can share everything, please do."

"I was coming back from the camp," Delores started. I noted a slight quiver in her voice. "They're doing so poorly. The residents, I mean. And I know we were told not to go into the camp until the doctors knew more about this virus, but I just can't ignore them, Mr. Carver. I can't. There are people with sores all over their bodies. They can't even get comfortable enough to lie down and sleep. Please understand."

"I do."

She continued, "When I looked outside, I couldn't... I just couldn't sit in the house watching my shows when I knew how miserable it was. How could I when I knew they were cold and suffering? This outbreak makes things so much worse. So, I made hot cocoa and filled a couple of thermal carafes and brought them down to the camp."

"You're a very kind soul," I said softly. "Did you go down to the camp alone?"

"Oh, yes. It was much too late for the other volunteers." She lowered her voice, almost conspiratorially. "We're not supposed to go down there at night and especially not alone, but I knew I would be okay. The residents are good people in bad situations. They're not trouble." Her voice grew louder, stronger. "Plus, I have an excellent Guardian Angel. She watches over me."

I wondered how Omen felt about being misgendered and figured he was too cool to get his wings ruffled over something so innocuous.

"It was at the camp that I felt... Well, I don't know how to describe it. Just... something." She paused and Billee mumbled in the background. "Yes. Okay. Mr. Carver?"

"Yes?"

"I need to be honest with you."

"Okay," I said, wondering where this was going. "What is it?"

"I'm not being honest about the camp," she said, and I could almost hear the shame drag her voice to a lower octave. "But I don't blame the residents. Please understand."

"What do you mean? What were you not honest about?"

She sniffed. "They were fighting, Mr. Carver. The residents. After I pulled into the parking lot to unload the carafes and get someone to help me bring them over, I heard the ruckus. Shouting. Yelling. So, I went to see. Have you been down there at night?"

"No, I haven't." I didn't want to tell her about the numerous nighttime stakeouts.

She *tsk*'ed. I don't think she meant it for me, but to embellish her next point. "The city does them no favors. They use light stands for the camp, which gives it a very... unsavory feel. Especially at night. Like they're in a prison yard or something. But the street and parking lot lighting is poor. Too many shadows. So I was already feeling unsettled when I got out of the car. For some reason, I couldn't shake the feeling I was being watched. As if someone was hanging out in the dark areas of the parking lot."

Oh, shit. Now I was understanding Billee's behaviors on the other side of the line.

"I looked as soon as I got out and almost didn't unload." She lowered her voice again. "Maybe I should have just done that. Got back in my car and left. But I didn't, and I can't change that now."

"I know society thinks it's cool, Delores, but victims should never blame themselves," I offered, not sure it helped. "What you did was a kind act, not something to be ridiculed."

"Thank you, Mr. Carver. Still, I should have known better. Even when I unloaded, I could have put the carafes right back in the case I used. The ruckus from the camp was loud enough that I immediately knew something was wrong."

"What was happening?"

"I crossed the street and was walking down the sidewalk, and…"

"Go on. Tell him," Billee's muffled voice said in the background.

"They were fighting each other. One man stabbed another. Two women had each other by the hair and were yanking and swinging each other around. They toppled a tent. One man raced by me, screaming. His eyes… oh, Mr. Carver. His eyes were crazed. That's the only way I can describe it. I don't even think he saw me. After that, well, I just couldn't stay. I felt terribly guilty, but it wasn't safe. My thinking was, I could get back to my car and phone the police. A man was stabbed and… whatever was going on, it looked like a riot and I couldn't have innocent people getting hurt. But when I— when I tried to cross the street… I don't know how it happened, but a car came out of nowhere. I never saw it coming." She stopped, hiccupping a cry. "I dropped a carafe. They're heavy and my arthritis is acting up. It slipped. Thankfully, it fell on the grass. I was so upset, nearly in tears from what I saw in the camp. I wasn't paying attention and turned to pick up the carafe. That's when I heard the car screech. Maybe from the tires popping over the sidewalk. My heart nearly stopped, I swear. The car couldn't have been more than two or three feet away, Mr. Carver. Had I not dropped that carafe…"

"You're safe," I said. "What happened to the car?"

"They sped off. Without stopping. No lights or anything. They just took off down the street and around the corner."

"Did you get a plate or give the description to the police?"

"I didn't call them," she said as quietly as a kid who got caught stealing a fist full of extra cookies.

"Why not?" I had an idea of her reasoning but needed her

to admit it. Information from a primed mind is no good. That's why anecdotal data is practically worthless beyond the individual's experience. In the end, that's all anecdotes are: one person's experience of their interactions with the world around them. They're not unequivocal facts.

Billee said something unintelligible but sounded much closer to the phone this time.

"B—because I didn't see a m—man driving," Delores Garcia finally answered. "Who—whatever was driving, they weren't human."

"What did you see?" I said, stopping my preparations to leave the apartment.

Delores exhaled slowly. The sound of her breath rippled across the phone's receiver. "It happened in a flash. But I didn't see anyone in the driver's seat. I was sure of it. Right as the car passed, it was also under the brightest lights of the camp, and they lit up the interior. And Mr. Carver, whatever drove that car, was not a person. Black and… fuzzy. That's the only way I can describe it. It had spikes of hair coming off its arms. Almost like an animal. And… I couldn't see a face. The thing had *no* face."

Delores' voice broke. I was about to ask where she was, if she was home and wouldn't mind company, when Billee spoke into the line. "Sorry, Rev. She needs a moment. Mind if I sit with her? I can call you back."

"It's okay, I need to make a call anyway," I said. "Listen, Billee, you know what she saw. That's why you had her call?"

"Yes."

"Smart move." I moved to my bedroom to grab my wallet and duster. "Keep her in the house. Don't go out for any reason."

"Rev, what if it comes here?" Billee said in a whisper. In the background, Delores was crying, so I doubted she heard Billee's question.

"One day I need to explain Guardian Angels to you, but let me just put it this way. You two are as safe there as anywhere. You're not alone. There's an angel there, watching over Delores. You too, though I've never met yours. Delores's Guardian is a good guy. He'll keep her as safe as he can. Keep her in the house. Okay?"

"Okay," she said, sounding more unsure than any previous time.

"Keep your phone with you at all times."

"Thanks."

We hung up, and I was punching Pher's number in before I had my duster on.

"What's going on?" Pher said tersely.

"Glad you're in town," I said, meaning the Overworld. "I've got a bite and wanted you to know."

"What kind?"

I gave him the low-down on Delores's experience.

"You be careful, lad."

Something wasn't right in his voice. I dressed and was snagging my keys when I asked him, in no uncertain terms, what was going on.

"Lots, that's all," Pher said. But I heard the catch in his tone. "Let me close my window."

He set the phone down and I heard the *thunk* of the window a few seconds later. I was outside and moving swiftly to my car when he picked up again.

"Rev, this is a mess."

"No shit."

"No, not the Penumbra Man," he said. "I mean, that's bad too. But my fear is that whoever is acting as the Penumbra Man, they're just a symptom of a larger problem."

"What are you saying, Pher?" I started the car.

He hit me hard. "The Safe isn't secure. We got the Council to open up a little. Something is going on with Yahweh. They wouldn't give more specifics than to mention the guards on the Safe are weakening. Not that just anyone can waltz up and get in, but it's not impervious anymore. The Council is scrambling to increase security until whatever is going on with Yahweh can be addressed."

"How vulnerable is the Safe?"

"No idea."

"What about the other artifacts? What about the six goddamn Bowls, Pher?"

"Everything is still there. We think."

"You *think*?"

Pher grumbled. "The Safe contains artifacts from the moment of the Creation, Rev. That takes time to inventory and we are all quite busy, the Order and Council included. But we're confident the Bowls are safe."

Well, there was that. At least I didn't have to fight an army of Nephilim posing as Penumbra Men. "That's how Arakiel got in, then?"

A sharp breath. "No."

"No? What do you mean 'no'? Who stole it then?"

"Don't you say a word of this to anyone."

"You know I don't enjoy talking to angels or people. Who took it and gave it to Arakiel?"

"We *think* the Four Horsemen are involved. One of them, possibly, got into the Safe and took the Bowl."

Well, wasn't that exactly the news I didn't want to hear? "How sure is the Order about that?"

"Eighty percent."

"Way higher than I wanted to hear."

"Me too, lad. Me too."

"You know what this means, right? If the Four Horsemen are involved?"

"We do. But until we have proof they took it, we can't move against Hellion. For all we know, one of them might have just gone rogue and is working with Arakiel for their own gains."

"Can a Horseman do that? Go rogue?"

Pher hummed. "I don't know. But there's been discussion at the table. That's exactly what we might be looking at."

"I thought they were a unit. All for one, one for all-type of shit?"

"Me too."

My phone buzzed. An unknown number. I sent it to voicemail and focused on my boss again. "Then someone ordered them to steal the Bowl. And that angel is the Lamb of God."

"We need proof."

I swung out of the parking lot and onto the main street. "Well, I hope someone is leaning on her and making her sweat."

"Above my pay grade, so it's above yours too," Pher said. "You've got enough on your plate. Take care of what you can and trust us to take care of ours. Just as we have to trust the Council to do their business."

"'The trust of the innocent is the liar's most useful tool,'" I said. "Stephen King."

"Rev," Pher warned, suddenly sounding like my father.

"'Trust is very hard if you don't know what you're trusting.' Marianne Williamson," I said in following up, peeling around the corner and feeling the tug of increased g-forces.

That got a snicker out of Pher. Hey, if you can't laugh when the Upperworld is going to shit, about to take the mortal realm down with it, you won't enjoy the ride to the end. "Go do your job."

"I am. Can I get an extension on delivering Ms. Garcia to the Veil Gate? And no, I won't give that assignment to another Reaper."

"No time for that stuff. Do both. Do *all* your jobs. That's why you get paid the big bucks."

"I'll try to call if I find Arakiel."

"Remember, we need him alive, if possible."

"I'll try."

"That's all we can ask," Pher said, sounding like he had to put effort into being patient. "But we're just shooting our efforts in the foot if we don't find out who is actually behind this."

"Gonna do my best, boss."

"I know, lad. Be careful."

"I'll call you."

I hung up, peeled around another corner, and checked the voicemail. The unknown caller had left a message. I sat in silence, gripping the steering wheel as I tore through the streets of Olympia at just under the speed of 'we're about to throw your ass in jail, mister.'

"S—sir? This, I'm... well, my name is Rick," the youthful voice in the voicemail said. "You came to see us at the old brewery. We were supposed to call you when he called. He wants us to go downtown. Tonight. We're supposed to meet outside a homeless camp and cause trouble. Not sure what kind. I—" the young man stopped, cut off cleanly, and then came back on the line in a rushed, breathy voice. "I have to go. My parents are paying attention. Please help us, mister."

The voicemail ended there. I called Billee.

"Rev?" she sounded panicked. "Is everything okay?"

"Yes. How about with you? Are you two safe?"

"Yes. You scared me. I thought something happened."

"Something is going to," I said. Billee didn't need to know about the bigger problems, not yet. I would tell her in time. Before she served as my familiar, I had gained, trained, and lost over three hundred others during my time as a Reaper. I know what I'm doing. Minds are easy to break if you know where to press. Billee was too valuable to not protect until she was ready to hear the true nature of the shit storm that is the immortal realm. If she survived the night, then I'd lay all the cards out. "Please get yourself and Delores ready."

"Now?" Her voice thickened like she had put her hand over her mouth. "Not tonight. Please. She just went through something traumatic. Don't make this her last night."

"I need to know exactly where she felt the presence, so she has to get the camp. You need to come too."

"Why? What are we doing?"

"We're going to throw fists with an agent of God."

22

THE FIRST OF THEIR KIND

"OVER THERE," DELORES SAID, LIFTING HER HAND AND extending a shaking finger that *dunked* my car window.

"Okay. And you felt the presence as soon as you got out of your car?"

"Yes," she said, her voice sounding fragile.

I shifted to include Billee in the conversation. I had already described my plan to the pair, but the drive from Delores's house to the camp wasn't long enough to detail every step and tactic. Hell, I still didn't know how I was going to do this. "Any questions?"

Delores shook her head. Tears rimmed the red shallows of her eyes.

Billee leaned forward, placing her elbows near the head-rests of the two front seats. "Are you sure this is the only way?"

I gave her a quick nod. Time was of the essence. I hated the thought of using them as pawns, but in the big scheme, that's all any of us are. "Listen, what's going to happen tonight will be distressing. Accept it, because once this kicks off, I'm going to control less and less of the situation."

The furrows of Billee's forehead deepened. "Can't we just take her home? I'll come back with you."

"I know you would." I looked at Delores. "What you've done for these people is remarkable, but it also might be what made you a target of that attempted hit-and-run. If my hunch is correct, it was. As horrible as it sounds, I need your help to draw him out. I wouldn't ask this if I could do it on my own."

"I'll help however I can if it will help these people, Mr. Carver." Lucky to be on the desirable side of five feet tall, Delores seemed even tinier now.

"Thank you. It will. If I'm successful." I looked across the parking lot at the expanse of public land that was once a vibrant blanket of grass but had been trampled into the muddy mess I now saw. "But they don't have a choice. If we don't intercede, circumstances will only worsen."

"They don't deserve that," she said with dark firmness.

I dug her attitude. "No, they don't. Nor do you. Ready?"

With a single dip of her head, Delores reached for the door handle and stepped into the night. Billee scrambled out behind her—an impressive feat from the back seat of a sports coupe—and I got out, drawing Maggie.

The night was chilly and wet, just like the other seven hundred and twenty-two days of the year in this part of the world. Delores cinched her jacket around her neck. Billee moved to her side and put an arm around her, glancing back at me as I made my way around the car.

Howls from the camp accompanied the chill and wet.

"My God," Billee said, her gaze fixed on the camp.

Admittedly, it was disturbing to hear those animalistic sounds coming from the makeshift hometown of Olympia's rejected population. Shrieks, screeches, and screams rose into the night, along with the howls. A concert of the platteland.

Arakiel had the camp properly roused for a fight. Now, the challenge was to win it while minimizing casualties. True success came with no one dying tonight, but I wasn't about to make that promise. Not Delores. Not Billee. To none of the homeless or the teenagers who should be lurking around the corner, ready to strike. I definitely couldn't make that promise to Arakiel or myself. Many will enter; fewer will walk out.

Delores repeatedly snapped her head to the corner of the parking lot. The lights blinked and hissed, struggling to stay lit.

"Did you see something?" I asked, moving to her side.

She shivered. "My mind is playing tricks on me, I think."

"Okay, come on. Let's get closer."

The women drifted alongside me as I made my way to the street. "Remember, as soon as we see it, get her to the car, Billee. I'll keep it busy. You get her out of here."

She swallowed and nodded.

I worried about my partner. Actually, I worried about both of them, but they faced very different futures and the long-term impact of tonight on Billee was something I was going to have to walk her through. Mortals just aren't prepared for this kind of stuff. My third eye said Billee wouldn't die tonight, but there was always the X factor. For every degree she was ready, I had to be three times as prepared.

We were at the grass when Delores yelped.

"Did you see it?"

Her arm raised, she pointed to where the chain-link fence touched the neighboring appliance business. Her arm rose and fell like a slip bobber on a tranquil lake. "Th—there. B—but it's gone now."

Of course. "Keep your eyes out." I crept forward, rotating slowly while trying to spot Arakiel and keeping my eyes on the distracted but incensed humans raising Cain in the encampment. I was doing all that while also wondering when Arakiel planned on releasing the small army of teen boys he'd been manipulating.

I heard the hiss at the same time the pair of women yelled

out. A flash of black shot across my vision and was gone, off into the night before I realized Arakiel was no longer hiding.

I spun, raising Maggie, trying to trace the Nephilim.

Out in the night, I lost any sign of its presence. It was quiet out there; a mockery of the chaos building behind me. This was going to get bad. My third eye saw death, more than just Delores's.

My head was on a swivel, trying to pick out anything that might give away the presence of the Penumbra Man. Sweeping to my partner and her friend, I saw something I didn't like.

Delores stood, hunched over. Billee wrapped her arm around the older woman while she leaned over to check on her.

I lifted the .327, sweeping it side to side as I moved toward them.

The noise coming from inside it drowned every sound outside the sphere of the homeless campout. Surely, Arakiel would use the advantage of the Penumbra Man while also making sure any attacks he made came while the noise from the camp was pitched. He had all the advantages. A single death tonight was too much, but if I couldn't figure out a way to level the playing field, Arakiel would make a clean sweep.

Billee looked back. "She's bleeding, Rev." My partner's mouth hung open like she'd just stopped herself. Then she mouthed, "Bad."

I growled under my breath, watching the night. "Come out, you bastard."

In the distance, I heard chittering. It could have been Arakiel or a nocturnal bird. But it was there, just below the din coming from the camp. I steadied my arms, holding Maggie true while recognizing the ridiculousness of aiming at anything in the dark.

Another flash of movement and Billee was sent sprawling to the ground. Her parka was shredded open in four neat slices. The rips exposed layers of insulating batting that fell in soft balls, tumbling along the mud patch as the scant wind carried it. Six more inches and the Penumbra Man would have turned Billee's back into something that looked like it'd survived an elementary school cheese grater project.

Delores fell to the ground, holding her injured arm. I started toward her, but she shook her head. "I'm okay, Mr. Carver. Please protect the camp. I'll be fine."

By the way the thin, red rivulets seeped from her arm between her fingers, I wasn't sure she was going to be fine. But with her injury and Billee narrowly escaping the same fate, I had to conserve my resources to catch Arakiel before he made his next move. The advantage was his. Of course, he wouldn't fight me mano a mano, the coward. That's probably why he chose the Penumbra Man form.

"Ladies," I said without taking my eyes from anywhere the street and parking lot lights didn't reach, "shout as soon as you feel or sense it."

I turned my back on the camp and faced the pair. A risk, but a necessary one. He was out there, somewhere. Waiting. Watching. Moving into an advantageous position. I wouldn't light up the night with my Angelfire, and he knew that.

Time passed. The shouts and cries in the camp rose. Somehow, a fire started and jumped from tent to tent.

"Come on, you bastard." I kept my growl low. A snapped twig might make the difference between plowing a bolt of Angelfire through his chest or having mine ripped open.

Billee cried out, her expression strained. "Rev, they're coming."

I sprinted forward to stand behind the two women so I could face the camp without turning my back on them. They were between me and the camp. From here, I could protect their backside while using the fires to help me pick out any threats in the darkness, including the supernatural type.

The city had corralled the camp with an eight-foot chain-link fence. In a single display of humanity, they left a split in the fence that was as wide as the sidewalk that served as the entrance and exit.

By the time Billee called my attention to the camp, a handful of its residents had streamed through the gap and were skulking in our direction. Those behind them, possibly frustrated at how long it was taking to squeeze through, decided that rocking the fence back and forth was a better use of their time. With so many bodies moving in synchronicity, the fence never stood a chance. It toppled within the first few swaying shoves.

The homeless stalked forward, their faces gaunt and crazed. Manifestations of the "sickness," the effect of falling under the influence of a Penumbra Man.

I tried to watch them while searching for Arakiel. He was the key. If I stopped him, I severed his influence. I'd only attack these mortals out of self-defense or two protect the two women on the ground in front of me.

"Come on. Come on," I mumbled, slightly rocking on my feet and looking for bolt cutter and his group of wrestlers.

"Can you use the stone?" Billee asked as she pulled Delores to her feet.

"Too many of them," I said. "It doesn't have that range. They'd be on us before it kicked in." I didn't want to tell her I could use it, but that'd put me at a further disadvantage against the real threat.

Smashing glass drew my attention away from the crowd of homeless. Toward the appliance store, now missing a window, fifty-odd teen boys emerged from the darkness.

Nearly a hundred mortals plus one cowardly Nephilim, and a Reaper and his Ruger. If that doesn't sound like an interesting night, I don't know what is.

"Come out, come out, wherever you are," I said in a sing-song way.

The two crowds of Arakiel's minions pressed in. Delores

was on her feet, but unsteady. Billee helped shuffle her back while I stepped forward. I could only do this for so long before something broke. I couldn't step in front of the women; that would expose our backs to Arakiel, and neither of the mortals would survive if he swooped in for a third attack if I was in front of them. But at the rate we were inching backward, the horde of zombie-like homeless would overtake us long before we made the parking lot.

The teen boys watched me. The homeless devoured me with their eyes like I was a succulent morsel.

A man stepped forward. In front of the crowd, he stopped and crossed his arms. His dark brown hair was thick on top and combed back. Broad eyebrows sandwiched his eyes between an obnoxiously long beard. Well-dressed and perfectly groomed, he was definitely not a resident of the camp.

Arakiel. In human form. Fucking Nephilim.

"What's this all about, asshole?" I asked.

He spread his hands. His cocky expression made me want to punch his father for having the desire to reproduce. His voice was silky. "As if I'd share that with you."

The Nephilim was stocky. I'd have my hands full when we tussled, but I needed to buy time for Billee and Delores. The latter might have her name in the Book of Planes, but she wasn't going out at the hands of a Nephilim or his brainwashed army. I couldn't take a shot at him either. That's why he was acting like he had the biggest pair on the planet as long as he had rows upon rows of mortals at his back. Any Angelfire I took him down with would barrel through the mortals behind him. Either Arakiel was hedging his bets that I was too nice of a guy to kill a few innocent mortals, or someone had told him of that fact. Both were problematic, but the latter was concerning.

I lowered Maggie, and his stupid grin widened.

I was about to catcall him, to provoke him into one of

those one-on-one duels you see in movies, back when mortal men believed in acting honorably. I wanted nothing more than to get him away from the crowd, but I never got the chance.

One second, Arakiel stood squared off at me, in human form. The next, his all-too human arm raised, finger pointed toward the sky, and as it dropped, it shifted into an extended arm with fingers nearly three feet long and as black as night. The arm, and the rest of him, was covered in spiky hair as his new Penumbra Man form wiped his previous features clean.

Arakiel raised his arm, now over four-feet long, a finger that made a jai alai cesta look like a Q-Tip.

"Shit," I said. Without turning my head, I told Billee, "Get back to the car. Now."

Arakiel's arm dropped. The homeless rushed forward, past their supernatural leader as if the lanky, spiked monstrosity wasn't absolutely terrifying. From the corner of the field, the teen boys broke out into a sprint. And Arakiel disappeared in the chaos he'd created.

Forces collided. Teens side-smashed against the wall of camp residents as I unleashed Angelfire from the mouth of my Ruger. My spell struck the mud in front of the approaching homeless, carving a trench fifteen feet deep. Placing it far enough away that they had time to pull out of their run and avoid stumbling into it and snapping ankles and maybe a fibula or two. The trench also cut them off from me and the pair of women. The teen boys did the rest.

Honestly, I sort of regretted Arakiel shifting into Penumbra form before he realized the boys were no longer under his spell. It would have been hilarious to see his douchey-bearded face twist in shock and probably a good dose of surprise when he discovered the betrayal.

I was denied that joy, but maybe I could make up for it by plugging him off once he stepped away from his crowd of controlled mortals.

I'd lost him in the chaos, but he couldn't be far.

As the battle exploded in front of me, someone screamed behind me. I spun to see Delores fall to the mud again. Billie rocketed five feet into the air. She landed on her side with a solid thud. The only thing saving her from serious injury was the fact that the ground was too sodden from what felt like four hundred straight months of rain.

Above her, Arakiel flickered into my sight. I fired Maggie.

The pure white beam of Angelfire zipped through the air. When he blinked away, the beam passed through where he had been standing, striking a tree two hundred yards across the road and setting it ablaze.

Flicker.

Arakiel, the Penumbra Man, stood above Delores, ready to slash with his disgustingly protracted fingers.

I shot.

Flicker.

Behind me, howls of rage and pain filled the night. Children, teens or not, fought adults. My brainwashed converts against Arakiel's. Innocents against innocents.

No one ever said Heaven was moral.

A last-second recognition of Arakiel's hiss saved my life. As I moved toward the fallen women, sweeping my gaze across the battlefield, I heard the hiss of Arakiel's approach. I dove forward into the wet grass just as he slashed at me in his sprint. The pain of searing fire raked at my back as my duster and skin were torn open.

I hit the ground, trying to ignore the misery spreading across my back, whipping Maggie toward the general area where I thought I saw the distorted appendages of the Penumbra form. I squeezed off a beam of Angelfire.

There wasn't time to see if I'd taken him out or not. I rolled away until I was sure he wasn't above me, and then got to my knees, squeezing off another beam. This one passed through the night, striking the brick siding of a building a block away and blasting a wrecking ball-sized hole through it.

To my right, I heard a cackle. Deep, edged. Taunting.

I swung around, lifting Maggie and blasting.

My Angelfire's sizzle and threat cut off Arakiel's joy, but sadly, not his life. Instead, it carried through the night, taking a satellite dish off a nearby apartment complex two blocks away.

I side-stepped closer to my partner as rapidly as I could without risking myself or them. I kept my eyes focused on the night, using the city's lights beyond the park to reveal any distortion in the murky nighttime shadows Arakiel used to his advantage. Oh, how I wished I could pull him away from the group and take this to a man-on-man fight. But he wouldn't do that. He was the coward I expected. Who else would choose the form of a Penumbra Man? It was the perfect form for someone with a devious mind, set on havoc, whose interest lay in avoiding responsibility. The second I moved away from the crowd of innocent mortals, he'd make his move on Billee and Delores, and then the boys. One of us was going to fall tonight, and we'd do it smack dab in the middle of these poor bastards who no one would believe.

A hiss from the night came from my side. I tucked and tumbled, still failing to avoid Arakiel's next attack.

I didn't need to see the obnoxiously long fingers to feel them rake my arm.

White hire fire seemed to scorch deep in my triceps at multiple points. Instinctively, I swatted the area, gripping it like I was trying to keep every drop of water in a leaky hose.

Arakiel's laughter faded off to the side, behind a large dumpster.

I shook my arm, letting it dangle. I could still flex my hand, which would be advantageous for firing Maggie any time in my foreseeable future.

I'm not bragging, but anyone who wasn't me probably

wouldn't have an arm to shake out after that last attack. One of the wonderful benefits of being a Reaper assassin who has sucked more immortal energy than he cared to think about.

Something in or behind the dumpster crashed. Metal against metal.

Taking tentative steps forward, I moved in. Maggie was ready with a chamber full of Angelfire.

Something crashed and splintered a few feet to my side. Nothing more than a wooden crate, but I realized my mistake too late. Arakiel wasn't tossing old boxes hoping to injure me. This was nothing more than a distraction.

He barreled into me, lowering his spiked shoulder. I flew backward and crashed to the ground on my back.

After the stars stopped popping in my eyes, I looked into the blank, black mask of the Penumbra Man. No eyes. No nose. No open mouth full of spiked teeth. A black mask of dread.

Hundreds of black spikes stuck up from his dome, and Arakiel drove his head down.

I cranked mine away and the Penumbra Man's slammed into the ground. Two of the spikes caught my ear, ripping cartilage that would leave a scar if I woke in the morning. The supernatural creature atop me shifted to launch another attack. With my arm under his legs, I couldn't do anything with Maggie. I had to get him off to have a chance.

Arakiel squeezed his Penumbra legs, digging the smaller spikes into my pinned arms. He sat deeper, driving spikes into my stomach.

I yelled out.

His shift of weight allowed me more freedom with my upper torso. I started to sit up, and Arakiel lunged forward, just as I hoped. Not only did his movement pull the spikes out of my stomach, but it also alleviate the pressure of those digging into my arms. For a fraction of a second, his balance was off, and I used that to my advantage.

Kicking up, I drove my thighs into his backside, flinging him over my head.

He hissed as he tumbled, now aware that I'd suckered him into the move.

I rolled and drew Maggie while still face-down in the wet grass. Even as I fired my Angelfire, the fuzzy form of the Penumbra Man shifted as if I was sleepy and imagining its presence.

The sounds of the battle raging between the camp's residents and a bunch of high school wrestlers covered Arakiel's retreating footsteps.

Billee and Delores were sitting targets. Three wrestlers lay on the ground, looking worse for having come into my life. The camp residents weren't faring any better. And Arakiel was using the night to blanket his attacks.

I drew a deep breath, ignoring the burning in my arm and back.

Shoving Maggie into my duster, I took a chance I didn't want to take. If I was wrong, I would hand Arakiel the opening he needed to kill the women and flit off into the night to raise chaos somewhere else around town, spreading the virus and the madness that came along with his influence. But if my only strategy was to keep taking potshots at his erratic form, I would be here all night while he broke the minds of the two women and the combatants who were tearing each other to pieces. Well, at least until he killed me.

The Ruger safely stored, I thrust my hands out, one aimed at Delores, the other at Billee. "Sorry, ladies."

White bolts of Angelfire flashed toward each woman's side. Aiming outside of them was the only risk worth taking. I might have been able to encase them in my shield, but when Arakiel flung Billee into the mud, he sent her out of reach of protection.

Crescents of white bordered each woman on their open side, where the Penumbra Man seemed fond of attacking. If

Arakiel wanted at them, he was going to have to come up the middle of my Angelfire shield.

Shield in place, I pulled Maggie out and lit the world on fire behind the women. A wall of white burst from the sidewalk. The flames spread thirty feet in both directions and crackled as they grew skyward.

The wall of fire would prevent Arakiel from attacking the women from that far side. If he was going to, he'd have to come at them from closer to me. That meant I'd see his flickering form before he reached his targets. More important than that though, I'd set the wall because it provided a gloriously phosphorescent backdrop that would illuminate a creepy Nephilim using dirty tactics to win a fight.

There, in the middle of the exterior shields protecting my mortal familiar and Delores, in front of the wall of Angelfire, Arakiel fell for my ploy.

The air flickered, his blackened form blinking in and out of my view. He stood in the middle of the women, probably deciding which he'd go for first.

I stripped him of that choice.

Squeezing Maggie's trigger with a firm, even pull, she roared. Angelfire swept Arakiel off his fuzzy feet, sending him toppling through the air. He spun, feet over head, head rotating over feet, landing near the wall of fire in his oldest, truest form.

Nephilim are fucking ugly. There are no two ways about it. The first of angel kind, they look nothing like us. Whereas One created us in the same form mortals would ultimately take millions of years later, Nephilim were their first attempt at life in this realm. Needless to say, they included aesthetic design flaws.

Eight feet tall and hairless, Nephilim are unsightly even to those who had somewhat regular interactions with them. Two inch-thick ridge bones where you'd expect eyebrows made their black eyes appear even more menacing. Long arms and legs only make their intimidating frame more dismaying. But the most utterly disturbing aspect of their appearance must be the vestigial wings. Yes, it's true, angels once had wings. That began and ended with the Nephilim. Generations after the first of their kind, one six-inch bone still protruded from the inner curve of each of their shoulder blades. The older the Nephilim, the longer and more curved the vestigial wing bones. Arakiel's stood about two inches above his shoulders, hinting at his relative youth.

"You're one ugly fucker," I said as I put myself between him and the pair of women.

Blood leaked from the corner of his mouth. A long, pale ivory hand held against his chest, he chuckled. "Lucky shot." His voice was so deep it made my skin itch.

I kneeled in front of him, Maggie still trained on him in case he made a stupid decision. The smart thing to do would have been to fire and forget he even existed. That would stop the battle raging behind him and allow me to check in on Delores and Billee. But Arakiel was dying, and I needed answers or Pher was going to be eternally pissed.

"Who's working with you?" I asked.

"Fuck you, Reaper," the Nephilim spat, literally. A wad of bloody mucus landed near my boot. Good thing for him it didn't land on my duster.

"Rev?" Billee called out behind me.

"Right here," I answered back without taking my eyes, or pistol, off Arakiel. "Are you okay?"

She grunted. "I will be."

"Can you check on Delores?"

"Yes."

I lifted Maggie, aiming at the Nephilim's foot, and fired. The Angelfire blew his grotesque tootsies off, splintering them into a hundred fleshy shards.

Arakiel howled. A skin-crawling-inducing sound. He

reached for his foot, but I was on my feet, swinging a boot at his head.

I should have known better. The Nephilim's skull was a size and a half larger than my own, and solid. I think I did more damage to my foot than him. But before I planted my foot, I had the satisfaction of watching his head fling back, his mouth spraying blood.

I shuffled toward him as I added steel-toed boots to my mental shopping list.

His black eyes were glazing over, but he still clung to life.

"Who are you working for? Who helped you get the Bowl?"

A deep chuckle. This time, though, it sounded wet. "Fuck. You. Reaper." The last word came out sounding raspy.

I squatted over his skull. "You piece of shit. I'm going to find out who started this and why." I grabbed him around the throat, pulling him up as high as I could. His head lulled side to side. His mouth hung open. Breaths came, but they were shallow and weak. I had enough time for a proper send-off. "You died for nothing, dumbass."

Placing Maggie to his temple, I fired.

The night fell silent except for a smattering of moans and cries. I cut off my focus on the Angelfire and my shields and firewalls died.

I kneeled next to Arakiel's corpse.

The swell of the dead Nephilim's energy rose from his chest, spreading toward his ugly head and his mangled foot. Within seconds, the hazy light encased him.

"Shit," I said, even though I knew what was coming. After all, this was why I'd taken a knee and stayed at his side. I couldn't outrun the absorption, and the mortals sure as hell didn't need to be exposed to what was about to happen. They'd have enough trauma to deal with if I didn't finish my job tonight. No need to add more.

Within the haze, fine bolts of white light radiated from the center point of the dome, arcing in every direction, igniting the boundaries of all that remained of the Nephilim's life. First, a single shot. Then another. Followed more closely by multiple bolts zipping across the hazy energy, smashing into the boundary, and zapping into nothingness.

The haze collapsed into a mass hovering over Arakiel's chest, growing too bright to look at directly.

I squinted and readied myself. The formed ball of essence wobbled before shooting into my chest.

I swayed backward, surprised at the strength of Arakiel's energy. Most immortals I've killed aren't this strong, but then again, most immortals I've killed also weren't Nephilim.

Instantly, I felt stronger, like I'd taken a great shit after a wonderfully satisfying meal, and followed that with an amazing night of sleep. The burning injuries in my arm and back evaporated. I bounced to my feet, ignoring the tingling in my fingers and toes, the residue of newfound youth.

I never knew how much my life was extended whenever I absorbed another immortal's energy, but Arakiel's had definitely just added a few decades, if not centuries, to my story.

"Fuck," I said to the still night, groaning and pushing my long hair back out of my eyes.

With Arakiel dead, the homeless wouldn't remember his touch. They'd be just as confused at what they were seeing as the teenagers I'd used the Soul Stone on.

Delores was too far injured to worry about things like supernatural creatures duking it out.

"Rev," Billee said, cradling the older woman in her lap. "She's…"

"I know," I said softly, looking at nearly a hundred mortals who were too stunned and confused to move. A handful of fighters still held others in headlocks or stood frozen in mid-punch.

After a moment, all across the grass, wrestlers let go of camp residents, hands up in the universal sign for 'we're cool, right?'. Those from the camp pulled back too, straightening their clothes, rubbing their faces, and staring around for answers. Both sets of fighters no longer looked to battle, preferring to tend to their injured.

Omen remained in hiding, most likely because there was an audience of a hundred mortals less than a football field away. It was for the best. His presence would just delay this departure.

Giving my partner a contrite look, I said, "I'll be right back. I've got to take care of them first, then we'll help Delores journey home."

Billee knew which 'home' I was referring to. There was no need to clarify.

Goddamn, I hate my job.

23

CROSSING OVER

B<small>EFORE</small> I <small>REPORTED TO THE</small> O<small>RDER ABOUT MY FAILURE TO GET</small> answers to the mystery behind the Bowl, I had a job to do.

An important job. The very reason for the Reapers.

"Does she have to?" Billee whispered at my side. "Isn't there anything you can do?"

I looked down at Delores, still cradled in my partner's arms. Arakiel had done a number on her, breaking her leg, and shredding her arm and side. She'd lost too much blood in an attack I hadn't even seen in the chaos. I could only hope Delores hadn't felt pain. "Billee, it's time."

Billee's lips quivered. "Call 911, dammit. Do something, Rev!"

I kneeled next to her, softening my firm response. "It's time."

We had privacy for this conversation, and all the time Billee needed. After dealing with Arakiel, I had gathered the teens and homeless under the influence of the soul stone. Because of the number of them, I had to break them into smaller groups, but set about my work quickly. The kids headed home. I told the residents of the camp to head to the nearest shelter. I had just enough energy left to hold the spell on the stone, thus keeping them under its influence for roughly the next thirty minutes. By that time, we'd be gone if anyone felt compelled to return to the camp to fill in the missing parts of their night.

I squatted in silence as Billee sniffled. Time seemed to slow as she held Delores as she passed.

When her energy residue stood and looked down at the other woman holding what used to be her mortal form, Delores smiled. "Billee is such a wonderful person. I'm crazy about her."

I smiled. "I am too."

Billee ignored me, stroking Delores's hair.

"You two should go out for dinner," the residue of Delores Garcia said, her aged cheeks cracking in a grin. "You'd make a cute couple."

"I'm a little old for her," I chuckled.

"Ah, nonsense," she waved a ghostly hand.

"So, young lady," I said, lifting my arm and cocking my elbow, "how about you and me take a walk? Are you ready?"

Delores's cheeks dropped, the smile gone. "I'm scared, Mr. Carver."

"I understand. But you won't be alone. I'll be right there with you."

She wrapped her arm through mine. Even though I couldn't touch her, she didn't need to know that. The gesture was more about creating the perception of comfort, not actually providing it—one of the cruelest aspects of being a Reaper if you ask me.

I snapped my fingers and opened the Rift to the Veil Gate. To Billee, I said, "I'll be right back."

She didn't look up.

"THIS ISN'T AT ALL WHAT I WAS EXPECTING," DELORES SAID WHEN we stepped through.

In fact, the Veil Gate rarely is what mortals—well, their residue—expect to see. I blame religion and fanciful imaginations.

I laughed, keeping the spirit of this duty light. It's already heavy enough. "What? You're not impressed with the bland, eternal emptiness?"

Blackness wrapped us. It was like being on the inside of a dark cacoon, I imagined. In every direction, every dimension. Blackness. Blackness. And more blackness. With one important exception.

Ahead, fifty yards from where I'd opened the Rift, stood the Veil Gate. On either side, twelve-foot-tall empyrean knights guarded the entrance to what lay beyond. Aligned to no one but the gate, these immense armored creatures with flaming broadswords and winged barbuta helmets presented one hell of an intimidating presence. Probably not the best customer-centric approach, but if thousands of years of escorting mortals to the Veil Gate taught me anything, it was that the All didn't care. The All just was.

Next to the arched gate, just out of reach of the empyrean knights, stood a single lampstand of green metal, wrapped as a vine, up and around itself. Broad, angular leaves complimented the twisted metal. A symbol of the eternal nature of life. The light its flame gave off was soft yellow. Comforting and calm. You know, to balance out the sizzling white rim of the forty-five-foot tall rippling gate and the two armored gargantuans protecting it.

Under the light of the lamp stood a Scroll Eater, an ugly creature that would have no place in the Upper, Over, or even Under worlds. In serious need of some vitamin D, the faceless beast administered the Veil Gate. Whereas the empyrean knights ensured no one, no matter who they were, approached the All's access point, the Scroll Eater kept a record of everyone visiting, escorting mortals, and those sent through. Named so because us Reapers picked on him—her? —it?—about 'eating' the scrolls we delivered. No one knows the origins of the creature, if there were more than one, or a plethora of other questions.

Harold, as I called it—and it never corrected me—was dressed in a white robe covering most of its body and matching his skin tone almost perfectly. Its seven arms and most of its long chest were exposed, as was the lump of its head. Seven mouths opened and closed in unison as it waited, its eyeless face seeing nothing and maybe everything.

Delores hesitated, casting a nervous eye at Harold, the knights, and the tall gate. It happens almost every time, even for those who are ready to cross over. She even took a small step backward, looking up and down the towering Veil Gate.

I think she might have been trying to see through the silent, rippling center, its only definition highlighted by the blaring white magic rimming the portal. She wouldn't be the first mortal to look into the true nature of what waits after death with a hesitantly skeptical eye.

These things take time, and I was going to give Delores every second she needed. She, like millions I'd already escorted, deserved it.

"Are you scared?" I asked, standing by her side as close as possible. At that moment, I would have loved to wrap my arm around her and hold her as she ran through the litany of memories of her life, regrets, joys, 'what coulda beens,' and more. But the All missed the boat on this part of creation, not allowing the material to interact with the immaterial. Still, I stood close and faced the silent rippling nothingness she would soon become part of, hoping my mere presence filled her with enough comfort to get her through this.

"A little," she said with a chuckle. She swatted the air the way grandmothers do when their grandsons tell an inappropriate joke. "Oh, I'm just being silly. Everyone goes through this, right?"

Her smiling eyes found me. I gave her a reassuring smile. "Everyone and everything dies in the end." I held up a finger, letting my mouth widen. "But you got to spend years of your life living it the way you wanted. It might surprise you to learn how many can't say that."

"It's a shame, really," she said. Her cheery radiance continually slipped as she forced herself to smile. "I wish nothing but happiness for everyone, and I wish they could find what I found serving the people of Olympia."

"Me too, Delores. What a wonderful life that would be." I took a small step forward, looking back. "Coming along?"

Her gaze swiveled between the two empyrean knights, who were as silent as Harold and the Veil Gate itself.

"Don't worry about them," I said about the knights. "As long as you're not a hell-raiser, they'll leave you alone." I pointed at Harold, lowering my voice. "Don't worry about him, either. He's ugly as hell, but a really nice guy."

Delores snickered. I noted she didn't take a step to join me. When she looked up, tears filled her spectral eyes. "Why, Mr. Carver? Why do I have to go now?"

Ah, the question of questions. The one almost every single mortal asks when not completely overwhelmed by what's happening. A fair question.

"Did I do something wrong?" She wrung her hands. I really wanted to wrap an arm around her.

"Not at all, Delores," I answered softly. "It's just your time. Your energy is needed."

Her face twitched. "Energy? Am I… am I not going to Heaven?"

Ugh. I moved closer. "Delores, what waits beyond the Veil Gate is the fate of every person. Rarely is there good and evil. The world is full of people simply trying to do their best to survive. I think you saw that with your work in the last few years. While many people denigrate the homeless, you saw them for who they are. It's really not much different for everyone else. Sure, there are always exceptions, but if you dig deep enough into someone's story, no matter who they are, you're likely to find they were trying to do the best they could with what they had." I half-turned, examining the Veil Gate. Fifteen feet wide and over forty feet tall, it cut an imposing figure. The All, if it cared, could have touched up the place so mortals weren't so overwhelmed, so it felt more welcoming. Maybe then, these last moments of awareness wouldn't be so daunting. "There's no Heaven beyond that, Delores. There's no Hell either."

"Wh—what is there?"

"Everything," I said, my throat constricting. I mean, come on, it's pretty intimidating to think about, even for an experienced Reaper.

"I—I don't know if I want to," she said, her voice sounding smaller than I'd ever heard from her.

I closed my eyes and focused. This was where I earned the big bucks, where I separated myself from those who just executed their duties. I squatted on the black floor, indistinguishable from any walls or ceiling the Veil Gate might have. I patted it. "Sit by me?"

Delores did. It was an enjoyable experience. She started to squat and extend her hand to the floor when recognition dawned on her face. In the afterlife, she didn't have the joint pains, the restricted and weakened muscles of her later life. Though she carried an older woman's body, she was as spry as a teenager. This part was always fun to witness.

"Oh, I feel good," she said when she sat. "My knees don't hurt anymore."

I chuckled.

We sat in silence for a while. Back in the realms of the Upper and Overworlds, infinitesimal seconds or days could have passed if not for the Interlude. Time stood still and no one would notice. Not angels and demons. Not Yahweh or Lucifer. Literally, time was ours now, and I had no problem giving Delores what she needed.

"What questions do you have?" I lifted my hand, palm out, and placed my other hand over my heart. "I'll answer the best I can."

"I can't go back? Even for a few days?" She sat up straight, looking pleased. "Oh, my. My back feels so strong." She blinked as she realized her thoughts were all over the place. It happens. My time to feel that would come too. I let her enjoy hers. "Sorry, Mr. Carver. That just surprised me. Anyway, I hate to ask, but I wasn't expecting any of this. Had I, maybe I could have taken time to see my children and grandchildren and say goodbye. There are a few women who work for CFC I would have liked to have had a moment with. And the people of the camp." Her hand snapped to her incorporeal mouth. "They're going to think I abandoned them."

"You didn't, Delores. They'll know because they knew who you were in life," I said. "If I had the power, I'd do whatever I could to make sure you got to say goodbye to your loved ones. I swear it. But I don't. Actually, I almost got myself in trouble so you could have as much time as possible." I explained my assignment, how it was delivered on a scroll I was going to hand to Harold, how her name was entered in the Book of Planes, and how I had a deadline to finish my assignment.

"You—you let me live *weeks* longer?"

"Yes."

"Why?"

I smiled at her. "Because you're a good person. And the world always needs good people. I would have let you stay longer if I'd been allowed. But I wasn't, and no one outruns the Reaper. I'm sorry."

"Thank you for that, Mr. Carver. I don't want to sound

ungrateful. I really don't." Her voice shook and tears refilled her eyes. "I—I just miss them and wish I had more time."

"I know. Look at it this way. What's important is that you wisely used the time you had. You lived a rich life. Loved and cared for others. You put good into the world. In your own small way, you left it a better place than you found it."

She sniffed quietly for a few moments. Her head dropped toward her crisscrossed legs. When she looked up, she drew a deep breath, eyeing the Veil Gate like it was a challenge. "What happens on the other side of that?"

"You, your energy, your spirit, if you will, return to the All," I said. "It becomes part of everything. You return to what birthed you." I cocked my head to emphasize my point. "You become part of birthing new life. The All needs balance, just as everything does. If too many shit people are called back in a short time, things get out of whack. The All needs remarkable people, like you, to stay balanced."

Delores snickered, her joviality holding the robustness of youth her visual presentation hid, though she was beginning to display fledgling features. The wrinkles around her eyes were smoothing. The loose skin at the base of her neck was tightening. Her brown hair, dyed for an untold number of years, was regaining its original pep.

She stared at the backs of her hands, noticing the regression of age, I think. Her head bobbed. "I didn't think angels could curse?"

I joined her in laughing at my expense. "My boss would tell you there are a lot of things I do that I'm not supposed to."

She tried to pat my knee. Though her spectral hand never made contact, she said nothing. With a big sniff, Delores Garcia stood, smoothed her pants, and extended her hand. "I'd offer to help you up, Mr. Carver, but I don't think I'd be much help. Still, it'd be rude not to at least make the gesture."

The chuckle was undeniable. Delores was a true champ. I stood.

"Before I go," she said, turning to me once more, "can I ask one last thing?"

"Of course."

"Can you please protect those people, Mr. Carver? The people at the camp? The others who might be hurt by that thing or others like it? Will you keep them safe? Will you look out for Billee?"

"Now that's a promise I can keep."

She faced the Veil Gate, straightened, and nodded her head that now appeared half as young as it did when we'd entered this realm. "Then it's time for me to go."

I nodded and walked her to the Scroll Eater.

"Hello, Revelation," Harold said as we approached, its seven mouths moving as one.

To this day, I still didn't know where to look at its face, since it had no eyes. I always aimed for center mass. Always an excellent tactic. "Hey, ugly. How's things?"

Harold lifted seven thin arms. "Quiet as always. One day, I might visit you in your realm and see what all the fuss is about."

"And scare the children? They'll make stories about you and tell them for generations."

"You mean I could become a legend?" All seven mouths grinned.

I don't think I'll ever get used to the sight of that. "Legendary."

"I like this idea," Harold said, extending its seven arms with no sign of which I should drop the scroll in. Harold never had, and never would. "Scroll, please."

Before I handed it over, I smiled at Delores, who watched the proceedings with what looked like nervous excitement. "You'll be fine. There is no pain. No suffering. You'll step through the Veil Gate as Delores Garcia and become part of all life."

"No pain?"

"No pain," I affirmed.

"Okay."

I handed the caring woman's scroll to Harold, aiming for the hand extended from the arm in the center of its chest. Taking the scroll, it promptly opened seven mouths and inserted it, swallowing the scroll whole.

"That's still gross," I said.

"I don't judge your diet. Don't judge mine," Harold said, seven mouths bouncing with laughter. "You may proceed."

I nodded to Delores, and she stepped in front of the Veil Gate. Pausing, she pulled her shoulders back and lifted her chin. And then she stepped into the rippling black.

The first touch of the All wrapped around her foot like a lover's caress. Up her calves, thighs, and hips. Over her hands, to her elbows and shoulders. Like a pair of soft hands, it embraced her chin and cheeks, draping around her back until it was nothing but what it had always been.

Except now, it was better because it had Delores Garcia.

24

MEATLOAF CURES ALL

MEATLOAF CURES THE STRESSES AND STRAINS OF LIVING LIFE.

Billee was discovering that now. Pher was hanging out for the free meal.

My boss stood behind my partner, rubbing her back in a grandfatherly way while I minced shallots at the counter—because not only did I buy the groceries, but I had to prepare and cook them as well. Pher is a cheap bastard. Or, more likely, he knows I'll do it anyway, so doesn't fight me on it. I prefer the former because I adore him enough to enjoy picking on him.

"I can't believe she's gone," Billee said, a thin hand tangled in her black and tan curls. "I mean, I knew it was happening. Despite that, it just feels... odd."

"I'm sorry, Sunrose." Pher moved away to refill his and Billee's wine glasses.

"Hey, what about me?" I asked, aiming the knife at him and then my empty glass as if it could compel him to pour. Side note: how nice of a superpower would that be?

"I don't want my chef under the influence. He might ruin the meal."

He and Billee shared a laugh. Hers was tepid.

"Keep your cook happy or he might add interesting ingredients to your dinner." I wiggled the cutting board as a not-so-subtle threat.

"That's gross, Rev." Billee snorted, covering her nose and mouth with the back of her hand.

"So is looking at an empty wine glass when I've got raw beef all over my hands."

Pher's nose flared. "For what it's worth, this smells wonderful."

"Thanks, boss. Now, chop-chop. Fill my wine before I chop-chop you."

One corner of Pher's wide lips curled up, but he did as ordered. He knew better.

"I hope you two don't think less of me," Billee said.

Pher stood next to his seat at the bar, carrying the wine bottle.

I stopped chopping the shallot and turned. "Why would I?"

She shrugged. "Because I knew Delores had to go, but I don't know. I think I fooled myself into thinking something was going to change."

"Once a name is in the Book of Planes, there's no undoing it," Pher said, lifting his glass toward the light, and inspecting its new contents.

"I promise, she's not suffering," I said. "No more stress, or aches and pains. No more heartbreaks. She doesn't have to worry about the residents of the camp and what's going to become of them or who will rebuild it after the fires. In a way, she's serving more life, making a bigger difference, now."

"I was naïve," she said, head dropping between her shoulders and her chin thrust forward. "But I'm a quick learner. Don't treat me like I'm clueless. She's gone. Her energy is back there." She rolled her hand in the air above her head. "Back wherever. I get it. Just don't have to like it."

"You'll get used to this. Plus, Delores was a friend. That changes the assignment for you. I understand."

"I guess." She sat straight as if the world's greatest idea had come to her. "But I don't want to become like you two. No offense."

"None taken," I said.

"How are we that you don't want to be?" Pher said.

"Jaded," Billee said. She had been lifting her wine to her mouth but paused halfway. "Rev, are you crying?"

"No, it's the stupid shallots."

"Sure," she said. "I don't know, Pher. I know you two. Neither of you is the type to not care. That's not the problem. But, to me at least, it seems you're so used to people dying that it doesn't affect you. This isn't just about Delores. Mostly her. But not just about her." She found my eyes, staring deeply like she was searching for the contents of my brain. "The way you killed that Nephilim, Rev. Don't get me wrong. After everything it did, the world is a better place without it. But still."

"He was dying anyway," I said, nearly taking a small slice of my thumb off with the knife. The shallots had irritated my eyes enough that a smarter cook would have walked away. But I was on a mission, and when I have a job to do, I see it through to the end. I'm stubborn like that. "Trust me, if I could have kept him alive and got him back to the Upperworld, I wouldn't have. But before I pulled that trigger, he only had a minute or two left, and I didn't want him pulling a last surprise. Arakiel did enough harm."

A dark feeling settled over the kitchen and bar.

The slight *whir* of Pher rotating his glass by the stem filled the silence between the three living entities who could do with a good dose of each other right now. He smacked his lips. "Arakiel caused a lot of problems for the Upperworld and the mortal realm. Problems we won't solve over this meal. Though I wish Rev had found a way to subdue him so we could have gotten answers." He fixed his gaze on me. I stopped in mid-chop, the shallots still torturing my nose and eyes. "I understand why he did what he did. Arakiel was not working alone. The Upperworld has a problem, and this situation with Arakiel and the First Bowl, and the spreading virus... All of it is just the beginning. I'm afraid we'll have to address many more problems, known and unknown, soon."

"Great," I said, drawing out the word and finishing the shallots. Meatloaf wouldn't solve my headache if I never finished preparing it.

"How bad could it get?" Billee asked.

Pher shrugged. I let him tackle that question. "No telling until we understand what we're facing."

"Just be real with her, boss. She can take it," I said, moving on to trimming the Brussels sprouts.

"Not a simple thing to admit," Pher said, shaking his shiny, bald head. "But if what we're hearing turns out to be true, all the treasures of the Upperworld are at risk. Bowls, the Arc of the Covenant, and the Halo. All of it."

"Whoa, whoa," Billee said, her palms turned down. She made a gesture like she was trying to shove more clothes into an already overstuffed suitcase. "The whats?"

"Bad stuff," I said, trimming, trimming Brussels Sprouts and not feeling a bit guilty about letting Pher take the lead on this discussion. I'd just killed a Nephilim, saved nearly a hundred lives, and escorted someone who was called by the All two decades before she should have been. I deserved a moment of decompression.

Pher was decidedly more pliant with his response. "I spoke out of turn, Sunrose. My apologies."

"I'm not tender, Pher."

"I know," he said, his voice hitching. What he'd brought up was heavy. The stuff you didn't bring up in casual conversations. "I mean no disrespect. What I should have said is there are enough vulnerabilities in the Upperworld now to have everyone on edge. Including me."

Billee patted his arm but said nothing.

"The Council has to stop it before the Overworld slides toward Armageddon," I said.

"We're having talks."

"Oh, good. More talks."

Pher shook his head. "You'll never make it as a politician, lad."

"Oh no, whatever will I do?" I said, faking distress and pressing the back of my hand to my forehead. Which was stupid. For one, it was my knife hand, and the snappy gesture caused chunks of leaves to dislodge from the blade and land on my nose. The bonus was that everything close to my face still held the scent of the shallots. My eyes were watering and my nose twitched with an oncoming sneeze before I realized my mistake.

That cost me a few minutes of dinner preparation as I dropped the knife on the counter to turn away and cover my sneeze. It fell to the floor and nearly carried all the Brussels sprouts with it. A few avoided disaster. The rest would need to be rinsed again.

Billee helped clean up. Pher sipped his wine and watched with a humored look.

"Thanks for the help," I said to him.

"You two have it handled." He smiled and lifted his glass. "Plus, I'm an elder and a guest. I'm pretty sure it's considered rude to have me clean up your messes. That's what the best Reaper in the history of the Upperworld is for."

"Keep it up and I won't be your Reaper for much longer," I said, taking the clean knife and sprouts from Billee with a grateful nod.

"You're not getting your morning star anytime soon," Pher said. "Too much work to do."

"I was afraid you'd say that," I replied, wagging my knife

at him. "But I will get my morning star. When this mess is over, I want out. The Order owes me that much."

A sad shadow passed over Pher's face. In my periphery, Billee sat up a little straighter, and I felt bad for being so heavy-handed. Dinner. This was about having dinner with the most important company in my life.

"I wish you didn't feel that way," Pher said.

"Me either," I answered honestly, before putting on a cheery face. "But hey, look at it this way. With Hellion using the Four Horseman to steal shit from the Safe, the Bowls being vulnerable, the Halo possibly compromised and bringing about the death of the universe if it falls into the wrong hands, you've got enough jobs to keep me busy for the rest of eternity."

"I'll drink to that," Pher said, giving me a smartass smile that said 'good to see you agree with me even if you don't actually agree.'

"I'm so confused, but I'll toast to anything right now," Billee said, lifting her own glass.

I set the knife down and joined the rim of mine to their nearly fused ones. "To battling the forces of evil, kicking ass, taking names, and to meatloaf!"

"To meatloaf," Pher said, smacking his lips.

Billee shook her head, her loose curls swaying. "You two are ridiculous. To meatloaf!"

We emptied our glasses, and get this, Pher got up to rinse and refill them with a new blend. Pher. Got. Up. It was official now. Wine was the only thing that moved him.

"Oh, I almost forgot," he said as he sat down with a bottle of cabernet clutched in his fist like he was trying to open it by squeezing the neck to pop the cork. "I've got something for you."

"A present."

He raised an eyebrow and held my gaze while he set the

bottle down to free his hands. He raised them in front of his chest, eyebrow still raised.

"No," I whined. "Not tonight, Pher."

"What?" Billee asked.

"He's about to be an asshole."

Truly gifted in the skill of perception. That's me. As soon as I shared my insight with Billee, Pher clapped his hands and a cloud of small sparks of white light sprang to life right above my Brussels sprouts.

I groaned.

"Another job? Already?" Billee said.

The scroll, once formed, plopped down on my cutting board. I found my boss's eyes. "Now I have to wash the sprouts again."

Pher winked.

With a sigh, I asked, "What's this one? Escort or fight another rogue Nephilim? Oh, wait. Do I get to stalk Hellion and see what she's up to?"

"Even better. You get to hunt a behemoth," Pher said in an annoyingly cheery voice.

"*A* behemoth?"

"Yes."

"Not possible."

Pher held up a finger. "*Ah*, but it is."

Billee's head swiveled between us. "What's going on?"

I scrunched my eyes at Pher as if I was mad at him. "Oh, nothing. Pher just wants us to hunt down one of the apocalyptic beasts."

"Uh, like from the Bible?"

"Yep."

Pher's wine glass rested on his thick lip. "We didn't want Rev getting bored with dealing with the Nephilim, so we thought he'd like a challenge." With his smartassery clear to all, Pher took an obnoxious sip of the new blend and smacked his lips.

"I swear to Yahweh," I said, reminding myself that meat-loaf cured all. *But could it kill a behemoth?*

"What?" he said, spreading his hands as if he was inno-cent. "You're the Reaper Minister. Isn't that part of your creed? To protect mortals and immortals. To hunt demons and monsters, small and big? To kill, if necessary, for the preserva-tion of the Balance."

I shook my head, waving the knife in his general direction without looking. "No, actually, it isn't. The Reaper Minister doesn't have a creed anymore."

Pher chuckled, the sound of triumph muffled by the wine glass around his mouth. "Yes, you do, my boy. Yes, you do. Your creed is as eternal as you are at this point."

"Open that bottle," I said. "I'm going to need another glass of wine."

THE END

MORE REV, MORE ACTION, MORE MONSTERS, MORE PROBLEMS FOR THE GRIM REAPER

Instead of getting his morning star, Rev gets to face a behemoth? The First Bowl has been poured on the Earth, and someone breached the Upperworld's Safe. Can Rev stop the world from barreling toward Armageddon?

Pre-order Rev Carver Book 2, *Angel's Creed*, now and find out!

ALSO BY PAUL SATING

FICTION

Urban Fantasy

Rev Carver Series (Same Story World As Zodiac)

Angel Assassin

Angel's Creed

The Zodiac Series (Same Story World As Rev Carver)

The Fall of Aries (Free for newsletter subscribers)

Bitter Aries

The Horn of Taurus

The Gemini Paradox

Cancer's Curse

The Pride of Leo

Virgo's Vigilantes

Libra's Liberation

Epic Fantasy

Hexed Heroes Saga

Thornbane Trilogy

Thornbane the Lost (Coming 2023)

Thornbane the Demon Witch (Coming 2023)

Thornbane the Free (Coming 2023)

Battleborn Books

Bloodborn (Free for newsletter subscribers)

Battleborn Trilogy

Fireborn

Rageborn

Battleborn

Bonebreaker Trilogy

King of Bones

War of Bones

Breaker of Bones

Crown of Thieves

Birth of a Thief (Free for newsletter subscribers)

Horror

12 Deaths of Christmas

The Plant (Free for newsletter subscribers)

Suspense

RIP

Chasing the Demon

Nonfiction

Novel Idea to Podcast: How to Sell More Books Through Podcasting

Podcasts

Audio Fiction Podcast

Horrible Writing Podcast

(Free for Patreon supporters!)

GET EXCLUSIVE CONTENT

More stories! Get exclusive Paul Sating fiction, including free audio books, in podcast form!

Get more stories each month by becoming a Patron! New exclusive fiction each month!

Become a Patron & enjoy more content!

NEVER MISS OUT!

Get the latest news, special deals, exclusive stories, first looks at book covers, and more by signing up for Paul Sating's newsletter!

Sign up for Paul's newsletter to follow all the news and special deals for upcoming novels, and to catch up on the latest regarding his podcast at http://www.paulsating.com.

ACKNOWLEDGMENTS

Rev was always the grown up version of Ezekial (Zeke to his friends) Sunstone (main character of the Zodiac books, of which this is a spin-off, but you knew that) in my head. When I started the Zodiac books, I made the decision to make Zeke younger than I like making my characters. The series is a long one (still ongoing as the writing of this book), and I needed to tell an epic-sized tale in an urban fantasy series (because I'm just that kind of rebel). Rev was always there, lurking, aching to be released.

Like a dutiful little author, I plugged away at the three-quarters of a million words of the *Zodiac* before I gave Rev life. And boy, did he bloom!

From the introduction with him and Billee, I felt this story down in my empty chamber of a soul. Rev just spoke to me. He's the kind of character I'd go out for beers with in a heartbeat. His charm, wit, humor, sarcasm, and jadedness speak to me (there's a bit of me in all of my characters, across all of my series, but Rev is probably the nearest and dearest to my heart). Suffice it to say, once I started putting words down, I got uber-excited... and probably annoyed a lot of people in my life. None more than the following:

Maddie, duh and or hello?! First and foremost. Always. Forever cherish. I know where I'd be if it wasn't for you... and it's *not* yet another Five Finger Death Punch concert. The earth may revolve around the sun, but you're the center of my solar-system, local galaxy cluster, and universe. GILU!

Nikki and Alex. Always remember, no matter how

sarcastic your dad is... he will die one day. There! Bet you never thought you'd see me put that in a book! Joke's on you!

Patrons, you crazy Epic Peeps do so much to help me keep plugging along at this. I can never thank you enough for you kindness, thoughtfulness, and general awesomeness. You're absolutely epic!

Having First Readers for this book was imperative. Lori, Alan, Tony, and, of course, Louis' mad editing. In my head, Rev sounded perfect. He's not, of course, because no one and nothing is, but he's pretty damn close—as close as I can get him. That's because of you!

Jason Burke. Okay, now I'm getting antsy when I don't hear your thoughts on a book a week after it's released. You have me spoiled! May I never burn you out.

Fellow urban fantasy author NM Thorn. A great friend, wonderful storyteller—even better human, and amazing cover artist. You've got too much talent to be contained in a single meat sack—and that's not even close to your best quality. Thank you for another year of amazing friendship!

ABOUT THE AUTHOR

Paul Sating is an author, podcaster, and self-professed coolest dad on the planet, hailing from the Pacific Northwest of the United States. At the end of his military career, he decided to reconnect with his first love (that wouldn't get him in trouble with his wife) and once again picked up the pen. Years on, he has published eight novels and he hasn't even screwed up his podcasts, which have garnered over a million downloads.

When he's not working on stories, you can find him talking to himself in his backyard working on failed landscaping projects or hiking around the gorgeous Olympic Peninsula. He is married to the patient and wonderful, Madeline, and has two daughters—thus the reason for his follicle challenges.

Find out more about his other books and free podcasts from his website: paulsating.com.

CONTACT PAUL

How to Contact Paul Sating

Published by Paul Sating Productions
   P.O. Box 15166
   Tumwater, WA 98511
   paul@paulsating.com

Follow Paul:

- Facebook: www.facebook.com/authorpaulsating
- Bookbub: bookbub.com/paul-sating
- Goodreads: goodreads.com/author/show/16982359.Paul_Sating
- Instagram: @paulsating
- Pinterest: pinterest.com/paulsating
- Twitter: @paulsating

BOOK 2 "ANGEL'S CREED"
CHAPTER ONE

Sneak Peak of Book 2 of the Rev Carver Series, "Angel's Creed."

1 – Run, Run, Just As Fast As You Can

What do you do when your latest target doesn't want to die?

You chase them, of course.

The problem is? I'm too old to find joy in running. If I'm moving swiftly, there better be a damn good reason. A Hell-hound chasing me. Something burning on the stove. A sale on wine at the local package store. Running is low on the list of my priorities. Chasing after a drug dealer whose name was on the scroll tucked away in my jacket was even lower on the long list of things I had to accomplish this week.

But, here I was, running through an empty home improvement store parking lot in Olympia, Washington on a bitter January night. Puffs of clouds billowed before my face as I panted. The blacktop flickered in the yellow light where ice patches waited to send me flailing to my ass. I swear, if I slipped, I would make Roger Baskin's last minutes alive a living hell.

"Stop running!" I shouted, shaking my head. "No one outruns the Reaper, you dumbass!"

What I didn't tell him was that I'm too old for this nonsense, and if he was determined enough, he just might.

"Leave him alone!" a voice screeched just as something slammed into me.

We tumbled to the frosty blacktop. Had it not been for a lazy customer and even lazier employees leaving the abandoned shopping cart in the middle of a parking spot, I would have met the icy surface with my shoulder. Guess I should thank them for their lack of initiative? As it was, the welded metal cart took most of the impact. My only injury came as one of its hard plastic tires poking into my hip when it tipped and I landed on top of it. At least my leather duster prevented the bolt from ripping open skin.

I rolled as a flurry of fists slammed into my chest. Even though my attacker threw them in fury, they were nothing more than an annoyance.

"What the hell is wrong with you?" I said as I deflected the fiery but meek blows.

Usually, I wouldn't complain if a woman straddled me. Not that I'd remember what the experience was like. I've been divorced for decades and remember little about the sensations of intimate contact with a woman. What I do remember didn't include fists. Alisha, my ex, wasn't into that sort of thing. Not that I was, to be clear. Not that I'm judging. I'm a Reaper. An assassin. Heaven's clean-up hitter and Mr. Fix It. I'm not an arbiter.

And this woman throwing fists didn't seem interested in any of that. Apparently, she had one thing on her mind; beautiful, glorious violence. By the twentieth punch, her square glasses flew off, rattling across a patch of ice. She squinted, still swinging. By the way she pinched her eyes, I think she was aiming for any blur that could possibly resemble the human form.

As another punch flew, I snagged her thin wrist.

I don't like being touched. At all. I'm not big on being hit either, no matter how light the punches.

I held her arm in-place. She tried to jerk it free, but couldn't break my grip.

This woman had the look of a librarian, and not the dirty kind. What the hell was she doing in this store's parking lot at one in the morning, and why was she attacking me? I hadn't pissed off a woman who wasn't my familiar or a member of the Order of Thirteen in a long, long time.

Unless good ole Roger was her supplier and my appearance had ruined an exchange, dampening her night?

This twenty-something didn't have that look about her. Instead, she was the type that hung out in coffee shops until the battery on her tablet died. The type that didn't know if her town had a home improvement store or not, and if it did, she wouldn't know what to do there. Not the type to throw fists with a Reaper.

"Get off him!" another feminine shout pierced the night.

I smiled. The voice belonged to an ally, my partner.

Billee came up behind the librarian-looking woman, grabbing her black, pinned up hair, and pulled.

My attacker stopped swinging and tried to grab Billee's arms. A pointless use of energy. My mortal familiar is a badass. The spunky librarian was no match.

Billee pulled the woman off, and they toppled to the blacktop.

I scrambled to my feet, seeing the dark of night beyond the parking lot lights absorb Roger's form.

"You going to be okay?" I asked Billee.

She had the librarian in a chokehold—I told you she's a badass. "Go get him. I've got her."

Billee wasn't even breathing hard. Damn showoff.

"Be careful, Sparky," I said, casting a wary glance at the librarian before dashing off to chase down a drug dealer.

Out past the protective shell of the parking lot lights, the night grew still. Sporadic cars and trucks raced north and south alongside the I-5 interstate, but they were the only signs of life in this small city, in the middle of winter, in the dead of night. Either Roger had gotten away or he hunkered down somewhere to avoid detection. The problem was, he wasn't fast enough for the former. So, I began my search.

"Where are you, Roger?" I called into the darkness over the din of traffic. "This ends with you and me heading off to the great beyond. It's cold, and I just want to get this over."

I did. I had more important tasks to complete besides escorting a drug dealer to the Veil Gate. Insignificant things like finding and fighting a behemoth. A giant beast. You know, the type spoken of in the Good Book? Yeah, that kind. And I wanted to get to it while this newest version was still in diapers. With that beast loose on the world for the first time in over ten thousand years, I wasn't interested in dragging out this pursuit. Roger Baskin was hiding, and that pissed me off. This task, to act as a Reaper to escort a mortal to their afterlife, was one more mundane thing to get done when time was already at a premium. That doubly pissed me off.

I crept toward the row of bushes lining the road and stopped. Streetlights provided enough illumination that I would have seen the drug dealer if he'd tried escaping along the road. That meant he was still in cover. I'd need to cross the street to explore the multitude of hiding places. That sucked. I'd be out in the open. Vulnerable.

I mean, I don't want to sound obtuse or anything, but a drug dealer not packing some kind of weapon was as likely as not seeing a single Confederate flag at a NASCAR race.

This was the Overworld, the one place where angels can

die. I was not taking chances stepping out into the street and being cut down by a lucky shot.

Reaching inside my duster, I slipped my hand into the specially made pocket where I kept my .327 Ruger. I named it Maggie. The revolver was small, just the way I liked it. I don't need the weapon to use my Angelfire Ability, but it sure is a lot cooler when you blast a jackass with a ray from a temporal weapon instead of using your hand. Plus, my aim is better with Maggie, and I don't look like a dork who'd just fallen out of a van carrying him and his buddies to some LARPing event when I tap into my angelic magic. Just the sight of Maggie often induced compliance. This drug dealer seemed more like a butter knife than a steak knife though, if you catch my meaning. I had a feeling he'd need more convincing than me just swinging the Ruger around.

Roger had proven he wasn't going down without a fight. He crossed the line when I first appeared to escort him to the Veil Gate, explaining what I was there for and that he was about to step into traffic and be struck down and killed. I was trying to play the considerate, nice guy. Billee had even tried to help with the explanation.

But Roger wasn't having any of it. He pushed Billee into the road, putting her in danger, and took off. After pulling her from the semi barreling down, I had a new level of determination to separate Roger from his crime-bound life. No remorse, no regrets. Plus, he was already a scumbag.

Staying low, I moved along the road. To the south, civilization gave way to the green of uncultured land as Olympia faded away and pockets of homes and farms sprang up. People like him didn't do well in the country. Not enough vulnerable people to take advantage of. They needed city life. They needed suburbia and kids with mommy and daddy's money to explore the mind-altering relief people like Roger provided. So I made my way north.

A loud clang drew my attention to the building ahead. The Great Wall of Dumpsters give it away as a Costco.

At this time of night, the store ha already been closed for hours, so either someone was rooting around and looking for an evening meal, seeking shelter, or they were hiding.

Using the sporadic spread of trees and blanket of black of the night as my cover, I moved toward the sound. The lid of a dumpster, one of those thick plastic ones, was closing so slowly it was comical. Roger might as well have called out to taunt me that I'd never find him in a million years.

Moving to stay hidden behind the closest tree, I shouted across the forty feet divide. "Come on out, Roger. I'm not going anywhere and, trust me, I can wait forever."

"Fuck you," came the reply, muffled by the container.

I shook my head. This guy had been sitting in a Corvette when I came to get him. A Corvette. Savvy enough to afford a car like that, yet no smarter than the steel surrounding him.

"You're coming out, buddy," I yelled back. "Now. In ten minutes. An hour. Tomorrow morning. It doesn't matter. This ends here. Don't make me come in after you. I already have to take my duster in for cleaning, but that doesn't mean I want to root around in trash. Especially to deal with trash like you."

The dumpster lid cracked open. The dark interior prevented me from seeing anything inside. "Fuck you!"

"Goddammit," I said, stepping out from behind the tree with Maggie in a two-handed grip, barrel pointed at the frost-covered grass. It crunched under my feet. The ever-present puffs of clouds formed around my face every time I exhaled. I was going to have to soak for an hour after this just to feel my toes again.

One foot into the open and the dirt near my booted feet split open just before I heard the pop coming from the dumpster. I jumped back behind the tree.

So Roger was armed, after all. A drug dealer with a gun. Shocker.

I leveled Maggie. Keeping the tree between me and the dumpster, I took aim.

The tree was wide enough to block most of me, but this was still a risk. Roger could be a crack shot, or he could be one lucky bastard and hit an exposed shoulder or my gut, and take out a vital organ. Imagine, the Upperworld's most senior Reaper, taken out by a dirt bag hiding in a dumpster? Good thing I didn't have children to shame with my potential demise. One more reason to be thankful to my ex. So level-headed, that woman.

"I gave you a chance."

Another pop. Bark flew from the tree.

I snarled and pulled the trigger.

Angelfire split the dark night. A beam of pure white, wholesome goodness—okay, I admit, the 'wholesome' part isn't necessarily true, but it makes me feel better about the duties I've been carrying out for eight thousand years. When the beam struck the metal dumpster, it didn't explode. The green metal simply became an ichorous mess, liquifying and plopping to the ground in molten globs. The metal container had no ridges, no sharp edges where I'd blasted the hole through it. Imagine a knife poking a through a piece of paper held taut. Clean, efficient.

I fired again, and again. Small beams; barely a workout. Each knocked another hole into the dumpster. With each, I reduced the room for the concealed dirtbag. By now, less than half the dumpster remained intact. With my next shot, I blew the last portion supporting the lid off. The black plastic clanged down into the dumpster.

Underneath my focus, someone howled. It could have been the drug dealer. It might not have been. One thing I knew for sure was that I wasn't losing focus and letting this bastard get a lucky shot. I knew what sort of mortal he was, and I knew the world would be better without him.

Pop.

More bark.

Pop.

The bullet punched the dirt five feet away.

I trained in on the far corner of the dumpster.

A howl rose in the air, closer this time. Behind me.

"Rev!" Billee, somewhere in the distance.

I fired.

The last corner of the dumpster evaporated. All that remained was the crumpled plastic lid, resting atop the bags of trash my focused shots hadn't melted into a goo.

No one would find Roger Baskin's body, not after tasting my Angelfire. But I doubted many people who didn't waste their lives smoking or snorting something would be worried about him. Beside the dumpster, looking down at a black trash bag sheared open by my beam of magic, was the energy residue in the shape of the former drug dealer.

An ethereal replication of his mortal form, he stood, looking at the spot where he thought he was safe, as if confused. Mortals usually are at this point.

He was no longer a danger in his bodiless form. His spectral body would linger next to the dumpster, waiting an eternity for nothing in particular, and terrorizing unaware employees on trash runs unless I finished my job. Sighing at the thought of his energy residue being added back to the All, I tucked Maggie into my duster's hidden pocket and stepped out from behind the tree. Halfway across the open lot, I heard footsteps.

I spun and stepped to the side, flinging my arm out and catching the back of my pursuer. Pushing, I propelled her forward, flinging her face-first into the remains of the trash.

Billee raced out of the darkness.

"Are you okay?" I asked.

She nodded. "You?"

"Yep." I tipped my head at Roger's energy residue. "He got off a few lucky shots, but nothing serious."

As a familiar to a Reaper, Billee could see the energy residue that had been Roger Baskin. When her eyes slid in his direction, she nodded. A normal reaction for a Reaper's familiar, even a relatively new one like her.

The most aggressive librarian impersonator in the world pulled herself out of the trash. Though she squinted—and probably would until she bought new glasses—she faced Roger's ethereal form.

That wasn't supposed to happen. Unless...

"You've got to be kidding me?"

"What?" Billee asked.

"She's a Guardian," I said, flicking a finger at the librarian. "A Guardian angel."

www.ingramcontent.com/pod-product-compliance
Ingram Content Group UK Ltd.
Pitfield, Milton Keynes, MK11 3LW, UK
UKHW040640080425
5372UKWH00019B/170